FOUND FAR AND WIDE

FOUND
FAR AND
WIDE

KEVIN MAJOR

BREAKWATER
P.O. Box 2188, St. John's, NL, Canada, A1C 6E6
WWW.BREAKWATERBOOKS.COM

LIBRARY AND ARCHIVES CANADA CATALOGUING IN PUBLICATION
Major, Kevin, 1949-, author
Found far and wide / Kevin Major.
ISBN 978-1-55081-632-7 (paperback)
I. Title.
PS8576.A523F68 2016   C813'.54   C2016-900766-9
Copyright © 2016 Kevin Major

We acknowledge the support of the Canada Council for the Arts, which last year
invested $153 million to bring the arts to Canadians throughout the country.
We acknowledge the financial support of the Government of Canada and the
Government of Newfoundland and Labrador through the Department of
Business, Tourism, Culture and Rural Development for our publishing activities.
PRINTED AND BOUND IN CANADA.

Breakwater Books is committed to choosing papers and materials for our
books that help to protect our environment. To this end, this book is printed on
a recycled paper that is certified by the Forest Stewardship Council®.

ALSO BY KEVIN MAJOR

FICTION

Hold Fast
Far From Shore
Thirty-Six Exposures
Dear Bruce Springsteen
Blood Red Ochre
Eating Between the Lines
Diana: My Autobiography
No Man's Land
Gaffer
Ann and Seamus
New Under the Sun

NON-FICTION

Free the Children (with Craig Kielburger)
As Near to Heaven by Sea:
A History of Newfoundland and Labrador
Printmaking on the Edge: 40 Years at St. Michael's

DRAMA

No Man's Land: A Play
Lead Me Home

CHILDREN

The House of Wooden Santas
Eh? To Zed: A Canadian ABeCedarium
Aunt Olga's Christmas Postcards

ACKNOWLEDGEMENTS

Found Far and Wide took shape over several years. The work was supported by the goodwill of many people and institutions, and by the writings of many more. To the following I am especially grateful:

For their encouragement and insight, Anne and our family, editors Marc Coté and James Langer, readers Luke Major and Linda McKnight.

For their research and writing, book and thesis authors Robert Carse, George J. Casey, George Allan England, John Gallishaw, James Glavine, John Hamilton, Jenny Higgins, Paula Laverty, Hilda Chaulk Murray, G.W.L. Nicholson, Ronald Rompkey, and John Tauranac.

Journal and letter writers Rhoda Dawson, John Gillam, Francis T. Lind, Jessie Luther, Howard Morry, and Owen Steele.

Magazine and newspaper contributors Norah Holden, P. Whitney Lackenbauer, Anne Morrow Lindbergh, O.O. McIntyre, and Robert Holland Tait.

For their resources, The Brooklyn Historical Society, The Centre for Newfoundland Studies and The Maritime History Archive, Memorial University.

For their financial support, The Canada Council for the Arts and Arts NL.

PHOTO CREDITS

FOR LINDA McKNIGHT

I

ONE

THERE were no pictures of his mother and rarely was she mentioned.

He could recall the first time he heard her name. Gladys. The sound of it had startled him. Just the fact of her having a name, and it such an odd-sounding one, as if attempting to be full of good things but held back from being that way. Once, when he was ten, someone at Sunday supper called her 'Aunt Glad' and the boy pushed away from the table and made for the step outside the back door. Sullen and lost for not knowing what to do until he turned and saw his father standing behind him.

Paddy wore stiff, wool trousers, their cuffs not reaching his shoes, in the days before Margaret was old enough to pay attention to his clothes. The cuffs were frayed and discoloured with dirt, the shoes salt-stained, missing their tongues, although laced tightly enough that it might have gone unnoticed had the boy not been so close. He didn't look up.

'What's wrong with you? Son.' The last word added.

'Nothin'.'

'You sick?'

He shook his head enough that it held back the tears. 'How come we never talk about her?'

'There's nothin' to talk about. She's been dead too long to talk about. We got enough to bother about here and now.'

'How come we got no picture or nothin'?'

'We can't be all the time moanin' over pictures.'

Paddy went back inside, shutting the door behind him.

Sam's mother had been young and slight, with russet hair that she tied back with dark green ribbon. He imagined that much as he grew older and needed to have an image of her to compare with the mothers of other boys. In his mind she was girlish and trim, different from the fleshy mothers of his friends, or the delicate, sickish ones.

He had assumed she had come from someplace along the Conception Bay shore, within walking distance of Harbour Main, until it struck him that no relatives of hers ever visited. Sam had thoughts of leaving home himself when he discovered deep in a drawer a hymnal with the inscription on its flyleaf: 'Gladys Carew. Conche.' Likely in her own hand. The first tangible connection he had ever made with her. In school the next day he asked the man who taught Geography if he had heard of Conche and if he could tell him where it was on a map.

It was tucked in the northern coast of the island, close to its very tip. So far away that Harbour Main must have been another world to her. How his father and mother met he would never ask, but assumed it was during one of the summer schooner trips his father made to fish the waters farther north still, off Labrador. Now Sam had another strand to add to the picture of her in his mind. She was a foreigner.

Never entirely fitting into her new home. And with a husband who must have been a dozen years older than herself.

It was forever someone other than his father who spoke her name. One of his uncles most often, recalling something she had done as a young woman. Once it was a prank she had played on Paddy, how it had been the cause of so much laughter. At those times Sam was silent. The mention of her gave rise to feelings he couldn't identify. Sorrow of a type. Not grief. He would have had to know her for it to be grief. Rather it was seeing something that needed to be touched but was out of reach. Like the time, as a five-year-old, he had lain against the warm body of a lamb, wanting to stroke her side, but didn't for fear of causing her to run away.

Sam was left with his father and his sister. An improbable family of three. With no thought ever given to the possibility of his father marrying again.

In his father he saw a man he was at odds to understand. Paddy was part of a long line of Kennedys who had arrived a century before from Ireland and settled in Conception Bay. Eventually they moved deeper in the bay, the whole lot of them, to Harbour Main where everyone was Catholic. Planters they were called, although they planted nothing other than enough root vegetables to last them through the winter. Their lives had all to do with fishing for cod, what anyone living along the Conception Bay shore ever did. It was a better life than they had known in Ireland, although Sam couldn't imagine it was much better.

They settled into a frugal and amenable lot. There was no reason to do battle with a neighbour. What few fights they had were with Protestants, and the prods were far enough away that life generally unfolded in obscure Catholic serenity, poverty-laden though it was for many.

Sam thought of his father as a simple, hard-working man, until Sam reached the age when he realized that, while everyone worked hard, no one's life was simple. The turns in his father's life had complicated the man, though he never spoke of them. He lived to complain and then he grew tired of even that. His lot was what it was. One day he would die and the world as he knew it would not have changed.

The times Sam saw his father stirred to life were when he drank. Rum or home brew on a Saturday night. He didn't need much and Sam came to think it was the idea of it, the ritual, that enlivened him as much as the alcohol itself. It made for his fondest memories of his father. The man could 'hold his liquor' as they all said. There were even times when his father would sing. 'Give us one from the old country, Paddy.' As if Paddy had ever been there or had somehow inherited the song from an unbroken chain of ancestors. His best was "As I Roved Out One Morning," a song that, as Sam dove into puberty and the latter verses become more suggestive, set him to thinking his father must have had a youth of some spirit, even though it was long lost.

From his father, Sam inherited what singing abilities he had. Good within a certain range. And likely his fondness for musical instruments, although he had never known his father to take one in hand.

His father's one night of indulgence led to successive days of grinding hard work. As Sam came to see it, the fishermen of Harbour Main stood ragged in the face of the merchant, as if circled by a lanyard, its knot growing tighter and tighter with each passing year. All-seeing, all-knowing, the merchant supplied the gear while the fishermen were paid in credit at the merchant's store, where their fishing profits circled back into the merchant's hands, where the fishermen never freed themselves from the immortal yoke of debt.

The fisherman was left beholden to a man no better than himself. Mere luck as to who was born on which side of the picket fence. The trial of circumstance was all.

Sam had his Mary Kavanagh to be sure. She in Avondale and he in Harbour Main. Five miles each way. Walked three times a week the summer he turned sixteen, for her father would never let Mary venture near Harbour Main on her own.

Walked both ways and that after a day at the cod. He was desperate to have her under him in some woods, his naked flesh lolling against hers, driving her arse in the cushion of moss, careful no twigs would stunt the fun of it. He had come close in the chill of May, but she managed to fend him off again. But teasing him all the same, leaving him to think the time would come, all well and good some summer night. He walked the five miles in everlasting hope.

And fear. Of Father Roe, another Irish priest. Did they breed like rabbits in Ireland? This one, meted out from County Kilkenny, prowled about the roads at night with a horsewhip, eyes peeled for young fellows and their girls kissing in the bushes. 'Johnny the Whip' the boys called him. Fouler mouths than Sam's said the priest's cock got more of a whipping than any of them ever would.

Mary was worth the chance. Sam liked the fact there was an upright piano in the parlour that he could sit at and attempt to play. He liked her mother's pea soup and still-warm bread almost as much. He felt comfortable with Mary's mother, though her father had no time for him. A railway station master after all, he wanted something better for his Mary and not the fisherman Sam was bound to end up becoming even with his education. That wouldn't get him anywhere, any more than it would the others of the Kennedy horde who lined the shores of Harbour Main. Still he couldn't lay down the law and stop Sam from spending time with Mary. He knew she might turn against him if he did. A stubborn sort, her father knew her to be, never one to take to being told. Just pray to God she didn't get pregnant.

No chance of that. Sam trooped back and forth every few days rooting around for more. Eventually Mary saw him for what he was—an impulsive sort who didn't know what he wanted, just knew it was more than what he had. One day Mary took the train into St. John's to stay with her sister for a week, and that was the end of that. Suddenly there were more fellows than Sam Kennedy in the world, and some courteous enough to buy her an ice-cream sundae at Miller's Restaurant and expect nothing but a smile in return.

The day that Sam, about to turn eighteen and clutching his matriculation certificate, freed himself from school and its unrelenting nuns was the day he figured he would take his world in hand.

Yet that summer he went cod fishing with his father, as he had done every summer since he was twelve, and when he had no schooling to return to in the fall, he stayed at it. As his father expected, as his father thought right.

Paddy had made what living he could fishing alone, fishing cross-handed, as he called it. He rowed his fourteen-foot skiff every day to his fishing berth, in the same way he had every year since his wife died. No oarlocks, only thole pins, the oars kept in place by a ring of twisted spruce roots slipped over each oar and pin. When the ice was clear he fished those cold spring months alone, until Sam was old enough and came aboard, after school closed in June. At fourteen Sam took over the rowing, without question, for Paddy was feeling the muscles turn ropey in his shoulders and back, even if he would never admit it, even if he was not yet fifty.

Sam didn't know whether to admire his father's stubbornness for working at the cod by himself, or to think him foolish at not throwing in his lot as a crewman on a bigger boat as he once did, a boat that worked a cod trap instead of hook-and-line. There had grown an obstinacy in Paddy that mocked logic, and he kept it that way even in years when his poor catches threatened the family with worse hardship than they already knew.

He had his fishing berth and no other fisherman in the harbour dared think anyone but Paddy Kennedy had rights to it. If there were years he did poorly, there were years he did better than most. And if he brought fish to shore when everyone else had nothing but a water haul, no one questioned that he should share the berth. 'Your turn will come,' was all the satisfaction he gave them. 'Then I'll be the one starin' at the bare bottom of the boat.'

Paddy's Shoal it was, and few bothered to think it used to be called Southern Shoal, least of all Paddy. Once, when he first went with his father, Sam made the mistake of asking him who gave it the name. 'It couldn't have been that. Not when you wasn't around.'

'Never you mind.'

Sam was about to ask what the name would be if his father ever gave up fishing, but caught himself. He had learned his limits with his father. Hour after hour in the boat, just the two of them, and Sam's youthful innocence was quickly displaced by a reluctance to say anything if it wasn't about the job they were there to do. He learned what it took to keep the peace.

There was plenty more going through his head, as there likely was his father's. 'The fish, Sam. Keep your mind on the fish.' An impossible boundary. One that one day would be broken, although Sam had no clear notion of how or when.

For now there was the routine of fishing for cod. Up before dawn, tea and two dry biscuits at a kitchen table set out the night before. Sam's eyes working to unglue themselves from sleep, his muscles to uncoil from the warm cocoon of the bed. The young fellow rarely made it home the previous night before midnight.

They walked, Paddy a few steps ahead, from the house to the shed in the dank hour to daylight. Not far, but far enough that a fellow had to watch his footing in the wet grass. By then just enough light making its way into the shed to haul on the oilskins and rubber boots, Sam every time faster than his father, using those extra seconds to take another leak over the wharf. For some reason he hated having to do it when they were in the boat, over the side, his father a few feet away from him.

Nothing said, nothing needing to be said. What gear they took with them—oars, gaff, bailer, dipnet, grub bucket—never varied. The bait box had been filled the evening before and, as Paddy lowered it down to him, Sam was thinking it had to be easier with two, though his father would not be one to admit it.

On the way out to the fishing grounds Sam wore mitts. Cuffs, his father called them. To keep in the warmth Sam had dipped them in the saltwater, wrung them out before slipping his hands inside. The saltwater had long ago shrunk them to half their knit size, had molded them to his hands, to the curve of the oars.

On calm days it was a steady half-hour of rowing, muscle-hard but not troublesome once he found the rhythm. Rare it was when there wasn't some wind, if not on the way out, then on the way back in. If it was enough to stir up a fair-sized lop, that could make it tricky, but Paddy was a good hand at forecasting wind and not one to take chances. If the sea was more than Sam was used to, he learned fast how to handle it. And one thing for certain, Paddy was never short on advice.

It was what they had to talk about—the wind, the weather, the fish. Mostly the fish. Sam couldn't deny the thrill of a lusty big cod snagged on a baited hook, of seeing it flounce over the gunwale, flop about vainly in the bottom of the boat. When they came fast and furious, as they did on more than a few mornings, there was a great deal of satisfaction all around. More than that, there was the feeling of refuge, of being able to look ahead to more food on the table, clothes to replace what should have been discarded years ago, kerosene when they needed it, a new bucksaw the next winter.

Fish wasn't money, but fish was all Paddy had, and by Sam being in the boat with him it came his way a bit easier. Sam was not prepared to deny him that.

Catching fish gave into chance and the weather, but once the fish reached shore Paddy had dominion. No one in Harbour Main did a better job of taking a freshly caught cod and transforming it to the gutted, salted and dried vestige of itself. When the day was done and all the steps had fallen into place, no one handed over to the merchant a better grade of saltfish.

Sam stood calf-deep in fish and pronged them one by one—through the head so it wouldn't damage the flesh—from the bottom of the boat, up and onto the stagehead, where Paddy directed them into the pound that stood alongside the splitting table.

Margaret showed up from the house in rubber boots and

donned an oilskin apron and cotton gloves. At the splitting
table she was the cut-throat and with a thin, pointed knife she
slit the throat of the cod, then inserted the tip of the blade in
the opening and sliced open the belly. Sam, the header, took
the fish and plucked out the liver, flinging it into an open
barrel nearby, where it would render into cod liver oil. He
saved the cod tongue and sounds before tearing away the head
and the guts and sending them down a hole into the sea.
He slid the fish across the table to his father. Paddy was the
splitter, whose precise stroke with the square-ended knife cut
down one side of the backbone. He lifted away the end of it,
then slid the knife deftly under and along the bone, extracting
it whistle-clean, without touching the flesh.

The fish were stored in a vat where eventually they would
be washed clean with saltwater, before being laid down in salt
inside the shed. When drying weather arrived in the summer
they were washed free of the salt that hadn't sunk into the
flesh, then carried to vast platforms of sticks covered
with boughs, elevated so air could circulate beneath them.
The fish would be spread to dry all day, then spread out again
the following day, and for more days after that until fine
weather brought the salted and dried cod to top grade,
merchantable prime.

In early fall came Sam's chance at cash. Squid showed up in
the waters of Harbour Main, in their thousands, teeming
schools prime for the jigging, as fast as a fellow could haul the
slimy buggers aboard, the air murky with their ink. Squid was
a godsend, what with a ready market, cash on the barrelhead.
Ships heading to the Grand Banks greedy for bait anchored
just outside the harbour and bought up all the fishermen could
catch. Some keeners had even laid down ice in sawdust over

the previous winter and sold that too. It was all a fine bit of excitement and Sam was eyes and ears into it.

He came away with a tidy sum in the tin box beside his bed. Though, when all was said and done, cod was still the business of the Kennedys in Harbour Main. As it stood, one man's price for fish set in stone the welfare of the other.

It was not something Sam was able to unravel. The merchant had set himself up in business a decade before. Now, besides the catch of the inshore fishermen, he had seven schooners going to the Labrador fishery. There was money being made, and Paddy Kennedy never saw one red cent of it. The merchant outfitted him in the spring, handed over food for the family through the summer. All on credit until, in the fall, Paddy's store of dried fish was carted to the merchant premises where it was culled and weighed and tallied. Most years it was enough to mark off the credit, and enough to supply the food and goods from the merchant's store that carried Paddy over to the next spring, when the wheel would start another turn.

Sam stood by and watched it unfold. He was not to open his mouth. This was his father's dealings and if there were words to be had with the merchant they would come from him. As it was, few words were spoken. Paddy had no dispute with the culler. His cartloads were generally top notch, as expected, and what wasn't, Paddy dismissed himself as due a lesser grade. The crowning moment came when the merchant revealed the market price for fish. It was prefaced with talk of how the markets were 'not bad' or 'not so good,' how Spain was not buying like it used to, and the West Indies was wanting more, but then again never taking the best grade. It was the merchant's word and Paddy had no way of knowing if there was more he was not being told. When a man had no head for the figures the merchant tossed about and enough schooling to sign his own name, but little else, his confidence lay vacant, surrendered to the taller, shirt-and-tie man with the pencil and tally sheet in hand. When Paddy signed his name to the sheet it was as if it was a renewed measure of the man, not to be signing with an X, as other fishermen had to do, signing an X and waiting while the merchant wrote the fellow's name after it.

Once they were home and drinking tea at the kitchen table, the fishing season over except for stowing away the gear, Sam couldn't keep it in any longer. 'He should be paying in cash, not credit. We got no way of knowing if his prices is fair.'

'He'll see us through the bad times as well as the good. He'll not have us starve in a year when there's no fish. You remember that. When the boats come to shore empty day after day, you remember that.'

To Sam's mind there had to be a better way. From other parts of Newfoundland came word there was.

'Coaker should be runnin' a man in the election,' Sam told his father, treading lightly, it being politics. 'He deserves a chance.'

'What's Coaker got to do with Harbour Main?'

As much as his father might pretend otherwise, William Coaker had a lot to do with Harbour Main.

He and his FPU. A union, Sam was thinking. For fishermen. For Christ's sake.

Coaker's Fishermen's Protective Union which cut out the merchant. Where fishermen bought their own supplies and sold their own fish. That alone should have been enough for Paddy to heed the man, to give Coaker a chance to get his foot in government now that he was leading nine men to run for office.

'A Coaker man in this district? Talk sense,' said his father. Meant to be a blunt end to the conversation.

Sam's focus shifted to his father's meager, unknowable eyes. Politics and religion, especially a mixture of the two, could cause them to slowly burn.

'Then vote Liberal,' Sam said, knowing the possible consequences of saying it, in some ways welcoming them. 'They've formed a coalition, the Liberals and the FPU.'

'What, and turn me back on me own. You're not bloody right in the head!'

Turn your back on the Church is what Sam would have countered had there not already grown so broad a gap between father and son, though he as much as said it with the look that passed between them.

The Catholic Church had come down like a hammer on the FPU. The Archbishop of St. John's said it all in the letter read at Sunday Mass. Said the FPU was "calculated to cause great confusion, and an upheaval of our social fabric; to set class against class, and to end in the ruin and destruction of our commercial and business system."

Horseshit.

Muttered under his breath when he got home from Mass the next day.

'Hold that tongue of yours, Sam. For Christ's sake, hold that tongue!'

Father Shean, the priest who followed Johnny the Whip, had quoted the letter even though the Archbishop had no authority in Harbour Main. Somehow the priest had gotten hold of the letter and read it out, as if the words were a papal encyclical, direct from Pius X.

Sam kept at it. 'Coaker's got a man running in Port de Grave.'

'For what bloody good that'll do ya!'

'I'm goin' to the rally. I'll hear for meself what he's all about.'

'Father Shean'll have something to say about that when he hears. Mark my words.'

'He's not gonna hear.'

Not unless his own father told him. Or Margaret blurting it to one of the nuns at school, as if it were a sin not to tell.

Margaret was so full of the Church that Sam told her she'd lost her common sense. She had all the makings of a nun herself and there was no doubt in Sam's mind that was where she was headed, even if she wasn't about to admit it.

Margaret was a nervous sort, for no sound reason as far as Sam could tell. She cooked and took care of the house, catered to her father hand and foot, and seemed to have no time for anything else, except schoolwork. And whereas schoolwork for Sam had always been something he made time for reluctantly, for Margaret there was no getting enough of it. Her one relief from the drudgery around the house. Sam doubted she was the smartest in her class, but she applied herself rigorously. Schoolwork became her constant source of pride and she never failed but come away with the top marks.

There was a lethargy to their conversations that only grew more pronounced when Sam had finished with school. The pair had even less in common. Sam willingly adopted the expectations of his father, of Margaret cooking his meals and cleaning up after him. She washed and dried his clothes, and Sam did nothing to dissuade her. In some ways she became more a servant than a sister.

If the talk at mealtimes was something beyond their fishing life, she might show some interest, but then again she was just as likely to nod and offer a half smile, before going back to her kitchen routine. He suspected Margaret had a world in her head he would never be privy to, that willfully excluded him.

Sundays were the one exception. On Sundays Margaret took control. It was she who saw to it that the two men in the house were up and fed and looking their best before the walk to Mass. It was she who made sure they each knew what day it was on the church calendar and what the Lord had endured on that day. Sam went along with it, if only because it allowed Margaret so much satisfaction to have her small enclave of Kennedys give a good account of themselves before the priest.

If Paddy was generally mute and did little more than mumble the responses during the service, it was no different than what it had been for years. And if Sam endured the service with hardly a change of expression, at least he was there. Margaret's devoutness and earnest singing voice more than made up for the rest of the family. When the service was over and they encountered Father Shean on the church steps, the priest fussed over Margaret without reservation. She swelled at his attention. It left her feeling that much closer to God, Sam suspected, and deservedly so, since she put so much effort into it. He just wished he had a sister who might laugh unexpectedly or find the nerve to contradict her father when he did something that irritated her as much as it did Sam.

TWO

SAM gripped the latch and swung open the door. A convolution of voices and tobacco smoke fell into him. The room was airless, sweaty, thick with fishermen, leavened with the smells of a day's work at the cod. All confirmation that the meeting was exactly what it had been billed—a rally for the common man.

Port de Grave was the electoral district that adjoined the district of Harbour Main along the southwest side of Conception Bay. William Coaker figured he had a chance there, where the FPU was stronger, where Protestants filled the voters list. He had a good man running from what Sam heard—George Grimes, an FPU man to the core, who grew up in the bay, in Brigus.

Sam did a morning's work before he washed up and changed his clothes, then started walking. It took him more than four hours to reach Brigus, where he struck in with a crowd going by boat to Bay Roberts. From the wharf they made their way to the Orange Lodge, the place brimming with men keen for a firing up.

Onto the stage walked a lanky, lackluster fellow in a navy blue suit, a size too big for him. The thick knot of his tie sagged between the collars of his shirt. There were bags under his eyes. He stood for a moment, expressionless. His saving grace was a robust mane of black hair, paired with a dense, uncompromising moustache. He set aside his jacket, straightened his arms and unhurriedly turned up each sleeve. He balanced his weight between his two feet. His hands, half-fists now, rose in the air.

'I don't have to tell you about the planks of the FPU! I don't have to tell you the fight we have on our hands so fishermen can make a decent income. Income, sir! Not credit, income! I don't have to tell Newfoundland fishermen where their bread is buttered. It is buttered, gentlemen, at the merchant's table! Not at your own table. Not where it belongs!' His epistle roared through the room, like a breech-loader through the ceiling.

An hour later the crowd was on the brink of exhaustion, fielding thoughts of heading home, when William Coaker himself walked through the door. The room erupted. Coaker dispensed with his hat and overcoat and took to the stage. A balding, blunt figure of a man. No stranger to raw, physical labour, at odds with his three-piece suit. His thick mitt of a hand gripped the candidate's own.

Coaker opened himself to the crowd. His convulsive testimonial drew back to the running ashore of their forebears from West Country England, through vast seasons of servitude. He was the man to rouse the frustrations heaped high by the centuries that had denied them a wage and an education. He was the fisherman's messiah, deemed to lead them out of the wilderness. He reveled in their expectations. Fair gloried in them.

In 1908 Coaker had signed up nineteen apostles at his first meeting of the FPU, at twenty-five cents a man. Within eighteen months he had organized meetings in dozens of outports and had come away with a list of a thousand such men.

Now Sam, of a generation with more education than most in the room, was no less in awe of Coaker. He eagerly laid hold of the torch. Looked beyond the impossibility of the man to the way he held the crowd. To the way a fierce light set into eyes long dimmed by debt.

'The question is simple, my friends—do you want the merchant class speaking for you yet again, or do you want your own voice ringing free in the House of Assembly? Do you want to stand mute, or do you want George Grimes, born among you, wedded to your interests, standing up and being heard. Yes, his voice, *your* voice heard. For once, heard!'

Sam hollered louder than them all.

When the speech ended—the crowd in Coaker's grip as steadfastly as when he started two hours before—Sam was coated in perspiration, an addict for the cause, lithe and limber in the name of change. He struggled to come up with words for the intoxication, for the sudden urgency to find a way into the fold.

The following day, walking back to Harbour Main, against every instinct in him he had to admit there was no way into the fold. Harbour Main didn't have a branch of the FPU and there was no hope it ever would.

His father asked him nothing about the rally, though he had to sense the change in his son. 'Don't get yourself worked up over nothin'. Don't let it make a fool of you.'

Sam planted himself in his father's line of vision. Looked at him behind thickening shoulders. A sharp uprightness matched with a keen pair of eyes. 'I'm no fool, father. That's one thing I'm not.'

'And don't be wishin' you were somewhere else when you're useful right where you are.'

It was his father's queer. way of saying he needed Sam's help, that it was hard on him to go at it alone. But in his head Sam had already made the separation.

His father offered no words to change his mind. What he did hold out was a heart gone sour. Unsparing in its frustrations, without as much as a stiff token of goodwill. Paddy turned and sat in the kitchen chair as if he had just come in from fishing, expecting Margaret to make him tea and cut him a slice of bread.

Sam said nothing, looked rigidly at his sister. Her face twitched slightly, her eyes wandering away. His life didn't fit into hers, any more than it did his father's.

Sam stayed away from Confession. It was his one mark of defiance against his sister. Besides which he wasn't about to disclose to any priest the torrent of desire that thrashed through him in his bed at night. Again and again and in such wicked rhythm that there was no recourse but to cast aside his guilt and be done with it.

He remembered her. The buoyant mistress of Victoria Manor, the rooming house in Brigus where he had spent the night, on his way back from the Coaker rally. Sally was her name, short, she told him, for Sarah. He was exhausted and feeling the effects of the rum that had come his way on the boat ride back. He fell on the bed immediately and passed out, still in his outdoor clothes. The next morning he detected the odour of her perfume lingering on the patchwork coverlet, as if she had spread herself on the bed beside him during the night.

He sat across from Sally over breakfast with the other guests—a humourless teacher with one straight leg and a chain-smoking dry goods salesman—before he set off back to Harbour Main. She had eagerly shared his excitement at what he witnessed of Coaker and his candidate. Her late husband, Vernon, had been a devoted supporter of the FPU. Her chest heaved about the breakfast table, her heart stirring at the mention of him. Sam reminded her of the dear man, suddenly taken from her, she said, so young and so able-bodied.

The more Sam thought about Sally and what might have been had he not passed out, the more it unleashed a hunger in dire need of relief. His thoughts led him where his prospects were the greatest, regardless of the fact that she was likely twice his age.

Brigus was out of sight and mind of Harbour Main, a favourable fact in itself. Sam set in motion plans to see Sally again, over Christmas, before his father needed help cutting wood for the next winter. He wrote her, requesting room and board starting on the 27th. He received a quick reply. *'Indeed, I shall be very glad to welcome you. I expect you will be my only guest as it is the holiday period. Wishing you a safe and contented journey, Sarah.'*

The arrival of a letter stirred Margaret's curiosity. Sam revealed nothing until the three of them were walking home from midnight mass on Christmas Eve.

'Someone you met on your Coaker trip?' Paddy said.

His father had taken to referring to it that way, with an added tone of disapproval once the election was over and it became clear that Coaker had won eight of the nine districts in which his party's candidates had run.

'Wasting away the rest of your squid money. Suit yourself.'

Margaret said nothing, as anxious as she was to know

more. The writing on the envelope had obviously been a woman's.

His option for getting to Brigus was again to walk and, now that it was winter, to snowshoe. The day broke clear and crisp, with little wind, and not particularly cold. He couldn't have wished for better. He strode away from the house, knapsack on his back that, in addition to clothes and kit, held several slices of buttered bread which Margaret had wrapped and tied in brown paper, together with pouches of tea and sugar. On the outside of his knapsack hung a small tin kettle.

All around him fresh snow lit the landscape. Sam's spirit quickened, set to embrace the day ahead. Once out of sight of the well-worn roads of Harbour Main his footing gave way several times in the soft snow, so he donned the snowshoes and in short order was able to keep up a dependable rhythm. The road took him past Avondale, which prompted him to hum loudly and defiantly, a tune he remembered from his time with Mary Kavanagh, brazen declaration that he was far from a schoolboy any longer.

As luck should have it, beyond Avondale he encountered a couple travelling by horse and side sleigh, heading to Kitchuses. They offered him a ride and he was more than pleased to take it, even though it proved a tight squeeze, the woman being rather stout and thickly clothed.

He was expected, of course, to explain why he was on his way to Brigus. 'A Christmas visit,' he said. 'And yourselves?'

The question set the woman in full motion, allowing Sam to escape relating the details of his own trip. In the midst of her chronicles the husband broke in. 'You're Paddy Kennedy's fellow, you are.'

Sam nodded, not entirely surprised.

'The boy who favoured our Mary?' his wife chimed in. It wasn't a promising note.

'Mary's our son's young maid.' Their much-loved, innocent granddaughter then.

'Yes.'

'You're at the fishing with your father?'

He nodded again. Only confirming what their son, the station master, had figured all along. Sam felt lessened in their eyes, as if Mary did well to be rid of him.

'For now.' They were waiting for more. 'Lots of fellows have moved away.'

Sure enough. There had been a small exodus of men to the States to find work, Harbour Main Kennedys among them and some not much older than himself. Gone to work high steel, as they called it in their letters home. They'd turned from catching fish to construction jobs, piecing together the skyscrapers that were spreading like mad across New York City, one over fifty stories high it was said. Sam could hardly think that part was true.

Maybe it would come to that, and sooner rather than later. In the meantime he had a mind and body of his own, and stolen pleasures far removed from Harbour Main.

'Give my regards to Mary,' he told the couple as he stepped down from the sleigh and they turned onto the side road to Kitchuses.

They waved and were gone, no doubt with a few things to say about the young man who was once favoured their Mary.

He called to them, the old couple out of hearing range, 'Tell her it was good while it lasted.' He smiled and walked on, thinking he might soon stop for a mug-up. He was getting a bit hungry.

The very first night in Brigus, Sam joined Sally at her invitation for a Christmas reception at the home of a Mrs. Bartlett, an evening of carol singing, sherry and mulled wine, and an endless array of fruit cake. Sally had landed him in the midst of Brigus society and he hardly knew where to turn. To Captain Bartlett and his stories of the *Viking* at the seal hunt? To the prattling Mr. Kent, a painter who had come from America and settled in Brigus because he was so taken with the landscape? Or to Sally, who rose from her place on the settee, stood beside the tree, and commenced a solo rendition of a carol. She introduced it as "The Holly and the Ivy."

Sam, who by this time had seated himself and retreated behind his sherry, had never heard it before. A Protestant carol most likely. English for certain, not Irish. Dear Sally with her sweet, sweet voice and constant smile, the flicker of light in her eye as it lingered on his. Causing Sam to smile guilelessly in return, as his stare intensified and he drank in the words. *The holly and the ivy, when they are both full grown,* as both of them were, especially Sally, beyond youth, bearing the *prickle* and the *crown* there was no contesting, and yes, *O the rising of the sun.* And yes, it was rising at the flicker in her eye. And it was the sun. Rising ever so surely that he thought he better place his hands in its vicinity to keep it from view, until Sally returned to the settee, the carol complete.

She advanced in his direction, her sherry glass sidling close to his, herself not far behind.

'You have a charming voice, Sarah.' And yes, he had convinced himself he was up to the challenge. 'May I call you Sarah?'

'Certainly.' Then in softer tones to him alone. 'Call me whatever your heart desires, Samuel.'

Beyond her formality was the charm of electric light on

her face. Sam had only recent and very limited experience of electric light. It excited him, the way it cast so evenly about her face and bosom, leaving little to chance. It took away the fitfulness of the candle flame or the oil lamp, baring so much of her charm, the way her necklace nestled between.

The rhythm of her breathing alone, how her bosom rose into the light and momentarily retreated, only to rise again. Sally was by no means a slender young lady and there was much to behold beyond the glass of sherry. She seemed to delight in her immodesty, though perhaps delight was too strong a word, giving Sam over to expectations beyond what was reasonable, what was decent.

'You don't mind if I call you Samuel?'

'Few people do,' he answered, his enterprise pushing beyond a slight stammer. 'And none so marvelous as yourself.'

Sally blushed. The colour seemed to descend from her face to her neck and beyond, at which point she chose to lay an open hand just below her throat and casually finger the strands of her necklace.

Sam shifted his eyes away to allow them both space to recover, and shifted their conversation to something more neutral. 'Do you know many Christmas pieces?'

'Yes, indeed so. They are some of my favorites, although I do like the more modern selections.'

'And what might they be?'

'Shall I sing one for you?' And quietly, near his ear, 'I would so love to thrill you with a favourite rendition.'

He swallowed his first attempt at a reply. 'Would you?'

Indeed she would. When there was a lull, and with the encouragement of the others, she returned to the floor. The lady began the song, without introduction, with just a clasp of her hands against her bosom, and exceptional concentration it seemed. '*I am dreaming, Dear, of you, Day by day...*'

Sam didn't quite know what to make of the composition, nor the occasional glance his way from the singer. He was thrown off stride. Sarah now appeared older than he had first guessed. And anxious, it seemed.

The applause was enthusiastic, outdistancing Sam's own, to his relief, since he thought it best if he didn't answer openly her call to arms. Sally reclaimed her place on the settee, blushing appropriately. Her bosom regaled its audience more exuberantly than ever.

'That was delightful, Sarah.'

'Thank you, Samuel. I like to be a tad expressive. It adds to the moment, Samuel. Wouldn't you agree?'

He nodded.

'Vernon so appreciated it.'

'Yes.'

'My late husband.'

Sam didn't need to be reminded.

'I have gradually recovered. One must move on. I feel something of my old self again.'

Her old self came to take up the whole of Sam's visit. She continued to call him Samuel and he thought he'd keep to the less familiar Sarah. Nobody else, she said, called her anything but Sally, and wasn't it tiresome. His choice of name, she declared, made her feel like a new person, a woman who managed her way out of the depths of despair, and into a new and brighter world. It renewed her faith in herself. 'It bathes me with confidence.'

She liked the word 'bathe.' And very much liked the act. In truth, she revealed to Sam, she bathed twice a day, sometimes three if she felt herself slipping into melancholia.

'Sinful, I know, and a waste of water, but it does me such good. One should not forego life's pleasures, not when the tenure upon this earth can be so taut.'

She also liked the word 'taut.' Samuel grew taut while in the process of lathering her back, and more so her voluminous breasts, and thus she was able to bathe in more of life's pleasures.

She extended a foam-shrouded hand to his. By the time Sam had discarded the remainder of his clothes and clambered into the clawfoot tub, his tautness was reaching the point of crisis and he had barely positioned himself to enter her, the water a foaming hindrance, his eyes stinging with the splash of soap, when his peak came, leaving them both rather sodden and unfulfilled.

'Damn.'

'Now, now.'

She looked into his anxious eyes and stroked his face. Her fingers slipped over his chin, smooth as butter, and it with a full two days growth.

Yet the ice had been broken.

And no odds. The opportunities for compensation came to be many and varied. The settee, the bed, the rug before the fire, the kitchen table, the clawfoot once again. His inhibitions dormant, he fell into the habits of a young man of profound experience, including, in her wisdom, the use of her late husband's 'French sheaths,' as she called them. And to think it all had come his way so fortuitously and in such profusion. Wasn't his the horn of plenty.

Sam returned home with a lighter heart. He was careful not to reveal the source of his high spirits, but his father had his suspicions. He took Sam aside.

'Is she Catholic?'

'She?'

'I weren't born yesterday, Sam.'

Sam's face began to redden, despite his urge to control it.

'Margaret would be heartbroken.'

What did Margaret have to do with it? Or religion? Or his father for that matter. Sam walked away. Jesus, he needed some breathing room. A fellow couldn't get himself a piece of tail but his old man had his nose in it.

He told his buddy Albert. Sam hadn't many friends he could trust not to spread it from one end of Harbour Main to the other. But there was Albert Woodford, who he had buddied around with since their first day of school together. Albert had quit school, years ago now, and gone fishing with two of his uncles.

'You fuckin' lucky bugger.'

There was that. Albert was envious as hell and it would have been foolish to deny it hadn't been one sweet time in Brigus, getting it so often he'd lost count.

'Like jeezley rabbits. What the fuck odds what your old man says?'

'You don't feel it, Al? You don't feel them crowding in on you?'

'Jealous, that's what. They're all wishing they was our age again. They had their fuckin' kick at the can.'

Albert had a carefreeness about him that rarely wavered. Sam couldn't understand it, for the longest time thought it childish, until Albert failed to grew out of it. It was his way, Sam supposed. Not that he hadn't had his share of misery. His father nearly drowned when Albert was twelve—fell through the ice of Doyles Pond. His brothers saved him, but he had been in the frigid water so long he was never the same. When

Albert was old enough to quit school he took his father's place in the trap skiff.

Was that all it was—a matter of paying his father no mind, of letting it all wash over him? A fellow needed to prove himself, on his own, away from his family.

'Think we could get a berth at the seals? Ever think of that, Al?'

'Sealing is a tough racket. Me uncles had their time at it.'

'Tough is right. Good and tough.'

Al was not so sure.

'There's money to be made.'

'Not a lot by the time you rigs yourself out.'

'Cash,' said Sam. 'None of this other shit.'

Cash sounded good. If they could come away with a decent few bucks in their pants pockets it might be worth it.

'Berths is hard to come by. The seal hunt is not what it was one time.'

But Sam knew someone who'd help them each get a berth aboard one of the vessels. In Brigus, at the Christmas reception—William Bartlett. Captained the *Viking* for the last ten years, he told Sam, since Bowring Brothers brought her to Newfoundland. Brigus was famous for seamen who knew the perils of ice. The Captain's son, Bob Bartlett, had gone with Peary on his expedition to the North Pole. He was a hero all over Newfoundland.

It had been an honour to meet William Bartlett. He hadn't been well, Sarah told Sam at the time, yet his hand was leather thick and his grip like a clamp. Sam had made a point of not letting it bury his own. The Captain would have noticed the young fellow was no scam when it came to hard work.

The *Viking* had brought home the fourth highest tally of pelts that year and paid out $72 a man. Bartlett himself wouldn't be aboard the *Viking* this spring, but he knew the captain who was. He'd put in a good word for Sam if he wanted a berth.

'And you, too, Al, if he knows I had a buddy who wanted to go.'

'A wooden wall is she? Steel vessels is taking over the hunt these days. If I got it in me head to go, it'd have to be one o' they.'

Albert threw up a condition he figured Sam could never meet. He wouldn't have it sounding like he wasn't man enough to go at the seals.

'What would your uncles have to say about it?'

'If I got it in me head to go, I'd go. Don't you worry about that.'

'Name your ship, Al.'

'Who was the head feller last year?'

'Abram Kean in the *Stephano*. Steel from stem to stern.'

'And what did he pay out?'

'$86 a man.'

'The *Stephano*, she's the one.'

Sam laughed at him, so cocky. Albert said show him a ticket and he'd be the first man aboard. Sam wondered what Abram Kean would say to that. He wondered what Captain Bartlett would say if Sam wrote him and asked if he'd put in a good word for them with the captain of a steel vessel whose catch year after year surpassed his own.

When, two weeks later, a reply came, he couldn't track down Albert fast enough. The Captain had written *Take this to Bowring's wharf in St. John's*, and then on a separate sheet of paper:

To Abram Kean, Captain of the S.S. Stephano:

These two lads are in need of a berth to the Hunt. I vouch for their willingness to do a good day's work and not complain.

Captain William Bartlett, Brigus

It set Albert on his ass. He wouldn't admit he'd been caught out, though he had trouble coming up with something to say, with Sam standing there full of himself, with a twisted grin that wouldn't let up.

'What do you make of it, Al? I say we go to St. John's…'

'What if we goes and nothing comes of it? Where will that put us? In the hole, that's what, and not a damn thing…'

'You're not up for it.'

'I'm fuckin' up for it as much as you're fuckin' up for it.'

Sam had a buddy for the hunt, even if he wasn't all he pretended to be. 'No matter,' Sam told him. 'We'll have our crack at it. We're good and tough.'

Come the second week of March they were on their way to St. John's. They had barely enough money for the train fare, what with fitting themselves out so they wouldn't be staring Abram Kean in the face, looking like they hadn't a clue what was expected of them.

A fellow needed a gaff for getting about on the ice and killing seals, a knife for skinning them and a steel for keeping it sharp, a tow rope for hauling pelts back to the ship. To keep warm they each had a thick wool guernsey and mitts, a canvas jacket and moleskin trousers, and oilskins to go on over them when the weather turned foul. They needed ice goggles if they weren't to go blind and sealskin boots with frosters on the soles if they weren't to slip and break a leg or end up in the open water.

Albert's two uncles who had gone to the ice years before fixed them up with some of what they didn't have. The rest they'd get in St. John's once they were assured of their berths. Bowring's would outfit each of them with boots and a tin pan and mug for meals, and they'd be wanting to add a few cakes of tobacco and some sugar for their tea. The cost would come off their sealer's share once the hunt was over.

The train was crammed with sealers, more so with each stop it made. From Bonavista, Trinity and Conception Bays they came, some with their tickets, guaranteed berths, but more on spec, although none would have a letter like the one that was carefully folded deep in Sam's pocket.

The hunt was the only talk, the experienced fellows regaling the younger ones with stories of the year before, and the years before that. It was a terrible hard way to scrounge a few dollars, no two ways about it, but still for all a rousing one. They were in it together—ice hunters, as they liked to think of themselves—on the move in the hungry month of March to do a job that, please God, would put food on their kitchen tables until the cod fishery started up.

'We's devils for punishment, the whole lot of us,' said one fellow, who could have been the age of Sam's father. He was resigned to it, but still bore a measure of satisfaction in his deep-set eyes.

Neither Sam nor Albert had set foot in St. John's before, the island's capital city, of legendary proportions to young fellows like themselves, from where all things good and evil seemed to emanate. It was the centre of the fish trade, the seal trade, the trade in merchant goods that trickled to the outports. From St. John's came the government regulations that set a tone for their lives and back to St. John's was sent their exasperation at the disregard their government had for them. There were stories of the great churches and merchant mansions, and stores where a fellow could buy anything he might ever want, had he the money to pay for it. And young women, the like they'd never have seen before. The anticipation stoked the fire in their guts and when they stepped off the train and onto Water Street, canvas gunny sacks on their shoulders, there wasn't a word from either of them, just a cut of pride that they had made the trip, an ardent pair of outport lads bracing themselves for whatever was about to come their way.

The sealers, in clusters of half a dozen or more, each on the same mission, strode up Water Street to the succession of finger piers that lined the north side of the harbour. It was an astonishing sight, the waterfront teeming with men and ships, masted schooners cheek by jowl with broad-funneled steamers. A man could step pier-to-ship, ship-to-pier the full length of the harbour and not touch water. It seemed as if half the male population of the city and all its sudden arrivals had congregated there. Most stood about, curious clumps of on-lookers and the stout, gaff-ready fledglings in line abreast of their chosen vessel, the one on which their hopes had been pinned for weeks.

The harbour was rife with uncertainty. Except for the fortunate few who clenched their tickets and the veterans whose faces alone were enough to get them aboard, there was no guarantee of a berth until the vessel's captain or his agent gave the nod. Doubtless there were some men who'd be heading back home on the next train, and a few, left in desperation, aiming to stow away aboard a ship undetected. As Sam searched for the pier that held the *Stephano*, Albert a step behind him, he pushed aside such worries. He was certain the letter would be all they'd need.

Their gaze fell on as big a vessel as either one of them had ever seen. A huge red X on a white background stretched almost the full length of the funnel, signifying a ship of Bowring's Red Cross Line. At 3,500 gross tons the *Stephano* was the largest vessel heading to the hunt. It was no accident that she was captained by the old warhorse himself, the man they called The Admiral of the Fleet.

The pair drew closer and stood behind a cluster of men peering at a sign hanging over the railing to the right of the gangplank. Their hearts sank. "Sealers list complete. All berths assigned."

The men, their hopes built on a bumper crop of pelts and on the captain who would surely deliver it, held firm, dumbfounded, with no thought to trying their luck elsewhere. It brought a querulous Captain Kean to the head of the gangplank.

Kean was a man of well-attended girth. Over a dark green waistcoat, he wore his black master seaman's jacket, tidily buttoned and braided. A matching captain's hat boosted his stature even more, as did a grizzled, substantial beard, neatly groomed. From the waistcoat hung a gold fob, at the end of which was a pocket watch that he consulted before he spoke.

'Off with ye, lads. The *Stephano* won't be taking another man. Yer wastin' good time standing there.'

Eventually one man turned away, then another, until the line disintegrated into small bands of disappointed sealers trying to decide what to do to salvage their prospects of a trip to the hunt.

'We're goners,' said Albert. 'No one is going to take us fellers when we never been to the ice before.'

Sam retrieved the letter and, ignoring Albert, guardedly

approached the foot of the gangplank. 'Captain Kean, sir!'

Kean lowered his eyes, with little tolerance for someone desperate to waste more of his time. 'You're deaf! Off with ye, I said!'

'A letter, sir, addressed to you, sir. From Captain William Bartlett of Brigus.'

With a thousand things needing his intention the man had lost all patience. 'Bartlett? Bring it here. Bring it here, you young poke!'

Sam scravelled up the gangplank. He carefully unfolded the letter, which, after so long in his pocket, had turned damp and limp. One of its creases tore in the wind.

Sam handed it to the Captain and stood back. Kean drew a pince-nez from the breast pocket of his coat and rested it on the bridge of his nose. He looked at Sam and then at the letter. It was still readable.

'Yes,' said Kean. And eventually again, 'Yes.' He handed the letter back to Sam, who refolded it, causing it to split into two pieces. 'Never been to the ice, have ye? Never had yer face and eyes in the fat?'

'No, sir,' said Sam, still fumbling to get the letter back in his pocket.

'A youngster then. That's what we call the likes of you crowd—youngsters. More sauce than sense.'

'Yes, sir.'

'Or that other one,' he said, looking down the gangplank, 'that leewardly laggard?'

'Him neither, sir.'

'You two got some gall. That's what I says to you. What makes you think I should take ye on? Answer me that. I don't pay no mind to letters. Not when ye knows nothing about workin' swiles.'

'We're keen, sir. We fishes, sir. We're used to the cold.'

'Like every other young cod hauler in Newfoundland. All thinkin' they could make a man o' themselves by shippin' aboard with Abram Kean.'

Sam struggled for something, anything to bring the captain around. 'I got my diploma. School, sir. I matriculated.'

Kean drew back, laughed loudly and shook his head. 'Did you now? You didn't learn much if that's the case. Not if all you got in yer head is fish and swiles?'

Sam held on. 'Family, sir. They need me to help out.'

Kean didn't doubt it for a second. What swarm of baymen couldn't use all the help they could get? Every last one of them savage for punishment. The Old Man loved them all. He thrived on men racked to their limit.

He looked Sam up and down and in the end, against his better sense, gave him the nod. And Albert, who had been waiting befuddled at the foot of the gangplank.

'Thank you, sir,' said Sam, offering up a thin smile. 'You'll not be sorry.'

'And you, Sam Kennedy. You'll not forget your trip to the ice with Abram Kean. No sir, that's one thing you won't do.'

'No, sir.'

'I'll keep eyes on you. Some days I might need you and your matriculation.'

By 8 a.m. the next morning the *Stephano* had steamed through The Narrows and was into open seas. Two hours later she passed to the outside of Baccalieu Island, exchanging the lead with the *Nascopie*, the other vessels not far off. Before many more hours had passed they had their first sighting of ice pans. Loose at first, but it soon thickened to pack ice. The ship pushed on, cutting through with little effort. All the same, Kean wasn't about to appear foolhardy, especially on the first day out, so crossing Bonavista Bay he gave the order to cut the speed by half. The other captains followed suit. The vessels held up about 30 miles to the east of Cape Freels and burnt down for the night.

Sam and Albert spent the second night where they had the first, in the dank and grimy sealers' cabin between decks. To get there they descended a steep set of stairs, icy slime covering much of it, to what had been a cargo hold, where now a double tier of wooden bunks was crudely pieced together. As the last aboard, the pair were out of luck for even one of these. They made do with the only space remaining, a leftover few feet of rough flooring coated in coal dust, a dark hole sandwiched between the end of the bunks and the curving hull of the ship.

They slept wedged back to back, on coarse brin sacks brought from home and filled with wood shavings from a Water Street cooperage. Each regular bunk housed four men, twisted together top and tail like fish in a can. According to the new regulations there should have been steam heating, but outdoor clothes and a half-moldy blanket was all anyone had to keep himself warm, together with the heat of so many bodies clogged into the narrow space.

The cabin was shared with everything they had brought aboard, from oilskins and rope coils to kettles and makeshift spittoons. Wet woolen mitts and long underwear hung from twine that crisscrossed the ceiling. Errant smoke trailed from a small stove, around which men were constantly congregated, pouring black-strength tea and making toast. All for all it produced a potent stew of odours, so dense at times that it was difficult to draw one decent breath after another. Little wonder the sealers often gave up their lair for the deck, ice-frigid and, in places, slick as a frozen pond. There they clustered with home rolls and cut-rate pipes they hoped would last the trip, careful as they were not to use up too much tobacco before getting into the fat, when they would relish a smoke the most.

Neither Albert nor Sam complained, beyond wary grumbling between themselves. They had their berths and they weren't the ones wandering back home penniless, tails between their legs.

'We're into it now, Albert, b'y.' Both standing on the foredeck, hands locked in their armpits, backs to the dying wind, shifting from one foot to the other to keep warm.

'Yes, we are so.' He bounced a stiff shoulder off Sam's, in the way he might have done standing around in idleness some summer night in Harbour Main.

Instead they were lying in the ice N.E. of Fogo, nightfall upon them, no more than 30 feet rail-to-rail with the *Nascopie*, and beyond it, within a hundred yards, three more iron-clads, all lit up like Christmas.

Some sight, they and their shipmates were thinking, as were the thousand more men in the other ships. Some wonderful sight. Made more so by the arrival from the bridge of Captain Kean, in his thick, boot-length fur coat and matching hat. He looked a great black bear of a man. The men doffed their salt-and-peppers, nodding slightly. Kean hardly took notice, his attention squarely on the men of the *Nascopie*.

'Heard you have William Coaker aboard,' he called across the ice.

'We have, sir,' came the reply. Not one of them with anything but veneration for Coaker.

'Then good luck to yas all.'

Sam had heard from others on the train into St. John's

that Coaker was taking passage on the *Nascopie*, to see for himself if his fight with the merchant bosses for new sealing regulations were having results. Better grub aboard the vessels for one thing. A fairer share of the profits. All to the good, as far as the sealers were concerned, not that Abram Kean saw it that way. From what Sam heard, his feud with Coaker had been on-going for years.

'Best place for that man is the lunatic asylum,' Kean declared when he turned back to an audience of his own men.

His words brought dutiful laughter. Sam turned aside as if he hadn't heard.

'That's yer buddy Coaker he's talking about,' said Albert, nudging him.

'Never you mind.'

'Then again Captain Kean's got plenty men cravin' to go aboard hes ship. Look at we fellers.' Albert chuckled. 'Coaker won't hold it against ya.' He nudged Sam again.

Sam jabbed an elbow into Albert's ribs and told him to bugger off.

Kean's animosity towards Coaker only got louder as the days wore on. Most sealers were cod fishermen, first and foremost, and Kean used every chance he could to undermine the FPU. The men knew the difference Coaker had made, even if they weren't saying anything about it in front of the Old Man, as they were calling Kean behind his back, still with respect.

Sam planned to keep his distance. Stay out of the Old Man's way and set his mind on the job he was aboard to do. And when the hunt was over, his share firmly in his hand, he'd be more than satisfied.

There was no one but himself to account for. He felt it in his bones, the separation from home. The satisfaction of being his own man, on his own terms.

The thicker the ice, the more fitful the Captain became.

'This'll rowse up yer blood, me sons, you crowd idling around the house in yer vamps since December mont'!'

In the barrel on the foretopmast—the parlour, as Kean called it—someone was on the look out for leads, channels of open water that would guide the ship through the ice floes, and further north, to where the sealing grounds would offer up their prize. Where the leads closed, the *Stephano* struck into the floes with hardly a quiver, butted and boomed and thrust aside the hulking chunks. Brine sloshed over the shattered ice, light catching the churning brew left in its wake, turning the water a brilliant bluish-green.

The iron-clad thundered on with a will as fierce as the Captain's own.

Five days out of port and they were into the seals, the sight every man aboard had been craving. The prospect of the first kill sent a pounding wave of expectation through the ship. Gaffs in hand, tow ropes coiled across their chests, the sealers stood five and six deep at the rail, waiting for the seals to turn thick enough to make it worth the scramble onto the ice. Waiting for the word from the Old Man.

Late that afternoon it came. 'Overboard, me sweet laddies! Overboard and good luck to every last one o' ye!'

It was all hands over the side of the *Stephano*, down the ladders, and onto the ridged, snow-crusted ice. They leapt forward in every direction, their spiked boots singing over the ice crystals, gaffs striding fervently through the air. A proven attack of like-minded men, out to set the floes ablaze for yet another spring.

Their rousing cheers were met with the terror-stricken chorus of whitecoats and their mother harps, like the everlasting screech of seagulls multiplied a thousand times. It stopped Sam dead.

'Sweet fuck!' declared Albert, rushing on. Sam steeled himself and chased after him.

His hesitation was nothing noticed by the ice watch, nothing that made the pair anything but sealers, there to strike the head of the pup with one fervid swipe of the gaff, killing it instantly, all the time with an eye to the mother, frantically rearing her head, worked into a devil's rage in defense of her young. Albert slid the knife across the dead seal's throat, down the belly, neck to scutters, and watching how the others did it, sculped the pup, sliced away the fat and fur from the carcass in one piece. The blood business lashed the crystal snow, a torrent so thick it held onto the snow undiluted, hot and steaming, a vivid red.

'Jesus, Al.'

The pelts they blood-trailed across the startlingly white ice to one spot and onto a communal pile. And though the herd wasn't endless it kept every man steady at it for an hour and in that hour Sam and his buddy turned into something more than youngsters at the hunt. They leapt from ice pan to ice pan and bloodied themselves repeatedly, and as brutish as it was, as mercilessly grim, they held fast to the habits of men. And of the generations before them who had seized it, and in doing so saved their families from the dregs of winter.

The day was done, and the men, raw with cold and bone weary, scaled the rope ladders back aboard ship. The pelts were winched up and heaped on deck, Kean looking on, a contented skipper. When the pair had cleaned up as best they could and sat themselves down to a meal of salt meat, spuds and turnip, and raisin pudding on top of that, only then did it all sink in. Their innocence purged by their baptism of blood and fat.

Albert fell in with the sealers' lot. He joked and laughed and worked himself into their revelry. He become one of them.

Sam did not, as much as it confounded him. Had he managed to escape the cries ringing desperately in his ears, he might have endured the meal. He might not have taken to a back deck and thrown his guts up and onto the ice pans sweeping by.

He was no better the next time, and the next time after that no better still. He forced himself to get used to the killing, learned what to expect from it. For his own good he did, and Albert's. He couldn't be an embarrassment to the fellow he had cajoled into making the trip.

Odd that it should be him and not Albert. Odd that he didn't have more nerve when it came to animals, because that was all they were, he assured himself, animals, no difference it was a mother and her pup.

After his third day on the ice, after a third supper retched overboard, the Old Man had words with him. Sam had avoided Kean however he could, but there wasn't much on the ship that went unnoticed. Kean had more eyes than his own.

'You're a poor excuse for a sealer, young Kennedy?'

'No, sir.'

'Waste of good food. Coaker got it aboard the ship. Least you could do is keep it down.'

'Seasick.' They both knew the difference.

'Good on figures, are ye?'

It caught Sam unawares. Kean meant mathematics. Yes, Sam told him, one of best when he wrote his finals. 'But I needs to be on the ice, sir, with everyone else.'

'Should never have took you laddioes aboard. Should have left you and that devil of a letter on the wharf in St. John's.'

'I'll do better, sir.'

'The tally-man's wrenched his foot. See the stow boss and he'll put you to work.'

'Yes, sir.' He sounded reluctant, if privately he was grateful.

'When you're not at that, have a gander in the parlour. Keep a look-out for swiles. You any good with heights? What about yer eyes?'

'Yes, sir. Good, sir.'

'And Kennedy, for God and heaven's sake, keep down yer next meal. The swiles is fat enough as they is.' He laughed as loudly as on the day he had given him the nod to come aboard.

The next morning Sam was taking orders from the stow boss, with more years at the hunt than his health should have allowed, the man in charge of stowing away the pelts once they'd been aboard ship long enough to cool. There were pounds below deck, holding bays that stored coal when the voyage started, that now, emptied and swept, were slapped down with pelts. Laid atop each other fat against fat, with shovelfuls of crushed pan ice between.

Sam was there when the pelts were slid over the lip and into the pound, a notch on the tally stick for every five pelts, a groove for every twenty. A fellow down below, doing a balancing act atop the ice and fat, prodded them around one by one. Sam never missed a pelt. Never lost count. Saw to it that he wasn't in the way, and when the stow boss needed help moving ice or shifting pelts Sam was johnny on the spot. So eager to get it done right that the stow man took a liking to him, against his will.

When the last pelt had been stored away, Sam cleaned the tally sticks of grease and blood, then with a pencil marked each one with the date. He copied the total onto a tally sheet, made his way to the wheelhouse, and presented it to Kean. The Captain had a rough total in his head, having kept a constant watch as the pelts were winched aboard, and scanned Sam's number only to see how close he had come. At the bottom of the sheet was the running total for the trip. This took more of his attention and he generally grunted his approval, comparing the figure to what other years had brought this far into the hunt. As much as it became him to complain, Kean found no reason to before setting the sheet aside, satisfied with himself, seemingly satisfied with Sam.

It was Sam's last job before crawling in bed for the night. There was still no getting used to the filth and the cabin stinking to high heaven, the snorts and snores coming from the oldtimers who could somehow sleep through anything. All a fellow could do was work himself into a spot, as satisfied as he was likely to get, accepting the fact that there was only the chance of it getting worse not better.

'Not that I minds all day on the ice,' said Sam.

Albert didn't think much of Sam's new station.

'Before the trip is out,' Albert boasted, 'I'll be as slick at sculpin' seals as any man aboard.'

Sam doubted it but let him have his say. As the days wore on he'd often slip Albert something he had held back from his own meals with the other crewmen. A couple of buttered biscuits, a few raisins, a folded piece of jam bread. Wrapped in a handkerchief he had managed to keep reasonably clean. Albert would scarf it down without a thank-you. He had come to expect it and somehow it helped to even things out between them.

Sealing had turned out to be one hell of a hard racket, whatever way they looked at it. But at least there were seals to kill and pelts to count and they hadn't been left leaning over the ship's rails craving the sight of the young buggers.

Most mornings Sam emerged on deck just as the light was breaking over the field of ice encircling the *Stephano*, and taking to the ratlines, more by feel than by sight, he clambered up to the barrel.

A fellow could get used to the barrel easy enough, frosty as it was up there, cramped as it was. A fellow could take a liking to it, peering down at his formless shipmates skimming the decks below, drifting together in scattered knots for a smoke and a fit of coughing to start another day.

Beyond the clogged and squalid steamer was brought to light an ice-prairie of mottled bronze and grey. Brightening calmly, steadily, to a glaze of arctic white, a thin, frosted mist hovering over it. A portion of the immaculate stage each day destined for the blood drama of the hunt.

Sam scrutinized it, first by naked eye, then by spyglass, all the while conscious of how much stake the Old Man had in him. There was sign of seals at most every point of the compass, but there had to be more than mere sign to launch a shipload of men overboard. There had to be a patch big enough that they would not return for hours.

It was easy to mistake one stretch of white for another. A man had to have a system, a way to be sure of searching every breath of ice until, closer to the horizon line, it narrowed into uselessness. Sam did two exhaustive sweeps, and although there were no sections crammed enough with seals to send him scurrying down the ratlines, there were pans that showed promise of a better run of seals somewhere further on.

Kean would be on deck, waiting word from him. It was up to Sam to make the move, when he had confidence enough in his own judgment, when he figured the Old Man had enough of waiting.

That first time in the barrel he only reluctantly gave up

the bracing, tonic air for the grime below. The Old Man was standing there, still the great burly figure of a man, when Sam set foot on deck. Gaulton, the master watch, brushed past him with a dirty look, and was halfway up the rope before Sam turned to Kean, realizing Kean wouldn't likely heed anything he was about to say.

'What do you make of it?'

'Starb'ard, about a mile,' Sam said grimly. For what it was worth.

'Not many men is made for the parlour.'

'Captain, sir!' yelled the master watch from up above. 'Young fat to star-r-r-b'ard!'

The Old Man roared with glee. 'Now then! What have you got to say for yerself, young Kennedy!'

Sam shook his head.

'Most aboard would sooner be dancin' about on ice pans than perched up there. Testin' you, that's what! And you come through the finest kind.'

'Yes, sir.'

'Go collar yerself some grub. And sharpen yer tally knife. We're in for a fine time at the swiles!'

The sealers could hardly break over the side fast enough. They took to it like men possessed. While he was waiting for the first load to be winched aboard, Sam made a hurried return trip to the barrel. He perched there for a few stolen minutes, seahawk's eye above the slaughter, a solitary man, witness to sealing men.

Six thousand pelts made for a wonderful fine time at the swiles.

Good luck and good judgment continued to the end of March. On March 30th the *Stephano* struck into the main herd, jolting spirits particularly high. Sam was steady at the tally sticks, notching them far into the night.

If the Captain had anything tormenting him it was whether his son Wes, captain aboard the *Newfoundland*, was having similar luck. Sam had noticed the Old Man raise the after-derrick. Sam suspected it was a signal to his son that the *Stephano* was thick into the fat and to set a course in his direction.

Sam looked in on the Marconi operator as he went by his station. 'What, no wireless aboard the *Newfoundland*?'

'Owners had the equipment hauled out. To save money. Skinflints.'

Kean took to the barrel himself, as slick up the ratlines as any of them, and when he descended he held no hope the *Newfoundland* would be able to maneuver any closer. The vessel was jammed solid in ice. While the Old Man's sealers were filling his ship with pelts, his son's had to be bound up in frustration. Kean could only guess at what his son would do next.

The following day the *Stephano*'s men were back on the ice as soon as dawn broke. At 9 o'clock that morning the Old Man had his answer to the raised after-derrick. The barrelman spotted sealers from the *Newfoundland*—by his estimate, more than a hundred—on the ice and heading their way. It was after eleven o'clock before they reached the *Stephano*.

'Come aboard, b'ys, for a mug-up!' called the Captain, peering down at them behind his fur coat, his sealskin mitts clapped to the rails. One by one the sealers scrambled aboard, dog-weary, but cheered by the expectation of food. They set their gaffs aside.

Hard bread and tea was all.

Sam stood before a stove, circled by steam rising from

several pots of steeping tea. A second crewman had the task of handing out cakes of hard bread. The sealers held together in a clump that shuffled rigidly forward. Sam faced one after another, a harried succession of disappointed men, no one among them with the courage to complain.

'Sam Kennedy.'

Sam looked into a face he recognized, though it was purple-red and raw from the walk over the ice.

'Mick Joy.' Sam smiled broadly, more in relief from the grimness of his task than any strong connection to the fellow. Although he was born in Harbour Main, Mick Joy had moved as a boy to Avondale. He was a few years older than Sam but they had encountered each other several times during Sam's excursions to Avondale to see Mary. Sam shouldn't have been surprised to encounter someone he knew. No doubt plenty more Conception Bay men had signed on with the *Newfoundland*.

Mick shifted to one side and talked on as Sam continued ladling the tea. He was fagged out from his long walk. It had taken them four hours and most of that over rough ice. Frustration had set in. They'd gone more than halfway when some of the men got it in their heads to turn back, panicked by the look of the sky, fearing they would get caught out in a storm.

'Lost their nerve,' said Mick. 'Not we fellers. A crack at the seals, that's what we's after,' sounding more resilient than he looked. 'Our trip's been pitiful so far, Sam. But we won't be goin' home paupers. Not if Abram Kean got anything to do wit' it.'

And right enough, it wasn't long before the *Stephano* steamed in sight of a herd of whitecoats. Kean glowed with satisfaction. 'That'll do ya, lads!' he called across the deck.

The few sealers left in line lost their chance at the bread and tea. The men of the *Newfoundland* made for their gaffs and were soon clumped together at the railing. Sam set the kettle back on the burner.

'Pan 'em, flag 'em, then head back to yer ship, b'ys!' Kean told them. Confident he had done his very best for his son.

Sam caught the eye of Mick Joy, caught the disbelief in every sealer about to descend the ladder, the last order ringing in their ears. The *Newfoundland* was a long way off. It had already started to snow.

'If the weather turns worse, we's supposed to spend the night aboard with ye fellows,' Mick said to Sam as he scuffed past him. 'That's what we been told. We can't be walking back if there's a starm.'

Not a single sealer questioned Kean. Not the second mate of the *Newfoundland*, in charge of the men. Kean was 'Admiral of the Fleet.' His words could just as well have descended from heaven.

By noon they were all on the ice, off in pursuit of seals, a few looking back grimly as the *Stephano* steamed off to pick up its own men. The wind began to rise and the snow grew thicker.

All day, hard at work, Sam felt his gut churning. Had Kean not checked the barometer? By the middle of the afternoon the *Stephano*'s men had panned and winced aboard a steady load of pelts. By the time the final man climbed over the rail the wind and snow had turned to a raging blizzard. It was late that evening before the last pelt was stowed away.

Sam was exhausted, but he couldn't put Mick Joy out of his mind. All around him men grumbled. Many had friends aboard the *Newfoundland*. Some had relatives. How had the poor devils fared? Getting caught on the ice in a blizzard would be a white hell. They'd never see their way back to their own ship.

Sam showed up in the wheelhouse and handed the Captain the tally sheet, his head clogged with doubt. Kean took the sheet, hardly looked at it or at Sam, and crammed it in a drawer with the others. He was in a rigid, foul mood.

Sam was about to, but in the end didn't open his mouth.

Back in the cabin word came from the master watch that the Old Man was sure the sealers from the *Newfoundland* had made it back to their own ship before nightfall.

'Got no fuckin' way of knowing!' Sam blurted out. No one answered him. Because every man aboard was thinking the same. Without wireless aboard the *Newfoundland* nothing was certain. Kean was making no bloody sense.

The men surrendered to it, struggled to settle in their bunks for the night. Suddenly the *Stephano*'s whistle blew. Then again five minutes later. And again five minutes after that.

'So there *is* fuckin' doubt in his mind.'

Sam ascended the narrow stairs, tightened his collar and edged forward, wind gusting fiercely through the deck. He slipped in among the few others near the railing. The ship had come back to the spot where the men from the *Newfoundland* had been dropped off. Torches cast light onto the ice, as much as they could through the squalling snow. Kean leaned past the rail and into the blizzard. He waited. Nobody around him moving an inch.

No men were sighted. No voices heard. Kean stood his ground, taking it as affirmation that no sealer from the *Newfoundland* had turned back, that they had all made it safely to their own vessel.

The grumblings in the bunks continued long into the

night, and resumed at first light the following morning.

The storm had not abated. Raging winds from the NNW lashed wet snow that turned to ice pellets. The weather was so poor Kean sent no one onto the ice until noon, and that through blinding snow squalls, and only to pick up seals that had already been panned.

The men of the *Stephano* spent most of the day waiting. They whispered the worst and in its gravity the resentment towards Kean intensified. Still no one spoke their minds to the Captain, not even the crewmen who served next to him day after day.

Sam had eaten his breakfast, as he had since he became the tally-man, with the stow boss, the bridge master, the master watch, engineers and scunners. A solemnness circled them all.

Kean sat at the far end of the table. 'Some wonderful black this marnin', ye crowd is!' He smacked down his mug impatiently, tea slopping over the table. 'Worried, are ye?'

No one answered. They ate breakfast without letup.

'Ye needn't be,' he said. 'Ye needn't fret like old women!'

He sat staring about the table, in his white collar and raffish waistcoat, its gold watch fob hanging loose. He smoked a cigarette, in an amber cigarette holder. From time to time he jerked ash onto the floor.

'Well?'

'Worried, yes, sir,' said Gaulton.

"Ye crowd don't know what worry is. Worry is goin' a week without seein' a sign of whitecoats. Worry is not fillin' yer hold when ye knows the seals be out there somewhere. Worry is stuck in ice and yer hold a quarter full. That's what worry is!'

He quit the table angrily. No one spoke. They finished

with their food and found work to do.

The day brought no news of the *Newfoundland*. According to the Marconi man neither the *Florizel* nor the *Bellaventure*, the two ironclads closest to them, knew anything more than they did. There was nothing to do but sit out the storm, locked solid in ice.

In the early evening, the storm ranting still, there grew in the cabin between decks the strains of "Will Your Anchor Hold." With each verse of the hymn the sealers' singing grew more and more robust. A bold, manful incantation refuting the uncertainty, defying the notion they could do nothing but sit idly by.

It riled Kean, though he said nothing. He shut himself away in his cabin. When he emerged he was, for the first while, oddly subdued, seemingly plotting the ship's course for when the storm finally lifted. He buried himself in his maps and charts and *Brown's Nautical Almanac*, maneuvering the dividers and parallel rulers about with the precision that came with his untold years at the helm. The man was in his element, indulging himself in the admiration of everyone who stood to one side and looked on.

The following day broke clear and frosty, with a stiff wind from the NW. The ice had slacked a bit. At 5:30 a.m. the ship began to move, though progress was slow.

The Captain was as keen as ever to get his men back to the business of sealing, but first he needed better sign of seals and a better channel through the ice to get to them. At 7:30 the barrelman came scurrying down the ropes. Kean was waiting for him.

'The *Newfoundland*, sir. She's flying a distress signal.'

'Are ye certain?'

'Yes, sir. She's much closer now.'

There was no argument. Immediately the Captain ordered two men onto the ice, to make their way to the *Newfoundland* and find out the situation.

They were back in an hour with the news.

'Not good, sir.'

'What is it, man?'

'The *Newfoundland*'s sealers, sir. They've been stranded on the ice for two days and nights. A few made it back this marnin' with the news. Captain Wes thought they was aboard the *Stephano*.'

The word raced through the ship. The men could barely deal with their anger. The Old Man dealt with it for them. He ordered every one of them onto the ice with food and drink and restoratives. The captains of other ironclads did the same.

On the ice the horrible news found human form. Deathly still and snow-swept, the man discovered by the search party Sam had joined could barely be distinguished from the white, ridged icescape in which they came upon him. Only his gaff, his mittened hand frozen around its shaft, set him apart. He was still alive, but barely, enfeebled by the cold and gravely frostbitten.

'Dead,' he mumbled, 'a lot of them. Frozen dead or dying.'

He'd been separated from his mates. Had wandered off on his own, or had given up and prepared himself to die, while the rest struggled on.

Pairs of searchers took turns lugging him over the jagged ice-field. A constant struggle to maintain their footing, but Sam and the others reached the *Stephano*, somehow got the fellow up the ladder and onto the deck, still alive.

The searchers took a quick mug-up of tea and bread,

before heading back to the ice again. By nightfall the crew of the *Stephano* had discovered and taken aboard four men of the *Newfoundland*.

Two were alive, two were frozen dead. The doctor helped the living as much as he could, gently thawing them and peeling away their piteous clothes, encasing them with heated blankets, as the pain of purple, frostbitten appendages took hold.

The ice-shrouded dead lay contorted the way they had died, frozen corpses beneath a frozen tarp on the deck of the ship, the corners weighed down to prevent the bodies sliding out from under it. The ship was in mourning and all the while its bow rammed against the massive wall of ice to get closer to the other vessels. It was a relentless pounding, a head butt ordered by a man who had gambled with common sense and lost.

The *Bellaventure* wired that it had picked up thirty-four men alive and fifty-eight bodies. The ship had no doctor aboard. By 10 p.m. the *Stephano* had managed to get close enough that the doctor walked over the ice to it.

All ships burnt down for the grievous night ahead.

The 3rd of April broke again with strong wind and heavy snow. A few hours later it turned to sleet. By mid-morning the *Stephano* finally reached the *Newfoundland*. Kean went onto the ice and walked to the ship to confer with his son.

Sam and Albert were at the rail when the figure of the Old Man reappeared on the ice, the cumbersome bear picking his way over the floes.

In the meantime the *Belladventure* and its gruesome cargo had drawn closer. The railing of the *Stephano* was thick with men anxious to lay eyes on what had now become a coffin ship.

Sam saw his chance and climbed the ratlines to the barrel.

The view through the spyglass slashed his heart. Dead sealers stacked on the foredeck of the *Belladventure* like pulpwood, body length atop body length, gaffs and rope coils ice-bound to them. Men clenched in frozen embrace, in their final, piteous effort to survive.

Sam brought his spyglass to bear on one face after another.

He stopped. There was no mistaking him.

The spyglass fell away and Sam's moistened eyes shut tight in the wind and the cold. His contempt was audible.

Kean shouldered no blame. Bore no guilt for not harbouring the men. What was he thinking?

Not four miles back to their ship! He thought it half that!

And no, ye crowd, the work of sealing must not falter.

Find another patch. Send men back on the ice. The *Stephano* will not turn for home with room yet in her hold.

'Not goin', sir. We has friends dead, sir.' A single man.

Then another. 'No, sir. 'Tis not right.'

Kean glared about the deck. Other men buckled under and jumped to the ice. Killed more seals. Dragged more pelts, hoisted them aboard.

Sam tallied them. Filled the tally sheet, handed it to Kean.

'And you, young Kennedy?'

Sam looked at him.

'Haven't the guts to back answer?'

Sam stood silent, his eyes holding off Kean's.

'A fellow yer age, he takes what comes. He bloody well makes a man of himself!'

The cabin seethed quiet. The first pelts aboard ripened, seal fat turned gelatinous, oil drained into the bilge, more with every motion of the ship. The stench was caustic, turned Sam to retching.

No one complained. A voiceless, damnable night. Dawn flared with fierce wind from the NW and heavy snow. The *Stephano* made little headway.

A week after seventy-seven men froze to death on the ice and the *Belladventure* had been ordered away with the bodies and the survivors, Kean commanded that his ship make for St. John's.

Sam and Albert went ashore with their gunny sacks to a city dumbfounded. Their share of the voyage—$59.17 each man. They paid off what they owed Bowring's, and each bought something to help drive the trip from their minds. The remainder tightly in their pockets, they found their way to the train station. They headed back as sealers, to the refuge of home.

II

THREE

ITwas an uneasy, disordered summer.

The weight of the *Newfoundland* disaster dissipated to no one's satisfaction. And then, when only a few months had passed, a potentially darker cloud began its slow passage over the island.

Neither Sam nor Albert had ever given much thought to war. They had no notion of it except for a scattered few stories of the Boer War. And now came headlines of something unfathomable: *The British Empire is at War and all Europe is Ablaze*. A sole copy of *The Daily News* had been sent from St. John's in advance of the recruiters, as if Harbour Main were so far-flung it needed proof. "*King George today addressed a message to all the British Colonies expressing appreciation of their spontaneous assurances that they will give the fullest support to the Motherland.*"

When the recruiters showed up Sam pitched even deeper into the fever of the moment. He and a dozen more were addressed by a stiffly uniformed, moustached officer of the St. John's Catholic Cadet Corps. Leather gloves, ash stick, braided visor hat, and leather Sam Browne strapped tightly across his chest, he paraded before them with no greater zeal than if he had actually been to a war himself.

Even so there was no escaping the vehemence of his message. 'You young men are part of the greatest Empire the world has ever known! At this very moment your compatriots in England, in Australia, in Canada and Singapore are queuing in their thousands, craving to fend off the German hordes who have invaded Belgium. Fiends who think nothing of chasing down innocent women and children and impaling them on their bayonets!'

Sam had known craving, had known its power over him, right and wrong. Now another craving muscled into his mind.

'They can have their wars if they wants,' said Paddy, one of the few dissenters. 'Belgium. I don't know no Belgium.'

'It's so far away,' said Margaret, who viewed with suspicion anything out of sight of Harbour Main. 'You'll miss Newfoundland something terrible.'

Their ignorance goaded him. Opportunity that promised space and comradeship and unimaginable times. So far beyond the finality of home that his mind leapt at the prospect. That and the promise of a wage of a dollar a day and whatever grub a man could eat. It left Sam desperate to once more feel the rogue.

Albert wasn't so sure.

'You can't be a slacker, Al. You can't be hangin' back when so many fellas is answerin' the call. You and me, together.'

'Sealin' is one thing…'

'You can't be missin' out. Not on the women.'

'What women?'

'There's bound to be women.'

'You don't know.'

Albert was seeing a girl, Cora. It wouldn't likely amount to much, not as far as Sam could tell, not if Albert had any sense. To Sam she was plain as a stump, and had about as much life in her.

'What about your old man, Sam?'

'What about him? I'll be sending money home.'

'He needs you.'

Just like Albert's father needed him was what he was saying. Not something Sam was willing to admit. He had his own life to live and he was needed in the Regiment as much as anyone. They were all leaving home, the whole lot of them.

'You got yourself, Al, when it comes down to it. That's what you got. You can't be livin' your life for someone else.'

Albert wasn't buying it. He made out he was wavering, but his mind was set. Nobody would think him any less a man for staying back to fish and feed his family. 'You go, Sam. If you got to go, you go.'

It would never be the same between them. When Sam left Harbour Main in the first week of September, to walk to Avondale and board the train, he didn't bother to search out Albert. It hadn't been enough that he had come to see that Albert was right, that Albert's family needed him.

As for his own father and Margaret, they would make do as best they could. They'd have his money. It would offset any help he could be to them. When he said his good-bye he handed his father the ten-dollar bill he had managed to hold onto from his time at the seal hunt, leaving Sam with enough to get himself into St. John's and little else.

Paddy held doggedly to the notion that it was all a distant, unknowable scheme to lure young men out of the outports and into St. John's and there trap them into thinking war was good for them. The man had struggled all his life for what little he had and now even part of that was being wrenched away.

'What has your Empire done for us, Sam? Answer me that. You name me one thing and I'll call you a liar.'

Sam cast it aside as the rant of an illiterate man. He stood in front of Paddy and shook his hand and wished him well. He embraced his sister loosely and told her to take good care of herself and their father. Then left home for the first time without knowing when, if ever, he would return.

Sam showed up at the Armory in St. John's as he had been told to do, to set pen to attestation paper and get poked and prodded and declared fit to wear the caribou badge of the Newfoundland Regiment.

On August 22nd had come a Proclamation of Enlistment and within ten days the list of volunteers was in the hundreds. Tents for a Regimental training camp were erected on the fields of Pleasantville, near the shores of Quidi Vidi Lake, which a few weeks before had been teeming with citizens reveling in the annual St. John's Regatta. Sam found himself in a city very different from the one to which he had arrived in the spring, found himself caught up in a furor for war far out of proportion to anything he expected.

'Isn't it all the greatest game and you have to be part of it, lad?' said the fresh-faced officer behind the desk. All starch and vinegar. Hardly any older than Sam.

Sam had no fear of war, no more than he did of heights. And that was all he knew to compare it to. That chance of falling, sure enough, of being killed, but as long as you keep your head about you, keep a steady hand, as long as you didn't take foolish chances, then there had to be a logic to it.

You learn your part and learn it well. You and your rifle. A steady hand, a steady eye. You make friends among the ranks, but all for all you have yourself.

'You won't be letting down your country, not you, not a strapping young fellow like yourself?'

There were those few—Coaker among them—who said their country had been the one to let *them* down. Beware of the shame of sending half-starved fishermen to fight. That's what Sam heard aboard the train into the city. But in St. John's, where life was a lot more than fish, Coaker's words were dimmed by Regimental fever and eventually even he succumbed. The outport recruits marched valiantly over the fields of Pleasantville with his blessing.

In the end Sam did the proper thing. He signed the papers and swore the oath. Stripped naked and submitted to the doctor's hands and his rant of questions. It didn't take long, not for a man who didn't hesitate on an answer, not for one in such solid shape. Had he been a Catholic Cadet he would have been a stride ahead in becoming an officer. As it was, they told him, he'd not be long in the lower ranks, as if it were a question that needed answering right away.

Pleasantville had once been a cricket pitch, and before that a city of tents for those left homeless by the great fire that ravaged St. John's some twenty years before.

Now it was a city of tents again. The recruits for the Regiment were under canvas, in training for the time it took to get them organized, outfitted, and aboard a ship for England. Bordered by Quidi Vidi on one side, Virginia Waters on another, and the rest by slapdash wooden fencing, it was a makeshift home for adventure-beggared young men, in their half uniforms, their ragged hats and home-knit salt-and-pepper caps. Wound about their lower legs, just above their hobnailed boots, were blue puttees, made of the only colour of flannel the Women's Patriotic Association could find.

Ten men to a tent in fifty white bell tents and fifty more of various frames and sizes. Sam showed up at a broad marquee flying the Union Jack, the tent he singled out as looking more official than any other. He was welcomed like a man blessed, shed of all his civilian sins. He was now sheltered in the company of comrades, in an enclave of guiltless innocents, resolute and ready for whatever the inevitable march-off would hand them.

What those in charge lacked in the way of the furnishings of war they made up for in boldness and efficiency. Sam was assigned to B Company, his name falling straight onto the list without hesitation, slotted consummately into the Regiment.

Sam cut a good figure even in the piecemeal khaki—the lank, rawboned outport lad, sporting still a lick of his black hair while most other men had theirs cut short. It ran errant across his forehead, out from under the fedora he had bought in St. John's on impulse when he came off the *Stephano*. His hair remained a mark of who he was and he would hold to it until the day some rulebook sergeant gave him hell and ordered it cut. He was Sam Kennedy, his own man, pliable enough to be recast by military life.

In his days under canvas the mate Sam drew closest to was not from Newfoundland at all, but from Labrador. His name was Johnny Gilbert.

Johnny was slightly shorter than Sam, and a bit stouter. Like Sam, he loved his fedora. And like Sam, found himself with a life very different from what he had known. In the case of Johnny Gilbert—half solitary trapper, half workman with the Grenfell Mission.

Johnny's father had come from Scotland, making his way down the coast of Labrador to Lake Melville, where it was warmer in summer and where there was soil for growing vegetables. There he found Johnny's mother and married her. He fished, of course, and trapped in winter. Johnny had done the same, but then in summer took work with the Mission. The summer before it landed him in St. Anthony, a few miles across the Strait of Belle Isle to the northernmost tip of Newfoundland, where the Mission had established its head-quarters.

Sam knew little of the Grenfell Mission, only the name, a passing mention of it by his father. From Johnny he learned a good deal more.

A young doctor, Wilfred Grenfell, had come from England in 1892. What he found was a string of isolated villages in northern Newfoundland and southern Labrador in dire need of medical care. The man had a frightful energy for change. 'He went off to New York and Boston and Montreal, and to London,' Johnny said. 'He raised thousands to build hospitals.' Grenfell altered the face of the coast. Johnny grew up hearing his name uttered in adoration that only grew in intensity with each hospital and nursing station that followed. 'And he's set up cooperatives for the fishermen.'

He told Sam how some places had done away with the need for a merchant, had joined together and bought supplies and sold their fish on their own.

'True, Johnny?' Sam devoured every word.

Grenfell set his mark, his Mission, deeply into the life of the North Atlantic coast. Indeed it was the Mission staff from England that roused the local young men to joining up, Wilfred

Grenfell chief among them. According to Sam he preached of a man's duty to England as staunchly as he preached of a man's duty to God.

It was Johnny's stories of his winter months in the woods that solidified their friendship. Johnny had held these stories back from Sam until he felt sufficiently comfortable with him. He liked the fact that Sam listened, that he didn't say much, just held on to the end, even if there was no great story to be told. They sometimes sat in silence, neither of them with a need to fill the space.

And when it seemed the trust between them was deep enough it led to other stories. Sam's turn away from his father, his time at the seal hunt. Johnny's capture of a silver fox and the great price it fetched, his time in New York where Grenfell had arranged for him to go, to the Pratt Institute for eight months to learn machine repair. It was where he had acquired his fedora.

'Johnny,' Sam said, 'you're no raw-ass recruit. You've been places.'

Johnny felt good about that. Felt good he had seen sights no other fellow in their tent had seen. He told Sam about New York, made it seem he half-liked it there. Over the days that followed, Sam could tell where Johnny's heart was, and it wasn't New York. Just like Sam's was no longer Harbour Main, although in Sam's case he didn't know where the hell it might truly be.

When enough time had passed Sam talked about women. When it was Johnny's turn there was no half-whispered swagger, which made Sam's exploits with Sarah seem all the more callow.

Johnny held out a photograph of a young woman, and

there was nothing fabricated about her. Johnny didn't say anything about the liking he had for his girl. It was all in him having the picture, in how he treasured it.

The photograph was small, cream-coloured, with a deck-led edge. When Sam held it between his thumb and forefinger his eyes deepened. Her name was Emma and she stood leaning against a doorframe, one hand holding a small book. She wore a printed summer dress that held to her in a way he had rarely seen on a woman, in an outport or anywhere. Her stylish good looks caught him unprepared, as if the picture hadn't really come from Johnny. It was her features more than anything, at once fresh and mature, elegant yet vulnerable, and benevolent, if he could judge by the simple smile.

She was all those things and it was only a picture. Sam held it for a long time, and when he looked up he could see Johnny was growing impatient to have it back.

'She's marvelous, Johnny.'

The fellow's smile returned and he placed the picture carefully inside its envelope and then slipped the envelope inside his breast pocket. Sam wanted to know more about the girl, but he knew better than to ask questions straight away. He and Johnny would need to know each other even better before the fellow would think him deserving of answers.

The photograph remained with both of them long after it had been put away. It did them good to think of a woman who had the Regiment in her mind, at a time when, contrary to what Sam had told Albert, recruits would likely not see much of women for months on end.

Their days now were all about themselves, getting in a shape to march off and board the ship that would take them across the North Atlantic. The open fields of Pleasantville were their first training grounds, their taskmasters keen to toughen them to the degree that they would prove no embarrassment to whatever English general would eventually take them on. It was a rigorous regime of calisthenics and route marches, target practice and, once they were up to it, games of dragging the iron weight of gun carriages over the rock-strewn South Side Hills. It shed what little fat there was, set in its place sinewy muscle, made of them hardened men of rank and habit.

At the end of the day, darkness settling in by early evening, any other life was a long way off. What they had was the lingering glow of the tents' white canvas, clumps of men outside, the light-smudge of their cigarettes marking the chill. And in the distance the fading outline of Signal Hill and its Cabot Tower, where Marconi had first pulled in wireless Morse code from across the Atlantic. One of the men had made the trek to the hill after it happened, then a boy of ten. England seemed not so far away after all.

Then the day came in October to board the S.S. *Florizel*, the very same vessel that a few months before had been to the seal hunt. They were ready to a man and the march through the streets of St. John's proved a tumultuous affair. The citizenry turned out in numbers that hadn't been seen since the visit in 1901 of the Royals, their King George and Queen Mary. The march routed them past the grounds of Government House where Governor Davidson stood on a platform and delivered his heap of praise, together with the expectation that the battlefield would produce heroes, in numbers to make their little Dominion stand as tall as any in the Empire.

Onto the *Florizel*, another dame of the Bowring's fleet of steamships, marched 540 men, the first contingent into the war, the Blue Puttees as they were called. A second contingent would be but four months behind them. Sam was every bit as proud as any man standing near him. If that should be Johnny, all the better, for the pair had made a pact to see each other through the war and turn up together back in Newfoundland, whenever that might be. They swore they would and there it was, as if just making the alliance would cause it to unfold the way they wanted it to.

Some distance outside the harbour their vessel joined three dozen others, a headstong brood of grey Canadian ships with 30,000 men and their 8,000 horses, bound for the coast of England. The *Florizel* tucked in with them, the last transport in the port column, determined to hold her own, suddenly the smallest of the lot.

Sam and Johnny stood together against the railing. They sailed into something for which they had made no allowance. Day after day they peered into the grey, roiling ocean and often nothing passed their eyes but the carcasses of horses. Three and four a day, dead in their crowded holds, cast overboard, sculpted giants awash in the swell, their vast strength ignobly spent. So many graceless hulks of flesh, led to so inapt and premature an end.

By seven most evenings, orders came for lights out, an ungodly hour to bunk down for the night. Most men did, even though what some had for sleeping quarters was little better than what had held the carcasses of seals a few months before. The lingering stench of seal oil uprooted memories in Sam, triggering a fight to escape them.

He and Johnny donned their greatcoats and drifted furtively about, finding their way on deck. The icy breath of the North Atlantic snaked into the gaps of the ill-fitting coats, the pair clenching tight the collars to meet their woolen caps. They managed to slink into a spot of shelter on the starboard bow. Out there somewhere was the rest of the convoy, confirmed only by the vague sighting of black smokestacks against a near black sky.

Some were still saying the Newfoundlanders would never get to experience any of it, that the war would be over before the turn into the new year. Yet who aboard knew anything for certain? And what the hell was the point in asking questions? The officers had no more answers than they did.

Officer—who would want to be an officer? Neither Sam nor Johnny thought of themselves as keeners who would rise through the ranks and get themselves ash sticks and bars on their sleeves, and look like they were on top of it all. The Regiment had plenty eager to take the role, men who back in St. John's had come through the ranks of the Catholic Cadets or the Methodist Guards or the Church Lad's Brigade. Some had merchant money in their step, though, it was true, not all.

Decent 'chaps,' most of them. Though to Sam and Johnny and the others of the lower ranks no one was ever a 'chap.' They were mates. Chums of a particular sort. Buddies and all of a Regiment.

They thought more of getting past what excitement was ahead of them and what they would be doing once it was over. Johnny would be back in St. Anthony and back to his Emma.

'You'll marry her?'

'We have plans.'

'Well then, you're all set. You sonofabitch of a lucky man.'

It left Johnny smiling.

'She's a looker, Johnny. Where's she from?'

'Labrador. From Red Bay. The Grenfells hired her to help with their children. When they're away she works at the handicrafts.'

Grenfell had set up what he called Industrials, to encourage the production of handmade crafts. The women along the coast had become particularly well known for the quality of their hooked mats. Sometimes Emma was the one to put together and distribute mat-hooking kits, collect the work when it was finished, and arrange for its sale in the States and Canada.

'She's got a head on her shoulders, Johnny.'

'She has.'

Sam winked at him. 'And a smart figure to go along with it.'

Sam was edging into private territory, but Johnny didn't mind. There wasn't a man who didn't like it when his girl was the envy of other men.

Johnny took out the picture again, though it was too dark to see. To tease Sam as much as anything. Sam reached for it, but Johnny slipped it back in its envelope. 'Get your own girl, bucko.'

'I did, and more than once.' Sam groaned suggestively.

Johnny didn't bite. He put the picture away with a grin and a playful curl of his fist in Sam's face.

'You're a decent chum,' Sam said. 'And a proper bugger.'

The next evening they teamed up with a half dozen others to sing a pair of songs for the amateur concert—"My Bonnie Lies Over the Ocean" and "Old Black Joe." Johnny had a new harmonica he had bought at a music shop on Water Street before they boarded the *Florizel*. He had a way with it too and he'd sometimes take it out and play a few tunes, nodding for Sam to sing along, which he did to what parts he knew, humming his way to the end.

They landed in England and with each day of training the bonds between the men grew even stronger—first on Salisbury Plain, then Fort George and Stobs Camp and Aldershot.

Getting themselves into proper uniforms was the start of it, stowing away any traces of their old selves, any bits and pieces of gear from their boyish brigades back home, their wool hats and sashes and the blue puttees that had only invited mockery. They turned themselves out as men of the Newfoundland Regiment in their regulation khakis, summoned into fighting trim, their caribou badge spit-and-polished to a gleam. Soldiers they were now, as fiercely independent as any other regiment to come in sight of them. Not Canadians and to a man as keen as any regiment of Brits.

A Ross rifle like another limb now, and if there was one thing that made them raw and restless soldier men it was their grip on that rifle, whether it be through the infernal rain and mud of Salisbury Plain or in the centre of the parade square in Edinburgh. In the end it was all alike to them. They made up Newfoundland's only regiment, odd men out in the grand scheme where a country's regiments measured in the dozens and, in the case of cocksure old Britannia, a hundred and more.

After three months on Salisbury Plain, the Regiment marched off to board a train for Scotland. They passed Stonehenge on the way, for the lower ranks their first and last sighting of it. It fell to Sam to tell Johnny what he knew of Stonehenge, which wasn't much. On the coast of Labrador Johnny had sometimes seen clusters of icebergs not far off that shape, without the horizontal slabs across the top of course. It wouldn't do to say he was no more impressed by Stonehenge than by icebergs, for that smelled of homesickness. What he did tell Sam was that he had come upon great columns of sea stacks once when he was walking a shoreline alone, hunting seals, and he'd never forgotten it, what with a stunted fir tree growing out the top of one of them.

'You'd never believe where a tree can grow, Sam.'

Johnny would say things sometimes with an urgency, after which Sam would smile but add nothing, thinking the fellow's mind was removed from every other in the Regiment. That it must have something to do with growing up in the way he had, that spending months alone put things in his head in private and peculiar ways.

Johnny had few other friends, except for those from the northern coasts whom he had known prior to the war and who had joined up at the same time he did. A fellow by the name of Archie Ash, a lance corporal in the other Company, another named Simms, and Wakefield, the English doctor who had served with Grenfell's Mission.

Wakefield had been to the Boer War and bolted up the ranks to Captain by the time they arrived on Salisbury Plain. He was chief Medical Officer and liked to display his starch every morning by standing naked in the out of doors, no matter how freezing the temperatures, soaping himself head to foot, then whipping away the soap with pans of rainwater from a barrel nearby. In Sam's mind he was a keener of the most irritating sort.

Johnny went along with the man's incessant attention to cleanliness and kept up a roughened soldierly façade in his presence, but he didn't show any disappointment when eventually Wakefield took a transfer to the Royal Army Medical Corps.

If there was a stint of their time in Scotland that Sam and Johnny took to, it was the Regiment's encampment in Edinburgh Castle. They were the only soldiers from outside Scotland to ever be garrisoned there, they were told, repeatedly, then warned to steer clear of any hijinks after-hours that might tarnish the Regiment's reputation. The barrack rooms were stone cold, but at least they were dry and for the most part free of vermin. Some days there seemed no end to the route marches and disciplinary drills, but when they found themselves with the freedom to roam about Edinburgh there was hardly a corner of it that escaped them.

Johnny lingered in places where the others did not, often taking time to make a record of it in his notebook. One Saturday he ventured into the Royal Museum and when Sam encountered him afterwards on the steps outside he was looking particularly intent, having only just put away his pen.

'Your girl then, Johnny, she's interested in museums?' Sam said to him, for no more than a chuckle.

Johnny didn't seem to hear. 'Skulls, Sam, they got skulls of Beothuks in there.'

'From back home?'

'Some fellow Cormack brought them from Newfoundland in 1827 it says. Beothuks all dead long ago and the museum got two skulls in a showcase.' Johnny could hardly comprehend it. 'So far from their home and no proper grave.'

Sam had never heard Johnny talk so much about anything.

'If I get killed, Sam, bury me. Put me deep in the ground. Promise me, Sam.'

Sam laughed at him and shook his head, but in the end he promised him. 'Yes, Johnny, swear to God.'

Sam was spending almost all his off-hours with Johnny. Nobody but Sam bothered to understand his moods.

Once he took him on in a wrestling match, in part to wrench him out of a bout of missing home. It was part of a succession of such matches to determine their company's champ. They wrestled bare-chested in an open field, encircled by the other men from B Company, jeering and cheering them on, the referee crouched to the ground to see who pinned who into submission.

They sweated and strained, grunted like they had the best of intentions, but in the end lost heart for it, until the referee gave up on them in disgust and called it a draw. They walked away, their skin smarting red, their muscle wrenched sore, the pair better friends than ever.

In Edinburgh—the only place where the Regiment had much luck with women—Sam had a night of it, but one only, enough that he came away thinking himself as canny at it as the next fellow.

Johnny held back, indifferent to trying to set himself up. Sam came to think it was better that way—to have someone waiting for you, to have that good a reason for getting past the pit of endless drill and training. The relief of stretching your mind past the distance, to fixate on so absolute a reason for making it back home. When the mere notion of seeing someone again was so strong it overwhelmed the worst of everything. Johnny had that much, and as for himself, he had family in Harbour Main. Needless to dwell on it. It wasn't the same.

Sam was shown the picture of Emma once more, and it was time enough to fix it in his head, fix the notion that so far away she could be as much his as Johnny's. He imagined her, just as Johnny imagined her, and there grew to be times he wrapped himself in her as much as Johnny did.

When there was just the two buddies, killing time, Sam asked more questions about her. Johnny's answers never amounted to much. It was his way and Sam expected nothing different. He liked it, the relationship between Johnny and the girl—an unknowable thing. That somehow sanctioned another, equally far-off right to her.

Johnny sensed that his friend's interest was more than a passing one. It was odd at first to Sam that Johnny would accept it, without jealousy or malice. Without the reflex of anger at the core. A favor for his friend, but something more than that—for Johnny a way of validating his choice of her. If he could win her he was the equal of any man.

Besides, he did not tell Sam her full name. Without it, and without the vow of her kiss, Johnny freely shared with his friend the woman he cherished. Sam couldn't ever come to know her in the way that Johnny did, wouldn't ever return to where she lived, would never be more than worlds apart. He'd let Sam imagine her. He'd do that much for his closest friend.

In an Edinburgh photography studio the Regiment's platoons had their portraits taken, groups of a dozen or more men stiffly uniformed, some bare-headed, a few in the wool caps they had worn aboard the *Florizel*, remnants of home to set themselves apart. At once fishermen and loggers, store clerks and men destined for the family business, men who had lived in hovels, men who had lived in mansions, and men who wrote poetry and men who couldn't sign their names.

They were set in three rows against a vaguely painted forest scene and a few wrinkled folds of a black, threadbare curtain. The back row stood, arms at their sides or behind their backs. The middle row was seated, two of the men perhaps casually on the broad arms of a middle chair to break the monotony of the pose. The foreground row sat cross-legged on the floor, arms folded.

In the portrait of their platoon Sam was seated in a single chair at one end of the middle row, Johnny on the floor just in front of him. Sam's two hands rested, one on each of Johnny's shoulders. The men were expected not to smile and everyone was able to, as hard as it was.

Until it was over, when they turned back to something of themselves. Never again would they be so formally drawn, nor expected to pose all looking so alike. They hoped it could be truly that, an indelible structure of men, woven together.

It still had not been revealed what lay ahead for them. As the weeks passed they grew more and more anxious to get to it, whatever it was. And in August of 1915, by which time they had moved to Aldershot for a final polish on their training, the Regiment stood for inspection before Lord Kitchener and were told, 'I am sending you to the Dardanelles!' The men cheered. 'Sharpen those bayonets for the Turks!' They cheered louder.

'Turks?' Johnny said when they fell out of formation. 'What the hell is a Turk?'

FOUR

SURE as hell it was different. The photograph showed them in shorts and wide-rimmed sun helmets wound with a muslin puggaree. It showed Sam atop the hump of a camel, the animal's legs knobby stilts, holding the soldier high above Johnny and two others of the Regiment standing in the foreground. Smiling idlers leaning against the thick necks of a pair of camels which had settled down flat to the sand. Crouched between them was a dark, bearded fellow in the sweep of a white robe, balancing himself with his walking stick. The Great Sphinx of Giza towered behind. And behind it—the colossal stone diamond of the Pyramid of Khafre.

In the heat of Cairo Sam clamored for the Dardanelles. It took the Aussies to set his prospects straight. The war-crusted Aussies were about to rejoin their regiment at Cape Helles, at the tip of the Gallipoli Peninsula.

'The flies are worse, mate,' said a Queensland sergeant. 'The heat no better. You can cool your arse in the ocean if the

Turks don't strafe a fuckin' piece of it first.' He shook his head. Lifted his beer in an exaggerated toast.

The troop ship *Megantic* had stopped in Alexandria, and the men transported inland to barracks in Abbassia, on the outskirts of Cairo. When they weren't parading in the sweltering heat, they had free run of the city. They fell in with Australians on leave, men who had endured hell on the Gallipoli Peninsula since April. First came decent beer—something other than the Egyptian 'camel's piss'—and then the eternal question.

'Where can a fellow get a good piece of tail?'

The Aussies had their laughs at that one and pointed them in the direction of Wazzir where brothels lined the streets—five and six stories high some of them. Half-naked, makeup-encrusted harlots lounging at the open windows, enticing the sex-starved soldiers of a dozen countries.

'Get all you want, mate,' another Aussie told the gang of Newfoundlanders who showed up. 'And more besides.' Then winked at Sam.

'The clap,' moaned Hughie Walsh from C Company who claimed he'd been the high liner when the Regiment was in Scotland. 'The jeezley clap.'

The Aussie told them there was an army hospital in Abbassia that treated nothing but blokes with VD.

'Jesus.' Sam felt every ounce of desire abandon him.

'You don't want your dick to rot and fall off,' grunted Walsh, his bluster suddenly deflated. The man knew his limits.

Johnny had been nowhere near the place and when Sam related the story he was met with a taunting, self-satisfied smirk that turned into the most raucous laughter they'd shared since leaving home.

A fellow needed a sense of humour to withstand the heat, which grew even more ferocious when the Regiment uprooted from Abbassia and marched off to encamp themselves in the desert near Heliopolis. So hot that parades were held only during early morning and late afternoon. At midday no one ventured outside, but occupied themselves with idle talk inside their double-roofed marquee tents that each held several dozen men. Idle talk that turned monotonous and made Sam and Johnny and every other man long to be done with Egypt.

'Give us the Front. We came to fight Turks, not dawdle about the Pyramids.'

The Front came in the dead early hours of the 20th of September, 1915. The thrust to landing on the beach at Suvla Bay aboard wide, flat-bottomed lighters. Each carrying two hundred men, shoulder-tight for hours, through blackness but for a pair of red and green lights far off their port side, a hospital ship anchored outside Anzac Cove. The mere mention of the cove roused them to a man. Then, as if the Empire had arisen from the Aegean in support, came flare and thunder from the Royal Navy, heaving the guts of its 15-inch guns inland.

The shells exploded, flashed alight a fraction of the landscape. Godless hill country, not the flat farmland they'd heard about from the Brits coming back from France. The twilight bared craggy, scrub-covered hills. No disappointment to Sam. Nor Johnny, who knew the like in Labrador. And now the desert heat was behind them. There was even the touch of a salt-water breeze.

The lighter grounded several yards from shore. Over the sides they jumped, as orderly as their knotted brains could manage. Up to their knees in water, piss-warm and promising, in the madness to get themselves to the beach. The excitement, clogged in the pit of their stomachs, drained out of them.

No show of innocence. They ploughed through seawater, loaded down with battle kit and three days rations. And ashore they were, but not a bad place as far as anyone could tell. Before the day was over they'd get a swim out of it, or someone said.

Nunns, orderly man for the day, made no such promises. Too much straightening away to be done. Daylight was abroad before the last of the Newfoundlanders struck Kangaroo Beach, while to their left and to their right were swarms of others still on the move. Aussies by the look of it. And colonials of another stripe—Sikhs they were told. Whoever the hell they might be. Bullying a herd of mules out of the water.

Onto the finger pier came the weight of war. Guns and ammunition, food, water tanks, horse troughs, hospital tents, and countless more adding to the jumbled stockpiles that already crammed the beach. An armory and depot for the thousands heading inland.

There were Turks in the hills for damn sure. Field glasses trained on the brazen commotion. On infidels strutting about the beach as if *their* God had confirmed a right to it. As if they were something more than thieving fools.

The answer struck Sam like the howl of a train over an iron trestle. Pitched with ungodly rupture. A squall of shrapnel burst overhead, striking out a hundred turns. Piercing whoever had the damned luck to be near it.

Sam cowered, then threw himself flat to the sand. He raised his head. The blare of mules filled his ears. Gut-cramping yelps where shrapnel had sliced their hides.

It was Australian troops who got it, and some New-foundlanders. Captain Rendell, the battalion adjutant, had hardly made it onto the beach when shrapnel sent him back from where he came, and straight to the hospital ship.

'Dig yourselves in, boys!' screeched Lieutenant Nunns. 'And be goddamn quick about it!'

They hauled off their packs. Each man mad at it with his entrenching tool. Sam flattened himself, squirmed into the sand, used his hands to clear away room for his head, capped his head and face with his helmet. Every man the same unless shrapnel got him first. Or one of the heavies. They struck the sand and obliterated everybody and everything, opening craters six-feet deep.

No one would lie there forever. When the shelling slacked, Sam jerked himself up and out of it, grabbed his pack and stumbled over the sand, chasing orders.

Baptism the boys in the other regiments called it. *Yer fucking baptism.* You Newfoundlanders are soldiers now. You got the open wounds to prove it. Now gripe all you want about the fucking war.

Numbers nothing like the Aussies and New Zealanders and Brits who came ashore at Anzac Cove and Cape Helles four months before, but plenty enough misery to earn respect.

Captain Rendell was gone and a couple dozen with him, though none dead yet. Two days later McWhirter was the first. D Company. Shell straight down on him. Then Hardy from A Company, bullet through the head. And Jack Blyde. Another sniper job. Sam and Johnny both knew Blyde, trained with him, did guard duty with him in Edinburgh. The first of their Company to get it. The stretcher-bearers passed Sam by on the way to the dressing station. But Blyde was dead by then, had to be with what the bullet did to his brains. The Turk knew what to look for. The boys had been careless, didn't know any better, paid the price.

Sam was on the Gallipoli Peninsula no more than an hour when he had it figured out. It wasn't any soldiering skill that would get him through. It was luck. The wrong place at the wrong time and it would be him to get the bullet with his name on it.

He'd keep his head about him. Nothing foolish. The Turk had his rifle cocked, his eye set. Heed the warnings, never trust the sly bastards for a second. The rest was luck, pure and simple.

On top of that, it was luck what the bullet did to a man. Got him to the hospital ship, or with the best luck, the hospital in Mudros and back then to England.

Sam learned it all quick enough.

That first day, when the Turks laid off their shelling, the Regiment worked its way up Essex Ravine and dug into the hillside, out of the eye of the enemy except for the few lads dodging back and forth to the beach for food and supplies. The Regiment soon had its own christening of the gully. Newfoundland Ravine it would be from then on. The Essex had moved out and, as the grubby few stragglers said, they didn't give a pinch of shit what anyone called it after they were gone. 'Yer welcome to it, boys, every fuckin' square inch of it.'

The dugouts were cut in the shadow of *Karakol Dagh*. The men had their own names for it, as they did for the other peaks that topped the rock-ribbed landscape beyond the beach and Suvla Plain. Sam memorized the Turk names, asking officers until he found one who said what sounded right.

There were generally two men to a dugout, home when they weren't in the front lines. Shoveled and shaped into the hillside, livable if they had the chance to make it that. A few scraps of timber to reinforce the walls, an empty wooden box scrounged off the cooks for a table and, as good fortune and persistence had it, a piece of corrugated iron for the roof. With sandbags on top of that not a scrap of shrapnel would make it through. Peace of mind for the men inside, except if one of the heavies dropped dead on top of them.

Compared to Sam, Johnny was more than used to roughing it in the outdoors. Building a lean-to of spruce boughs after an all-day trek through the Labrador woods in heat and blackflies was hardly less a sweat than cutting through clay soil to fix up a dugout. What they both wanted was comfort, in whatever measure was possible. If nothing else, what they got was clean and respectable. Each of them naively determined to keep it that way.

Two days after their landing on the beach at Suvla Bay, B Company was marched into the front line trenches, to spend time with what was left of the Dublin Fusiliers, whose job it was to prime them to take over the firing line. The Dublins were an easygoing crowd, charmed to discover that a good many of the Newfoundlanders, like Sam, had names and accents freely traced back to Ireland. When Johnny told them his father came from Scotland, it was almost as good. At least it wasn't bloody England.

The first thing Ryan did was land a hand firmly on Johnny's head and leave it there until Johnny felt the pressure in his shoulders. Sam looked on. It was as much for him as it was for Johnny. 'That bit between yer eyes and my hand,' Ryan told them, 'that's what the Turk is after. Before yer eye catches him, he's had hes sights on that much of ya. The careless ones— that's where they get it.'

No harm being reminded. Sam told him about Hardy, about Blyde.

One of them had been wearing the bowl-shaped sun

helmet. Dead give away. To a man, B Company stowed away the fool things before heading to the trenches. It was back to their regular helmets and their caps when they were out of the line. They liked it when the caribou head was showing, their cap badge, with *Newfoundland* embossed under it. Nobody had to ask where they were from, even if they had to be explaining where it was exactly.

The Regiment showed up in the trenches with their notions of the Turks, but here the buggers were now beyond the lip, in gunsight, in some places but a few dozen yards away. Sam caught sight of his first one that first night. Or what he thought was one. While he and Ryan were on sentry duty, Ryan half asleep. Sam couldn't be sure at night.

Ryan had a quick look, and slouched back 'That's him.'

Sam gripped his rifle, his training taking hold.

'Leave the bugger be,' muttered Ryan. He crouched down and lit a cigarette, covering the flare of the match as best he could. 'Part of a buryin' party. We give 'em that much. They'd do the same for us.'

Not what Sam thought would happen when he saw his first Turk.

Nor the bullet that cracked past his head.

'Jesus, Mary, and Joseph! Don't listen, do ya! Sniper'll have yer fuckin' brains splattered on the trench floor!'

Sam had the luck that first time. Paid more mind the next. Had a way about him after that, never trusting to reason, or to anything but his wits. His senses sharpened as if he'd inhaled a lungful of icy, spruce-scented air. He shrugged off Ryan, though they were trench mates still for the couple of days. Sam drew into himself. In the end, if he got through, it would be fucking luck for sure.

On the 30th of September the Newfoundlanders replaced the South Wales Borderers, in the centre position of the five-mile front. To one side of the Brigade were the Anzacs, and to the other the impossible hill of *Kiretch Tepe Sirt*, then beyond that the Aegean Sea. Ahead of them, in the eastern sky, towered *Tekke Tepe* Ridge, infested with Turks and impossible to penetrate without sacrificing whole regiments. The Anzacs had tried in August, and pulled back desperately depleted. Sam overheard a pair of officers eagerly debating the possibility of the Newfoundlanders mounting an offensive to take the Ridge. Commanding Officer Burton had proposed that very thing to General Hamilton, head of the forces on Gallipoli. 'Single-handedly' Burton had said, according to what the officers recounted, hardly able to contain their disbelief. The General denied the request. And choked back a laugh, Sam suspected, given that Hamilton knew firsthand the hell the Anzacs had suffered.

Sam and Johnny had been on the Peninsula less than a week when they themselves encountered Hamilton. The General showed up near the front lines from time to time, entourage in tow, making his way through the safer sections of the support trenches. They could see straightaway the man was no ordinary brass, but it was only after a scramble of words from the duty officer that they realized exactly who was coming their way. Sam, bare-chested, in short khaki pants, stiffened to attention, his other hand gripping upright the shovel he'd been using. Hamilton strode tall and lean, his moustache the most robust feature on an angular, worn face. When he spoke he was mild-mannered and forthcoming in a grandfatherly fashion, not in the least what Sam would have expected.

'From Newfoundland are you, Private?' he said to Johnny.

'No, sir, not exactly. From Labrador, sir.'

'I've heard of Labrador. Gallipoli is a bit of an oven for you then?'

'We have our hot days at home, sir, but nothing like this.'

Hamilton turned to Sam. He looked him over.

'You take to the heat.'

Sam was well-tanned, his skin conducive to the sun, unlike most in the Regiment.

'You remind me of the Australian lads,' Hamilton said. 'In physique I mean.'

'Yes, sir,' came Sam's dutiful, uncomfortable reply. He felt Hamilton's eyes lingering on him.

'Labrador,' the general said, turning back to Johnny. 'I seem to recall something about a doctor, a missionary of sorts. He has written several accounts of his time there.'

'That would be Doctor Grenfell.' .

'Yes, that's the man. As fine a Christian as the Empire has produced.'

Johnny smiled, and eagerly claimed Grenfell to be his good friend and employer.

'He's hoping to serve, sir. In the field hospitals in France.'

'I'm not surprised. When you return home extend my best wishes to the Doctor.'

'Yes, sir.'

Hamilton and his troupe moved on. Hamilton was known to have a deep-seated admiration for the Australians. From what Sam knew of the Aussies it was hardly returned. They had suffered horribly under the command of the Englishman, and while many would attribute the numbers of their dead to the terrain and to the fierceness of the Turks, Sam had heard more than a few barbs about the orders emanating from Command Headquarters set up on the island of Imbros.

Nevertheless Sam couldn't help but be persuaded by the

General's eagerness to plant himself among the ordinary
soldiers. In training Sam had only once set eyes on a general,
perched on a horse across a vast stretch of troops on parade.
Sam's encounter with Hamilton had turned his head, set it to
mulling over what it took to be in charge of a whole battle-
ground, the Navy at your back, men from a batch of countries
filling your trenches, none knowing the fate about to be
unleashed. It was a passing curiosity, and so far from what
stared him in the face—widening the rut of a trench—that it
was soon out of his mind again.

The Regiment was long in the trenches without any sign of the
Turks being whipped up enough to attack. Routine settled in.
The first hour after dawn was spent on the fire step, rifles at the
ready, bayonets locked, sights fixed to the enemy positions. It
set the day in order. For the Turks it was the same, and rarely
did it amount to anything except affirmation that there was a
war on.

The sector the Newfoundlanders held included a pronounced bulge in the route of the trenches, one that brought
them closer to the Turks than any of the other troops along the
line. Clamped against the dirt, Sam's concentration invariably
fell away to the constricted stretch of ground between them
and the enemy. The terrain was strewn with dead Turks, a
consequence of weeks-old battles. On the hottest days the
stench was relentless and turned more than one trench-hard-
ened soldier to retching. Night parties had buried some of the
dead, but countless humps of corpses remained, the cesspool
flesh a breeding ground for flies and vermin.

Even for Johnny, a Labrador man used to swarming black
flies and mosquitoes, the buggers were an ungodly aggravation.
The same flies, laden with disease, infested their mealtimes. An

open tin of jam proved the most hideous lure. As soon as the lid was cut and bent back, the inside went black with the demon masses. Sam had scrounged a piece of muslin large enough to cover his head and his food, but still there was no escaping the flies completely. He had mastered the timing of the route from the jam tin to the biscuit to his mouth, but knew better than to try even that in the middle of the day.

Most fellows were not so particular, and suffered the consequences. Within a few days of landing there was a steady stream of men back to the shoreline again, to a field hospital, or to await transport to the hospital ship, praying in their misery to escape the Turk shelling during the time it took to get there.

The bloody flux it was—what medics were calling dysentery. The constant diarrhea was bad enough, but it was the stomach-wrenching cramps and fever that laid them waste. Only the most iron-gutted wanted anything but a place to lie down, to outlast the agony made worse by the lack of drinking water.

Both Sam and Johnny dodged it, leaving them to do what they could for those who hadn't. Hughie Walsh, who had prided himself on being one of the few in the Regiment to knowingly get himself a Turk, was suddenly so fever-stricken and delirious that at his worst it took two men to restrain him.

'Easy, Hughie. Save your energy, fella.' Not that the plea did any good. If his fever were to break, he might have calmed enough that he could have been transported to the field hospital on shore, but as it was the commotion would only ever be a magnet for the Turk shells. Sam and Johnny together cursed the heat and lack of water, and watched Hughie slowly quiet down and die.

Dysentery and jaundice severely cut their numbers and soon it was no longer four days in the front lines, and four back in their dugouts, but eight up front and four in the rear. Even that turned to dull convention. Trench work grew to something to keep bored men occupied. A stretch of most afternoons was spent picking lice from their clothes and crushing them between their fingernails, or, in the case of Johnny, stripping and turning his clothes inside out, then meticulously running a candle flame along each seam. The monotony lulled men to carelessness, making it easier and easier to fall victim to snipers.

The snipers became the face of the enemy. C Company had the worst of it. Sam only came close to getting it that one time, but on several more had witnessed the scurry of a sniper to his post. More than once he and Johnny had been forced to draw back against the trench wall to allow passage of two stretcher-bearers and a sniper's quarry.

Johnny had struck Gallipoli with the mind of a trapper, a woodsman who'd been known to carry a rifle for months on end. He was keen with his hands, and possessed ears and eyes that sensed the slightest change in the landscape. Johnny had the makings of a sniper himself.

Captain Bernard had said so from the outset of his training. Johnny resisted, never giving it much thought, other than the vague notion that sniping was the business of a coward. After he passed his first nights in the trenches, only then did the notion start to rework itself into something worth considering, something he was willing to talk about with Sam.

'You got the eye, Johnny. You got the nerve.'

When Johnny again encountered the Captain, the man said much the same.

'Yes, sir.'

'I'll fix you up with one of the Australian lads the next time you're out of the front line. See if *he* thinks you got what it takes. Are you game, then? You and Sam, the pair of you. Sam would be your spotter.'

'No harm considering it.'

By that point, no harm at all.

Sam looked at them both and shrugged. It was up to Johnny. If Johnny was able for it, he would be too.

'Take up the rifle and match the blaggards man for man,' Sam said to Johnny after the Captain had gone.

A rifle barrel crammed with the Turks' own medicine. That's how Johnny needed to see it.

The Aussie's name was Billy Sing. From the moment Sam laid eyes on him he knew Johnny would drift into the fellow's confidence. Not that Billy Sing made any effort to befriend him. Sing was obviously tired and out of sorts, having only that morning left his post and made his way to where the Fifth Light Horse had their supply base.

It had to do with the fact they were near the same height, of the same stoutness.

'Where you from?'

Johnny told him. Then had to explain it.

'Me,' said Billy, 'I'm half-Chinese.'

'Me,' said Johnny, 'I'm half-Scottish.'

The fellow didn't crack a smile. Captain Bernard hadn't told them, not that it mattered, that the man who had been nicknamed 'The Murderer,' who had made more than a hundred confirmed kills, was not the six-foot Digger Sam or Johnny had expected. He had a father who was born in Shanghai.

'You a loner?' asked Billy.

Johnny said little at first. Gradually it came out of him that he'd been a woodsman since he was a boy, that it took a keen shot to strike Arctic hares on the run, that he had worked at perfecting his shot every chance he got. There were lots of chances in the woods, alone for a full winter.

For Billy it was kangaroos, and somehow a white-furred hare in the snow seemed to Sam a tougher target. But that wasn't the point as he found out, from the monotone tendrils of advice dispensed Johnny's way.

The bastards don't know you're ever there. Come before daylight, go after dark. You're the colour of dirt. You smell and sound like dirt. You see nothing except through the fuckin' loophole.

As if it was common sense.

Johnny had a doubt, the one he'd never ask about. Sam knew it. So did Billy.

I don't lose no sleep. You're dead if it makes you lose your fuckin' sleep.

Johnny told him about the silver fox he trapped, about the hand-deep pile of its fur, how it was the fur he was after, what he got paid for it. How he would have left the animal alone if it wasn't for that, though there was no forswearing the thrill of finding it in his trap.

Billy claimed his kangaroo hunts were all to stop the bastard hordes from feeding on grass meant for sheep. Johnny didn't have to ask what fun was in it for Billy. Johnny could tell there was plenty to keep him going back for more.

The pair parted friends of a sort, though they never laid eyes on each other after that. It was enough of a meeting to get Johnny figuring he had the guts of a sniper, if not yet the skill. That, too, would come.

Sink yourself in it. Billy's parting advice. *Hardly come up for fuckin' air.*

On their way back to their dugout they discarded their fetid clothes on the beach and, like hundreds more, ploughed into the saltwater at Anzac Cove. The Aussies were keen swimmers and swarmed the water, a boisterous crew, second nature to them, even those whose faces and forearms stood in black, sun-burnt contrast to the rest of them.

They wallowed chest-deep in the hedonistic comfort of soaking skin that had not known the touch of water for weeks. Every crack and crevice was coated with the cooling salve, its salt a stinging balm. Johnny had never learned to swim, unlike Sam, but dove in regardless, anxious to vanish totally into the war-less world below.

Even that was not to last. The Turks in the hills lobbed shells into the water, if but a scattered few, a warning that nothing escaped their notice. As if they were boys, too, envious of the fun, and didn't have the heart to ruin it for more than a handful.

Following the literal edge of the war, the pair walked back along the coastline crammed with men and supply tents, and across the neck of land to Suvla Bay, bare-chested, thirsty as they always seemed to be.

Johnny was feeling alone and out-of-sorts, even after the meal that evening. Ordinarily, he would have fallen into the routine of complaints and foolish banter about the heat and flies and what there was to eat. He left Sam and the others to it, walked on until he reached the dugout. He stretched out, ignoring the erratic din of shellfire.

Captain Bernard showed up the next day. Sam was lying about outside, having a smoke, but it was Johnny the Captain was keen to see. He stuck his head in first, and then the rest of him, found a place to sit across from Johnny. His feet to the dirt, Johnny saluted, then rested his elbows on his knees.

'What are you thinking, Johnny? How was it with Billy Sing?'

'Fair enough,' said Johnny.

'Give it a go, then?'

He didn't say yes, but he didn't say no, not that Sam heard.

'You got your spotter.'

The Captain was clearing a path for them. The truth was Johnny's mind was already made up. It had been by the time he'd crossed back over Suvla Plain, after seeing Billy, after he and Sam had their swim.

The letter had settled it.

A letter had arrived from home, another from Emma, both forwarded from the depot in England. Johnny raced through the one from his mother to get to the other, several tissue-thin sheets in a small, faded mint-coloured envelope. He read and reread it, while Sam glanced at him from across the dug-out, reading his own letter from an anxious Margaret.

When Johnny was about to put the letter away he passed a single page to Sam.

Doctor Grenfell is about to join up with the Royal Army Medical Corps in France. No doubt he will get as close to the front lines as he can. Mrs. Grenfell is worried for him, and so has decided to accompany the Doctor to England and remain there until his three months of war duty are up and they can return to the Mission. In the meantime, I am still in St. Anthony, while the Grenfell children remain with Mrs. Grenfell's mother at the cottage in Massachusetts.

My days are filled with preparing the rug-hooking kits to be distributed to the women along the coast. The long winter days ahead will see the creation of some beautiful rugs I am sure.

Oh, Johnny, I think of you every hour of every day.

I want nothing more than to see you step down the gangplank to the wharf in St. Anthony and into my arms. I long for that day with all my heart and soul.

If Johnny had passed Sam the page to arouse his envy, he easily accomplished that. The few words, the memory of her in the doorway, foiled Sam's sleep and set him to stealing her into the night.

And the next, and the next. At first no more than a vision drifting through. But gradually, assuredly she took form and Sam held her in his arms.

It was the touch of her, his hands against the back of her thighs, slowly drawing up, his face sunk into the hollow of her neck. Building to the moment, his heart frantic, when his lips fell to her breasts, brushing lightly, given to more and more fire. He trembled fervidly and strained like a tethered beast.

There were days after Johnny joined the Regiment when he wished he had never left Newfoundland. Those days had passed. Like every other man he was so thick into it he couldn't think of the war without him. And now, suddenly, in thicker than ever. And more determined than ever to see his way through to the other side. Turning himself into a sniper was suddenly his safest bet.

'You're good for it?' Sam said.

'You?'

'Rather kill another fucker 'fore he kills me.' Sam playfully slapped himself on the top of his head, the place where the Turk had almost put an end to him.

Together they spent hours sizing up the Turk trenches. The next time they were in the front line Johnny worked a loophole between the sandbags and set into it the end of a telescopic sight. The sight alone, not the gun.

Sam proved an equal keener. He'd be the one to use the sight. He'd find the target, pinpoint it exactly. Johnny would have a wider loophole, wide enough to fit the barrel of his rifle for the split second it would take to fire the bullet, and have it down again almost before the bullet blew abroad the Turk's brains.

The gun the Captain got for him was a SMLE—Short Magazine Len Enfield Mk. III. A proper sniper's rifle. That's what it took—the telescopic sight, the rifle, the patience. The Captain's promise they could come and go as they pleased.

And a nest, a womb, a quiet, well-positioned spot along the front line where the pair could disappear. For Sam and Johnny the closest thing to solitude, while the machinations of war encircled them.

The spot was crucial. They took their time ranging through the trenches, eventually fixing on a position partway up one of the steeper sections of the trench route, one that gave Johnny a good angle on the part of the Turk line that had constantly proved a bugger. Of course they wouldn't know for sure how good the position was until he and Sam were days into it. If they played it carefully the spot could go undetected for weeks, until there came the warning signs and the time to move on.

The first kill was simple. The fellow's blood bursting in the air, his arms thrown back, his rifle dropped. Not a doubt he was dead. As dead as their own men killed by Turkish snipers.

A simple lowering of the rifle and the scope. It was the moments afterwards that dug into them. The faint signs of

Turks scurrying about the trench, traces of shallow, rasping voices. The desperate crack of return fire, flagrantly off target. It was the crudeness of death, of the skull defiled, of an unsuspecting man, ravaged and smattered into dirt. Their imaginations clenched the consequences of a single bullet.

The pair said nothing, even as they stared at each other. They didn't look across at the spot a second time.

They considered how careless the Turks had become when there was no one keeping them pinned in place. Likely a raw recruit who didn't know the difference, who took the bullet in the skull, in the same spot Sam would have been hit that first time but for luck.

The sniper and his spotter finally mumbled confirmation that the intended deed had been done. There would be no congratulating each other. Only silence again to the time it took to find a spell of breathing right, enough to set their minds to starting over.

At one point Sam hinted to Johnny that he might notch the butt of the rifle, but Johnny said no, he didn't want to be keeping count. Sam did so anyway, quietly at the end of the day, a stroke from a blunt pencil wetted at the corner of his mouth, on the end page of a water-stained notebook. A single upright stroke.

On some days there were strokes lined up in a row. Followed by the date. On one day, a row of four strokes notched across by a fifth.

The killing was never routine. The waiting was routine, each day settling invisibly in place, a stretch of peering across the gap until the eyes lost focus. A rest, light talk, then another stretch. Again and again. Until that moment of the kill. Silence. Until the time it took to be breathing right again.

When it was getting dark and soon safe to leave the nest, the pair were more likely to talk. Especially on days when there had been no targets. Sam constantly wondered what might be in Johnny's head when his finger was on the trigger, though he realized he'd never get far putting the question to him.

'You'll have your time at the seals, Johnny, when you get back.' Said as if it were likely to be soon.

They'd had the same talk countless times before, but there was comfort to be had in familiar recollections, in the same way of saying it, the echo. They lived to get back to what they left at home.

'And, dear God,' said Johnny, 'do you think it will be the same?'

'You're a crack shot, if you wasn't before.'

'I was. I always was.'

'In the cold?'

'Find an air hole, and I could wait for hours. All it took was the second he showed his face.'

'No more to it than that.'

'No more to it than that.'

The Turk's loophole, squared by bricks, where he looked through thinking he was invisible, that was a breathing hole. Johnny's bullet, the answer to his own long wait.

When Johnny wasn't around, Sam supplied the details to the others in the Regiment. Sam's steady column of strokes made them shake their heads, week by week, and soon they were bragging to others in other regiments. Every one of them impressed, except for the Australians, who had their own man.

Johnny kept it to himself, as if it were his secret, even though there wasn't a man in the Regiment who didn't know. Peculiar, they all figured, and it came to colour how they saw the man from Labrador. Some of them had caught no more than a glimpse of a Turk. Only knew the Turks were there by the shelling, and for certain had never stared into the eye of one the way Johnny had.

They held a picture in their heads of Johnny, of the man with his rifle sighted directly into the eye of that Turk. What they didn't have was a picture of Johnny making the choice to put a bullet into it, or to ease his finger off the trigger and leave no one the wiser, not even the Turk. Killing by his own choice, no one else's.

Except that the Turks were sniping killers, too, with callousness equal to Johnny's own, they might have thought him a coward. Peculiar just the same, something of the madman in him. To kill that many men, Turks or not.

What madness, no one could say. Likely it had something to do with how well he slept at night, with none of the nightmares that broke their sleep, even those who had never shot a man, and likely never would before their time on Gallipoli was done.

In daylight, out of the front lines, Johnny looked much the same as he always did. Sometimes he offered a scrap of a smile when they congratulated him. The men never knew, except Sam, that it wasn't the tally of dead Turks that brightened him. Rather, it was the security of the nest, of escaping the careless slog through the trenches that might earn him a bullet. It was the notion of returning home.

He wouldn't be writing anything about it to Emma. There was no reason for her to know.

At the end of each day he and Sam waited out the time until darkness crept around them and grew deep enough they could make their escape. Some evenings the silent wait seemed endless, lying back in the narrow confines of their nest, the decreasing light baring their fantasies, the stars emerging in the night sky, markers of the minuteness of their lives. It was the time of every day when they ached for the war to be over, when in truth it had barely begun.

There swirled an absurdity about it all, the killing, the escape. The lust that filled them whenever the night was silent and they were as safe as they could hope to be.

One night, the blackest one, they had overstayed the time. They loosened their breeches and released themselves into the open air, allowing memories of what it was to be a man, not to be bound in the dirt and filth and nights of deprivation.

Sam stroked himself, craving the inner flesh of a woman. Johnny, startled for the moment, followed suit. Both of them imagining Emma, their quiet moans nearing the sound of her name.

They allowed themselves all the time it took to ease back into their uniforms, then rose to their feet, and started a silent night walk back to where the others were slouched against the trench walls, in semblance of sleep.

FIVE

THE daily tally rose and leveled off. Then sank to the point Sam and Johnny figured they'd better be moving on, that the Turks were on to their position and it would only be a matter of time before a shell pitched their way and that would be them done for and dead.

It took a few days to find another spot that satisfied them. Then, just as they were getting settled in, the two of them were called away.

. They had never seen Captain Bernard wound so tight. 'Orders straight from the General, lads. Major Drew picked men from C Company, then added you two.' Intensely efficient, nodding his head stiffly towards Johnny and Sam. 'It's a sharp eye we're after.'

'Yes, sir.' Both of them, practically the one voice.

'We all know the godforsaken knoll,' declared the Captain. 'Rabid with snipers since the day we arrived.'

Other regiments had taken on the Turk stronghold between the front lines, never with much success. Now the General wanted the buggers rooted off the spot once and for all.

'And not soon enough,' added the Captain. 'The crowd back home have heard enough about the Aussies and the Brits. Time for us Newfoundlanders to show what we're made of.'

His face stiffened again with the weight of the orders. He put Donnelly in charge, a lean lieutenant from St. John's, of stout Irish Catholic background. Green for such a task, like every one of them, but steady for all that. There was no one who served under him who didn't admire the man.

Donnelly took three of the men assigned to him and scouted the hill in advance, first by day and then after dark. Back in their trenches, he gathered them all and laid it out. 'We have our chance, lads. From what we've seen the Turks make their way there a half-hour after sunset. We stow ourselves away in the nest and give them bloody hell once they show up.' Simple enough.

The lieutenant split them in two lots of eight men. Sam would be part of the second lot, reinforcements once the first had control of the hill.

Donnelly, Johnny and the others slipped out of the trench at three that afternoon, a keen and wary crew. They edged over rock and scrub toward the knoll, out of the sightlines of the Turks. Johnny had never been beyond the lip of trench, though he had scanned and scrutinized it so many times that nothing about the terrain surprised him. What they all dreaded was sinking a foot in a rotted corpse. They counted on the ungodly stench being enough to steer them clear.

Each man kept Donnelly in sight, and each matched his slow, deliberate and silent pace. After an hour longer than the lieutenant had allocated, with darkness falling over them, Donnelly and his band of eight finally made it to the top of the hill and into the pod of snipers' posts. Spent shells were scattered everywhere.

They had barely taken a breath when the lieutenant held up an opened hand. They listened. For certain it was the noise of Turks coming their way, what sounded like three or four men, the small pack assigned the hill. Donnelly motioned to spread themselves out. Each took a position, the landscape near black.

'Who's there?' Shouted toward Lance Corporal Snow. Factious words. Dead silence.

In seconds bullets flew. At what might be men.

Errant fire ripped the air. Johnny was the only one to take it slow and deliberate, as if the dark were his sniper's nest. Felled one of them he figured. Impossible to tell for sure and impossible to follow any who weren't struck.

Had it been daylight the Newfoundlanders would have slaughtered them all. But one of the Turks had slipped aside, taking his time, like Johnny. A lull, then two shots more. One struck Snow and the other his cartridge case, exploding it.

Johnny's ears gave a bearing on the Turk. One shot and Johnny put an end to him.

'You all right, Snow?' A loud whisper across the knoll, as if someone knew how to throw his voice. They waited, tested the Turks with a brazen shout. Nothing. They were all dead, or shrewder than the Newfoundlanders gave them credit for.

Snow croaked enough to curse the bullet that had sliced his neck. The second bullet did him no good either, and for a while the others thought he might be done for.

He proved a rugged bird, with neck skin like leather. He jammed a wad of bandage against it and passed it off as nothing. The exploded ammunition—that, too, could have done in a lesser man.

'You make it back, Snow?' uttered Donnelly. 'Get word to the Captain? We've not seen the last of the bastard Turks.'

Sam and the others had heard the shots, but Captain Bernard needed to know who'd come out the victor. He had the second lot of men primed to make the leap, waiting on word from Donnelly so they wouldn't surge off blindly in the dark.

Snow made it back, his wounds piercing his stride, his willpower in battle with the pain. He'd been calling out for five minutes thinking he must be near the line. He fell over the lip of trench, landed flat on his back next to Sam.

'First Aid!' Sam yelled along the trench. 'First Aid!'

Bernard got as much of the story as he needed before Snow collapsed in exhaustion, a medic on the run to him.

The lot were off, Lieutenant Ross in charge. They had no fixed orders except make it to the hill as quickly as they could, to get there before more Turks showed up.

Not so simple. In daylight Sam had taken a sound sighting of the hill, fixed it clearly in his head, but what none of them had was judgment in the dark to get back on course once they veered around the rough bits that couldn't be scaled or forced through. They put their faith in Ross, as naive as them, though he did well not to show it.

They were better off, at least, for not eyeing some of what they smelled. For the most part they managed past it, though not every time, in which case all that could be done was curse and curse again and slog their way through.

They had reached what they figured was close to the knoll when they stopped dead in their tracks.

'Who is it?' came a voice.

It was Donnelly or one of his men, or a Turk who knew enough English to fool them. The sole choice was to call back.

'Newfoundlanders!' Ross yelled.

'Newfoundlanders.' One of them tried and didn't get it right.

Ross bellowed, 'Bastards!' and fired into the dark, in the fellow's direction, with scant hope of striking anyone.

Black silence then.

The slightest crack. A twig? A shift of weight?

Sam drew a breath, hardly dared let it escape. A mere rustle. Wind? Another crack. The dullest of thuds. The thud of his heart inside him.

All hell erupted.

Outnumbered, Sam figured. But nothing was reason, only chaos, gunfire streaking in the dead of night, out for whatever target it had luck to find.

Lieutenant Ross took one of the bullets. Pitched him reeling to the ground. Two more men fell.

Sergeant Greene seized command. The young daredevil stood up, recklessly willing to die. 'Shoot the bastards! Now! Now! Keep it up, keep it up!' Shouting until they'd turned it to a louder screaming rant of gunfire.

Bullets found their Turks. For no reason but chance and a shooter's ear for the queer groans of the wounded. The Newfoundlanders turned into madmen, and held them off until shouting confirmed the Turks were in retreat.

'Thank God,' Joachim Murphy said before he took a bullet.

Young Murphy had stuck with Sam during the advance to the knoll. The fellow needed someone he could count on, who had more confidence than he did. Agitated, shit-scared, Sam could tell, but he was a solid soldier, a good follower. Needed a role to play. Not keen when anarchy filled the dark, though he fired his rifle as rapidly as any man. Chance it was for sure, all too much of it.

'Stay down, man,' Sam had yelled. 'For fuck's sake, stay down!'

The dark had lured Murphy to his feet, when all he had ever known was true cover.

The bullets stopped, and it sounded as if the Turks had gone, back to their own lines, dragging their wounded with them. What was left of the patrol made it to the knoll. Donnelly and the others took them in.

'Thank God, Sam,' Johnny said. Sam stared vacantly, hardly believing himself that he was alive.

In daylight Sam went in search of young Murphy.

He found him crumpled on the ground, crazily angled. Oddly, a bullet to the head, when there had been so much more of him exposed. He must have died instantly, Sam knew, not to have made for himself a more comfortable position. Sam turned him over and gazed into his bloodied face tilted skyward.

For the first time Sam saw close-up what a bullet could do to a skull, how it had blown a jagged channel above the right ear. How bloodied brain tissue had oozed out the cavity, dried through the hair and fallen onto the dirt between the mangled head and useless helmet. How past the rivulets of blood down his face there was still an expression on his lips. Though none in his eyes. These had long been vacant.

Sam stiffened his instincts and on his own began dragging Murphy back to the trench, not getting him far before stretcher bearers showed up and did the rest.

That day, while the Turks came out and dragged back their own dead—without a bullet fired either way—Sam stayed by the body of the fellow, to be there when he was buried.

A hurriedly dug hole in the ground, near a dozen or more of the Regiment who had been killed since they landed on

Suvla Beach. Regiment, name and number in his breast pocket, for when he would be dug up again and given a proper burial, when the troops pulled away from Gallipoli and the war was over. Not that any one of the men standing limply at the gravesite could think of that happening, not the way they rushed the prayer in the scramble to be done and out of the open. They expected some Turk just might get it in his head to lob a shell in their direction. Always in their minds was the notion that some callow, cock-eyed troublemaker might be behind the gun on any given day.

An hour after Sam made it to the knoll, thirty more men, under the Captain's orders, showed up. From that day on the Newfoundlanders owned the spot. Caribou Hill they christened it, and it was all the story anyone back home could want.

Sam started to put to paper the story of Joachim Murphy, in a letter he intended to send home, agonizing his way through his urge to record the raw truth of Gallipoli. He had hardly begun. It was better they didn't know, Johnny told him and he agreed and tore the page to pieces.

Johnny and Sam were left without time to dwell on it, and they never did get to settle back in their sniper's nest. Without warning, late in November, came the worst weather to strike the Peninsula in forty years. It left every man—Brit, Colonial, Turk—in a fight to save himself from drowning.

It started with a fierce gale of cold northeast wind. Wind that reeled and rattled between the hills and skimmed across the top of the trenches like a whirlwind playing games. Then the rain struck, in mad muttering torrents until it vehemently proclaimed itself in thunder and lightning, rain no Newfoundland soldier ever thought possible. All the Regiment's men who had escaped the dysentery and jaundice were in the firing line, there for too long, awaiting word of troops to relieve them, word they gave up thinking would ever come. Suddenly every one of them was washed violently awake, standing soon in water pooling deep in the bottom of the trench, turning clay to viscid mud.

Sam tried to pass it off, but Johnny knew weather enough to know it wasn't about to turn quickly, that it was not the water battering them they had to worry about, but what lashed the hillsides rising up on both flanks. It wasn't about to stand still, and within minutes the laws of nature channeled it straight for the Newfoundland trenches.

'Jesus,' shouted Sam through the uproar, his eyes squinted past the curtain of rain, 'what the fuck is this?'

The parapets were collapsing all around them, brewing the trench to quagmire, making it hell-hard to move about. The water and mud wrapped about their knees, the rest of their bodies as saturated as if they'd been submerged. Already what little they owned had turned to sodden clumps, about to be caught in the surge of water, their rifles torments impossible to keep clear of it.

They slogged a way out of the trench, to where the water was only calf-deep, where, for the moment, they escaped the grip of the surge. They slung their rifles across their backs, a hand on each other's shoulder, and stood like youngsters at a macabre fairground, heads constantly twisting about, not knowing to what freakish sight they need give their attention. The decision was made for them—dead Turks eddied face down in the black trench waters, blankets, empty ammo boxes, kits, food, whatever water could move.

The scene failed even Johnny, habitually sane at the worst of times. He helped his own, what men of the Regiment who had yet to free themselves of the trenches. Fools, waist deep now, trying still to salvage scraps of belongings hoarded for the two months they'd been in Gallipoli, lugged back and forth between dugout and trench, all they had to their name.

'Forget the goddamn stuff!' Johnny shouted, extending a hand down to another of them. The fellow gave up and grabbed onto Johnny's arm, and, with the trench wall caving in at every step, managed out of it. Johnny dragged him up the rest of the way and to his feet. Gathered him with the others, huddles of sodden rats.

At least they were alive. More than could be said of a good many of the Worcesters, the Dublin and Munster Fusiliers. The Turks, the most of them on higher ground, must have it better, Sam decided. They weren't much the enemy now. Just men saving themselves from what God decided was worthy of them all. That was it, he shouted, God having back at them all for their foolishness. The other boys shut him up. They wouldn't be hearing that. They had enough pitching through their brains as it was.

It got lost anyway. Frozen to death. That evening, with the rain stopped, it turned colder. Only to rain again, and by morning—believe it if they could—snow. A perfect layer of snow. Laid upon the rugged rock, upon the mud-spent battlefield, hiding ice-skimmed pools of rainwater, as if God had changed his mind and brought Christmas early.

If they weren't so bloody frozen in their clothes they might have found something to remind them of home. What sleep they had was snatched standing up, or, when they got there, leaning against the outside of their dugouts nearer the beach, all flooded, the water now with a half-inch of frozen sludge across the top.

When Johnny opened his eyes and first saw the snow he thought himself dead. His spirit back to Labrador. Encased in a calm he had not known since he left. He closed his eyes and dreamed himself deep in the woods, a man rapt in his trapline. With the makings of a good season, an evening of wood heat inside his cabin, so warm he had to strip to his underwear and open the door a crack.

Sam, one of his feet frostbitten or he was demented, laughed at him. Sam had the cynic deeper in him, but Johnny had long ago learned how to take Sam, because Sam, in the end, still knew when to shut up.

No one was surprised when word of evacuation came down. Every last man would be pulled off Suvla, where the first troops had landed ten months before. Word was the British generals were calling for full evacuation of the Anzacs, too, further down the Peninsula. Gallipoli was about to be abandoned.

Relief overwhelmed the moment. Only later, alone with the nightmares they would be taking with them, did anyone question what it had all been for. What had been gained by the thousands dying, where now was the self-respect? With what logic remained, they kept their cynicism to themselves.

The self-respect for every man was in getting off alive. Everyone, in his own way, consumed himself with the logistics of escaping the Peninsula without the enemy suspecting it. The challenge was figuring ways to fool the Turks into thinking they were still in the trenches, when in fact they were on the beach, boarding lighters that would get them to the troop ships. Only gunfire from the trenches and exploding grenades would do it, and the keenest minds fell deep into the workings of devices to accomplish exactly that.

What won out in the end was simple enough. A rifle wired in place, its muzzle poked through a loophole in the sandbags. Its trigger weighted with an empty biscuit tin half filled with sand, and above it a can of water. A slow drip of the water steadily increased the weight of the lower can, until, several hours later, the trigger snapped, sending a bullet somewhere near enemy lines.

A wick stretched between a lit candle and the fuse of a Mills bomb made a second device, one more precarious. But more than likely some of them would discharge, more evidence there were soldiers about.

After dark on the 19th of December the evacuation was in full motion. Suvla Beach was alive with it, ghostly rhythms of men tuned to the steady pace of lighters back and forth between the piers and the troop ships. Over it all hung the dull hum of orchestrated commotion.

The wounded had already been shipped off. Everyone who was left—except for a small rearguard—had made their way silently after dark from the trenches to the beach, in single file, following trails of white flour laid down that afternoon.

On the beach they held together in companies, awaiting their time to move along and board a lighter, anxious for the muted shuffle of their own boots over sand and the blanket-covered piers. They numbered twenty thousand, pockets of soldiers ordered into strict silence, their war in retreat.

Scattered among them were huge piles of munitions, crate upon crate of food and medicine, stockpiles of unissued winter uniforms, tents and carts, heaps of timber, formless metal. None of it going anywhere. On one section of the beach had been corralled mules and horses. None of them going anywhere either, their throats slit that afternoon before the men showed up.

What tormented any man the most were the graves he was leaving behind, never to be seen again. For days after Murphy died, Sam had gone to where he was buried, to bring some order to the grave. He had laid out a rectangle of rocks, made a cross and drove it with the back of a shovel into the ground. Like them all, Sam reveled in thoughts of seeing the last of Suvla. Like them all, he bore the sting of disloyalty.

The night scene of evacuation was not war. No Turk shells dropped among it, no man died, no one was left unaccounted for. Soldiers gloried in an astounding deception. They stole away, leaving the Turks to creep dumbfounded to the deserted beaches where a storm of fire raged throughout the stockpiles.

In the course of the loading their Company was split and it was after midnight before the twenty who were left, Johnny and Sam included, boarded the lighter that got them off Suvla. Just minutes before the lighter pulled away, Lieutenant Steele and a clump of thirty men who had made up the rearguard came aboard, the last men to leave the support trenches.

'Dead quiet,' one of them told Johnny, as they stood up in the lighter, on their way to the *Barry*, an Isle of Man paddle-boat. It would take them to Imbros. 'Turks,' the fellow said soberly, shaking his head. 'Not a fucking clue we've gone.'

'Good work, men,' said Steele, a precise, regulation display of satisfaction. Johnny liked the look of the officer just the same, the way he carried himself. There was no show to him, no nonsense. He did the job and engendered loyalty.

Leaning against the ship's railing, Johnny stood a few feet away from Steele, who, like himself, watched in silence as life on Gallipoli receded before him. Sam sat silently, nursing his frostbitten foot.

Someone to the other side of Sam spoke up. 'Fuckin' glad to see the fuckin' tail end of that lot.' A cigarette in the corner of his mouth wobbling with each word. An Englishman, although it was too dark to tell from what Regiment.

Sam nodded, said nothing.

The fellow tried again. 'I lost me best buddy. Poor bugger.'

Sam would never have called Murphy a buddy. But a poor, unfortunate bugger, Murphy was that.

'Like us all,' said Sam. It was enough to encourage the fellow.

'Makes you wonder, don't it? Makes you wonder what the fuck we got to show for it.'

Sam knew he and Johnny had dead Turks to show for it, lots of them.

'Trench-digger or collier?' the fellow said. 'I think now I'd take the mine.' He had the good sense to laugh.

Johnny glanced at Sam. Sam half smiled through the pain still rising in his foot.

'You're the sniper,' the fellow said, catching a look at Johnny for the first time. 'We all heard about you. Never got a Turk, I didn't. I wanted to get one back for me buddy.'

Have one of ours, Sam thought.

'Your buddy don't care,' Johnny told the fellow.

'But I do. I wanted to have something to show for being here. Something to tell me missus.'

'You could lie. She'd never know.'

'I could at that.'

'Or say nothing. Your buddy'd be no better off.'

Johnny and Sam found a place on the boat to slip into their heads, thinking the chaos of the past months was behind them. Now that they had time to sleep they failed to, each brief lapse cut short by the wakefulness of a sniper shot, another Turk slumped out of sight. They longed to get back to themselves, to set each other right, to share the strain, the tally, to get back their sleep.

They wished the Turks a motherless breed, but could claim no sense in that. Sense they still had. When all else failed, what they clung to was the belief that Johnny's tally saved their own men. There were those in the Regiment who had walked the trenches because he had put bullets through Turks who would have put bullets through them. None of them ever thanked him for it, but there were times when Sam and Johnny would stare at some kid they were sure had lied about his age, who should have stayed home and played at war instead of lying crumbled against a trench wall, frozen numbly to a rifle. They would stare at him and think they might have saved him from a bullet exploding in his brain.

Anytime they had doubts, anytime the Turk Johnny killed had a mother, had the face of a kid himself, they would that night find someone and stare themselves back to peace. Just as they did now, aboard the *Barry*, on their way to Imbros.

A fellow had to like Imbros. The relief of it more than anything. By the time they landed it was three o'clock in the morning. Steele led the way to where they might find something to eat, Johnny and Sam bringing up the rear, slower than the rest, Sam's foot giving him more trouble. But what was there to greet them when they did arrive but a hot meal, as welcome as a mother's own, no flies fighting over it.

The pair settled with their mess tins into a spot not far from the Lieutenant. The whole Regiment knew who Johnny was, and Steele was no exception, although they had never spoken directly to each other before.

'I've not been to Labrador, but they tell me it's a fine place.'

'Yes, sir. For any man who likes the wilderness.'

'I expect I'll get there some day. Our business has had dealings with Grenfell's Mission.'

'And what business would that be, sir?'

'The Steeles deal in crockery and china, cookware and the like. I've travelled to many of the outports, but not yet to your part of the world.'

'Then you'll have to make a point of it, sir.'

'Are there places a fellow can walk and see the country?'

'For days. Come in September, sir. The country is at its best for walking.'

Sam admired Steele's ability to put the war aside. The officer liked to hum bits of songs, seemingly moved by some other life surfacing inside him. He was a good singer, the man behind the concerts aboard the *Florizel* when the Regiment made its trip across the Atlantic.

They were about to go their separate ways, off to find somewhere to bunk down for the night, when Steele's attention was diverted across the water to Suvla. One of the fires had erupted, likely a new stockpile of ammunition lost to flame. The night sky and the ocean were suddenly alight with an unbelievable, ferocious intensity, towering above the beach. Steele took it in his head to get a better view. He started in the direction of a nearby hill, having put aside the desperate need for sleep. 'Johnny, ' he called as he stood up, 'let's have a look.'

Sam's voice came out of the darkness behind him. 'Go on, Johnny. I'll rest the foot.'

The freedom to move about at will, without any thought of an enemy, revived something lost for months. Johnny followed the urge to throw his shoulders back and give one, long, unencumbered stretch of his torso.

Atop the hill the sight was astonishing. In one final stroke the retreating army savagely laid waste to the potential spoils of war. As if it were possible to triumph in defeat, as if all the

Turks had been left was a fiery hell, and were somehow worse for it.

Conversation fell away. The mood turned sober. As everyone had, the Lieutenant left behind someone who had been a friend. Steele began to sing, with no great volume, but enough to deaden the distrust that lingered at the edge of their thoughts.

Enough that Sam could hear it as he stood, his foot throbbing, in darkness as close as he could get to them without being seen.

The sea was full as the shore could tell,
With mine, entanglement, shot and shell,
And we stormed Caribou, as we knew we should,
And we fought and won as we knew we would.
We fought and won as we knew we would.

SIX

THE retreat to Imbros lasted two days.

As it turned out, a beggarly two days. As chummy as Steele had been with them, they weren't officers. The lower ranks were left to fend for themselves.

The next day it rained like mad, and turned cold. There was no proper place to sleep and nothing more to eat that didn't sit a cold lump in the gut.

Suddenly rumour had it that they were about to be shipped off to Cape Helles, on the tip of the Peninsula, the Gallipoli bridgehead, the only section of the Peninsula that still held Allied troops.

Spirits plummeted. After all they had just gone through on Suvla? Did Headquarters not have a bloody ounce of mercy?

'Orders. Outright fucking orders,' Sam said, his feet back in marching shape, or close enough to it.

Orders never came with a choice. It was a steady march to the shoreline at midday, and load themselves again aboard a lighter and out to a steamship, the *Redbreast*. Aboard were more weary men of the unflinching 29th Division. Bloody stalwarts. Doubtless there wasn't a man among them who could have done without the reputation, who would have traded it for sleep.

And what was their job this time? Do what had to be done so Cape Helles could be evacuated. 'Get the hell off Cape Helles,' was how every second man put it. 'What idiot Turk would fall for it a second bloody time?'

And don't believe for a second, Sam said to Johnny, that the question wasn't in the head of every officer who smoked and caroused and filled the lounge of the *Redbreast*. Steele included, him leading them, one rousing song after another.

Sometime after ten o'clock that night the troops went ashore, where nine months before the Turks had butchered a battalion of Lancashire Fusiliers, who had fought like dogs to get through barbed wire and mines and rifle fire, just to make it to the beach. The poor sots earned three VCs 'afore breakfast.' And that 'wasn't 'alf enough,' Sam had been told in Cairo, from a fellow who'd been there.

The Lancashire Landing where the Newfoundlanders came ashore was no longer bare beach. Now it was piers and breakwaters, and mounded everywhere with stockpiles of God knows what. Rutted paths and slaving horses. Thirty-five thousand men had to come off the beach, and whatever supplies that could be salvaged. And in the end, another inferno to destroy what was left.

A few miles inland, men of four Divisions crowded the trenches. The 29th had been called in to fill the gap left by the French, who had buggered off to another part of the war. The Hants, the Essex, the Worcesters, and the Newfoundlanders—88th Brigade all of them—back into the dirty thick of it and no man meant to complain.

There was plenty to complain about. For starters—the worthless march off in the dark to find some place to sleep. And when they were marched again to somewhere that wasn't already thick with men, what they got was some vile dugout. 'The fucker breeding vermin in a fucking foot of water!'

And, on top of that, no proper rations drawn for them and not half enough to eat.

Sam spent the next few days trying to get it out of his head that he could have been anywhere but Helles. Johnny took him aside and talked him down from his fever pitch. 'Sam, we're in it and we'll bloody well get through it.'

Digging ditches and fixing up roads, swallowing orders from the engineers. And when it wasn't that, it was carrying shovels and picks back and forth, back and forth without cover, so other bastards could do the same. The shelling then, as if a fellow's nerves weren't raw enough already. Always on the wait for it, the dread driving Sam rabidly over open ground, one hopeless spot to the next.

He complained some more, did what he was told to do, and did it right.

In the midst of it all came Christmas Day. It had its moments—turkey and chocolate filched from the Brigadier-General's Mess, no cook the wiser, at least until the lads were well on their way back to the dugouts. Christmas Day was a reprieve from bully beef and biscuit. An extra tot of rum to keep them bloody civil.

A few hymns marked the day. There was "O, Come All Ye Faithful," which everyone agreed was a miserable one, especially the 'joyful and triumphant' bit, then "Silent Night," from a young fellow from Trinity Bay who no one ever heard sing before. It trounced them in a way they never expected. By that time the Turks had stopped their shelling, it was calm for sure, and the stars were out. The trenches had been drained, and for the first time since they arrived they were dry. The night held silent and warm and they were bloody sick for home.

'What hell odds?' That was Johnny's verdict, when orders came down that they'd be taking up duties on the beach as long-shoreman. Sam nodded reluctantly. The Greek Labour Corps, sick of being shelled by the Turks, had refused to work. Brigade lost patience and had them shipped off, back to their islands, and called in the Regiment.

Dog labour, a lot of it. That was bad enough, but the living quarters they took over from the Greeks, set on rock terraces jutting out from a cliff face, had been hopelessly knocked together from biscuit boxes and scraps of wood, roofed with blankets and canvas. The squalor inside was enough to make any one of them gag ten times over. Blankets reeking with vermin, festering scraps of food, wet and mangy clothes. Strewn everywhere.

They spent the morning scraping out the rot and filth and dumping it into the sea. In the end they made the quarters livable, more or less. They had a view—straight over the Aegean—and some consolation, the sea in front and the cliff soaring up behind. A shell from the left flank was all that could reach them, and that not often. Besides, not far away was Corps Headquarters, where the brass had buried themselves in the cliff. A more enticing target. A more deserving one, they all agreed. 'Cavemen, b'ys, bloody cavemen. Wit' a front porch,' Sam quipped, the clean-up finished, the shelters halfway decent. Johnny pleased to see him that way. Sam's exaggerated accent got a good laugh, despite the disgust that was still sunk deep within them all.

Johnny had roughed it as much as the next fellow, endured

as much mud and filth as anyone since the day they ploughed ashore in Suvla. Straightening himself out inside the shelter, stretching out in the bunk, all led him back to the Mission. Cleanliness next to godliness, the Grenfell rule, as if it were a quotation from the Bible. Odd how, given a break from the trenches, the words came back to him, how easily he pictured Sunday dinner with the Mission staff, the gentility of it, the crisp white tablecloth and patterned china. He had fit in, more than a regular fellow from Labrador, one who'd been to New York, more sure of himself by then. Queer, he said to Sam lying on the other side of the dugout, how that picture had bored into his head when there were so many other things crammed in with it.

Sam pictured it too. Emma at the table. In white, her hair tied back with ribbon. Her easy manner, turning to him, sharing her stories, her hand resting on his for the moment. Quickened, unspoken intimacies. The look in her eyes that told him to rest easy, that all would be well. Sam closed his eyes and let himself be swept into her and when he opened them again they were moist with the beginning of tears. He quit the dugout before Johnny knew.

When they encountered Lieutenant Steele later that day Johnny said he was sure thoughts similar to his had settled in the officer's head. Of Sunday dinners, of the orderly arrangement of china, if that had been his working life before he joined up. Johnny could almost feel certain of it, just by looking at him. He liked that about Steele—the knack he had of not giving into the grime. He admired an officer who kept himself tidy and kept his manners, who swore only when it made a point.

'You're no worse for it, Johnny?'

'Worse for it? Always worse for it, sir.'

'Complaining?'

'No, sir.'

Johnny never complained to an officer. There was never any satisfaction to be found in that.

The two stood together for a moment on the stone ledge in front of the shelter, peering out to sea. Sam taking it all in, the fact that someone among the higher-ups had gone out of his way to befriend Johnny.

'You'll like Labrador,' Johnny said to Steele. 'You'll like it very much.'

'Every man should know his own country if he's willing to die for someone else's.'

'I never thought of it as will, sir. Chance more than will.'

'Then you *have* thought about it?'

'For what good it does, sir.'

Steele had nothing to add.

'I write about it.'

'Write about it?'

'I copy poems. From a book.'

From the pocket of his tunic Johnny took a small book, its red book cloth embossed with Greek columns and the words *The Golden Treasury*, one of a pair of such books he had bought in New York, he had told Sam, a copy for him and another for Emma. A book they shared across the thousands of miles. Johnny removed it from the waterproof pouch he had stitched especially for it. The book had endured the worst of Gallipoli. With it was a small notebook, and a tiny pencil.

'I copy the ones I like. A line or two, only that, so I can repeat it in my head, think about it all day.'

'Do you have favourites?'

'It would be hard to choose.'

'Would you tell me some?'

Johnny thought for a few seconds.

'*How like a winter has my absence been…*'

It held in the air, vacant, in need of what came after. But Johnny wasn't about to add to it, and chose instead to take up another line.

'*So true a fool is love, that in your will / Though you do anything, he thinks no ill.*'

'A bit melancholy.'

'*There's not a joy the world can give like that it takes away.*'

Steele waited.

'*She walks in beauty, like the night…*'

'That one I know. Byron died near here, in Greece.'

Johnny seemed pleased to hear it had been so close.

'He died fighting, a poet turned soldier.'

'*Yet did I love thee to the last, / As fervently as thou/ Who didst not change through all the past / and canst not alter now.*'

It was an odd trait in a soldier, Steele said, this penchant for lyric. But no odder than his own, his journal writing, done so faithfully, sometimes under the most wearisome of conditions. And, like Johnny's, protected at all cost against the water and the mud.

'Have you written your own?' Steele asked.

'I've kept only a few.'

'The worthy few.'

'They're saved for home.'

Steele didn't ask to hear any of what Johnny had written. It was like Steele's own journal. People would read both someday, would know something of their minds, what they had been on Gallipoli.

Sam overheard it all with suspicion. A fellow could never be true friends with the higher-ups. Rank would always cut a line between them, and at the end of the day the private would go one way and the officer another.

That Sam understood. It buggered him up that Johnny didn't. Buggered him up to see the fellow share that piece of himself with Steele. To see there was a part of Johnny he'd never truly know.

In the end all anyone had in his head was getting through each day.

Some buried themselves in pier repair, slaving over rock quarried and rushed under shellfire to the beach on rail trucks. More slogged supplies from the beach into horse and mule carts, from the carts onto lighters, from lighters onto ships offshore. The miserable animals themselves would not be so fortunate. When there was nothing left to haul, like on Suvla, each would meet a ruthless end.

The Regiment wasn't alone. Their cohorts in the drudgery were the British Labour Corps. Washed-up soldiers and volunteers too old for active duty. At one time, which they didn't remember, primed and eager to do their bit. Their aim in life now was to make it off the Cape in one piece, without being bluntly rooted off by shellfire or shrapnel.

If nothing else the Brits were a diversion, queer enough for a laugh when the Newfoundlanders could find a way through their accents. Asiatic Annie showed them for what they were. Bloody well good at saving their own skin.

Asiatic Annie, a gun on the Turk mainland, fired across the mouth of the Dardanelles and directly onto the Cape. A bugler on watch in one of the hills overlooking the beach sounded a warning the moment the gun went off. That gave a man an unwavering count of 27 seconds to race for cover before the shell struck.

The old Brits, like scurrying rats, never failed to bury

themselves away with half the time to spare. They had their favourite spots and everyone else knew better than to encroach on them. Practically knocked themselves out getting there, but they'd had relatively few casualties in the months they had been on the beach. They weren't about to chance anything now that evacuation was in sight.

'The Old and the Bold,' the Newfoundlanders called them. Sam could forgive them their sluggish work, for who'd ever want to think he'd be in the middle of a war at that age. The age of Paddy. And older some of them. Sam couldn't fathom it.

On evenings when the shelling stopped, the Brits and the Newfoundlanders had ways of turning bully beef into something other than what it was. It became their common ground. Though it wasn't enough to satisfy Sam. He brazenly led raids on the stockpiles of food intended for the higher-ups, and regularly showed up at the braziers with something more— canned ham, canned puddings, prunes and raisins.

One time three bottles of Old Orkney whisky.

'Jesus, Sam!' crooned one of the old fellows. Sam smiling and playing it like nothing could have been easier, when the truth was he had come damn close to getting caught. Their eyes lighting up like the whisky was bloody gold. Which it was, only better.

They were primed for a rousing few ditties after that. "The Petty Harbour Bait Skiff" making way for "Burlington Bertie." "Has Anyone Here Seen Kelly?" giving in to "Old Brown's Daughter." Not one of them had a mind for the songs that came out of the war. Not the ones they sang on the marches that got them all to Gallipoli.

In the first days of January the evacuation was in full motion.

Night after night troops emerged from the front lines and support trenches, and stood together, desperate for the word to board a lighter that would take them to the ship lying offshore. As was Sam the night he left Suvla, they were racked by the thought of abandoning dead comrades and of quitting a job undone.

They swore the Turks had no notion of what was taking place, the enemy action on the front lines plainly no more zealous than usual. Yet most expected it would erupt at any time, and on the afternoon of the 7th it did. The men on the beach cowered at the intensity of the artillery fire inland. Eventually a fragmented line of nerve-worn troops emerged with the story. They had been rushed by the full weight of the Turk infantry. *Allah! Allah! Voooor!* But then within yards of the British lines, the Turks had abruptly halted. Their men refused to advance any farther. They gave up and, with the vacant shouts of their officers dogging them, retreated past their dead. 'As if they'd had too bloody much of war.'

The sting of the Turks had been squandered. Or so it seemed. But nothing was ever sure, and as more and more of the men escaped the Cape, including the British Labour Corps and most of the Newfoundlanders, Sam and Johnny turned increasingly restless.

Word got to them that they were to report immediately to Lieutenant Steele. Hand-picked for special duty, again.

'Two dozen of us. On orders from General O'Dowda,' Steele told the lot of them, slouched over their rifles, nobody with any enthusiasm for whatever was coming next.

The following day, the final one, barbed wire would be strung across the access paths to the beach, to stymie the Turks further, in case they attacked in the last hours of the pull-out. Steele and his men were to station themselves at the two gaps in the wire, at the two forming-up places, where the last troops coming off the front lines would be heading. The assignment was to guide them to the beach and close off the gaps when the last man made it through.

'We'll be the last to board a lighter,' Steele told them. Not said like anything to be proud of. Sam gave him that much.

'Yes, sir,' Sam said, like they all did.

Steele waited for questions. They stood unresponsive, their guts churning.

'The last off the Cape,' one of them uttered, desperate to add weight to it, 'The very last off Gallipoli.'

'Yes, private.'

A grandiose scene somewhere, in some minds.

'The General thinks we're the best for the job,' Steele said.

A bloody well dangerous one. Not to be dwelt on, or they'd go mad in the hours remaining.

There was plenty to glut the time. The routes between the forming-up places and the piers. The unrelenting artillery bombardment at the head of Gully Ravine. The fuses trailing the stockpiles ready to blow to kingdom come.

Letter writing. Sam's hasty few lines to his family in Harbour Main, Johnny's longer, more considered lines to Emma in St. Anthony.

Each in turn pressed the letter he had written into his friend's tunic pocket and buttoned it. They stood aside and renewed the pledge—if one didn't make it to the shores of France, the other would mail the letter. Then Johnny, half turned away, withdrew a second envelope and, turning back, passed it to Sam. Without a word, Sam unbuttoned his pocket and slipped it in beside the other.

A 100-pounder screamed into B Company's cookhouse. It came

with no warning from the lookout.

Steele bolted toward the mayhem, the others tight behind. The cookhouse had been flattened. They scrambled to unearth two men cut to pieces by shrapnel. One of them, Morris from Fortune Bay, was dead. The other lost an eye, had raging open wounds to an arm and leg. Three of his fingers were a bloodied mangled mess, barely part of his right hand any longer. He gasped frantically for breath. What he managed caught in his throat, fouled with phlegm and blood.

Neither Johnny nor Sam had ever seen a man so badly sliced by shrapnel. If Steele had, he wasn't letting on. The fellow railed in pain on the stretcher, about to be rushed to the beach and transported to the hospital ship. With any luck he'd make it and never know the war again.

Then, suddenly, came the faint screech of another shell heading their way. Sam glanced in the direction of the lookout. Where the fucking hell was the bugler?

'Evacuated! Christ Almighty!' Everyone who could dove to the ground, thinking themselves done for by a second shell as accurate as the first.

They dragged themselves under what little cover there was. The shell landed a few yards beyond, hurling dirt on them all. Shrapnel again sliced the poor bastard on the stretcher, crudely aborting what little life was left in him.

It sobered them all severely. On their way back they said nothing, not even Steele, though no one had doubts what anyone else was thinking. Every minute stood in balance. Every minute to boarding a lighter, this time absolutely and forevermore not to set foot on Gallipoli again.

That night 16,000 men escaped the Peninsula from Lancaster Landing, many with the help of the Newfoundlanders. The front lines and support trenches were empty, the gaps in the wire closed. By 2 a.m. the number left on the beaches of Cape Helles was 200, Lieutenant Steele and ten more men of the Regiment among them. For the first time they were tasting an end to it.

They were about to forge their own escape when a telephone message came through that the boat taking the last men off Gully Beach, two miles away, had run aground. The men would have to make their way to Lancaster Landing, an hour-long march overland. That would still give plenty of time before the huge stockpiles of ammunition left on the beach would blow. By 3 a.m. most of the men had shown up. At 3:15 the fuse was lit as planned, timed for 45 minutes.

Commanding officer, General Maude, and a dozen others were nowhere to be seen.

General O'Dowda was beside himself with the wait. 'Where the hell are they?'

'General Maude, sir. He forgot his valise aboard the boat, sir. He went back for it.'

'He went back for it!'

'Yes, sir. With a few of the men. We were only ten minutes along, sir, when they went back. They should be here now.'

'But they are damn well not here, Lieutenant, are they?'

'No, sir.'

More time passed. O'Dowda's patience had stretched beyond all reason. 'The load blows in fifteen minutes! Where the hell are they, Lieutenant?'

He cursed, then spit his question to those around him. 'Who here knows the grounds over that fucking hill?'

Steele stepped forward.

'Go like hell, Steele, and see if can you find the bloody General,' and only half under his breath, 'the goddamn slug.'

Steele ran off, motioning to Johnny and Sam to follow him.

'Be back in ten minutes, Steele!' O'Dowda yelled after them. 'We're leaving in ten minutes with or without the bloody General!'

The three of them raced up the hill. They had traversed the terrain many times. It was not easy to cover with only moonlight to show the way, but there was only one route from Gully Beach.

They began to call out. Lightly at first, given the months of doing everything possible not to alert the Turks to their presence. There was nothing between them and the Turks but silence. With only minutes to detonation they had nothing to lose.

They shouted his name. 'Here! This way!'

With time rushing by there came a call back. 'Here! We're here!'

Steele shouted louder, 'Quickly, sir. We have to get off the beach before it blows! The ammunition dump, sir! We have to hurry.'

Johnny, who had the better instinct for the terrain, rushed ahead to the General's party.

The dozen of them slogged along, weighed down with kit from headquarters. The General held his valise vice-like in his hand.

'Sir, we have only a few minutes.'

'Very well, private. We are doing our best. We had to cut our bloody way through the bloody wire. Lead on, man. Lead on.'

If the General seemed unruffled by the prospect of being blown to hell, his carcass destined to remain on the Peninsula forever, his men were not.

They pushed ahead, leaving the General in their wake, paper flying loose from them.

'Here, here! You're losing kit. These are valuable papers. It's the record of what we've done on this godforsaken Peninsula. Someone pick them up!'

Steele had joined them. 'We have no time, General.'

'Then lead the way, damn it!'

Finally Maude grasped the urgency of the situation. He huffed along until they were in sight of the beach. The General shuffled down the hill, Steele steadying him as best he could without marring the man's dignity, Sam leading the way, desperately urging them on.

From aboard the lighter O'Dowda and several others shouted their way.

'It detonates in four minutes!'

Sam positioned himself behind General Maude and practically lifted him aboard the boat, O'Dowda at the receiving end, neither man paying any mind to the general's protests.

'You made it, General,' O'Dowda barked as the lighter pushed away. 'You and your valise.'

'The man's fucking valise,' Sam uttered, sitting exhausted next to Steele, his words loud enough to reach the General's ears. Maude had no energy to respond.

Sam leaned against the railing for a few seconds to recover his breath, then turned to find Johnny.

At that moment Johnny was rushing full speed down the hill, his arms filled with wads of the General's papers.

The lighter had left the pier.

The explosion obliterated Johnny's voice, then obliterated him.

III

SEVEN

At that moment there was no more precarious a perch for any workman in New York City. The riveting hammer, thrust alive by a hose of compressed air, had the will to judder straight through him, through the pair of 2x10 planks on which he stood, planks that stretched out into space, nothing but fresh air between them and the ground seventy-seven stories below.

The vibration started and stopped in his arms. Sam had been on similar ledges hundreds of times, and while he didn't relish it, he could sense the least unsoundness in any plank which he trusted with his life. The planks were braced to more 2x10s, makeshift flooring, weights scattered about as insurance, including the weight of his cousin, Charlie, the man with the wide-mouth bucket, the catcher.

They were a team—he and Charlie from Newfoundland, Joseph, a Mohawk from Québec, and Ray, the only genuine American, from Pittsburgh. They had been together since the start of construction in March, an inseparable unit, swearing by each other's every move, never for a second doubting they'd get the job done and done safely. If one man failed to show up for work, the other three quit for the day rather than take on a new man. The bosses accepted that without question. They had forty such teams in their stride, raising the Empire State a story a day. On its incredible schedule and then some.

The work of raising the steel started with Ray, the heater, the passer, situated somewhere below them, sometimes as much as fifty feet below. He fished a red-hot rivet from his portable forge with a pair of tongs and in a sweep of his arm tossed it overhead to Charlie, the catcher. You had to have a good arm, and an even better eye to be a passer. Ray had both. His baseball days had done him good.

Charlie took to catching rivets because he wasn't the man for anything else. It was the job he had the first day they teamed up and he stuck with it. He never missed a rivet when Ray was in form, and could pluck it from his bucket with his tongs, tap it against a girder to clean it of cinders, and have it into the waiting hole of the steel plate, all in a couple of seconds. As slick as the best man at a splittin' table, Sam said, a cod fishing reference only he and Charlie understood.

Joseph was the odd one out. Not part of the Mohawk gangs that came down from Kahnawake. He showed up a day late and missed out, until Sam spotted him and asked if he would team up with them because they were short a man. Joseph, afraid he wouldn't get hired at all, agreed. He and Sam liked what they saw in each other and within days had molded as if they'd been together for years.

The bucker-up and the riveter, a twosome joined liked brothers, or it didn't work. One man at either end of the rivet, on either side of the steel beam—the bucker-up with his dolly bar braced against the rivet's buttonhead, the riveter with the pounding hammer to drive his end abroad and into a cap that fused over the hole. The pressure of one man in visceral balance with the pressure of the other. The pair of them so trusting in each other that sometimes they exchanged places, a break from the constant crouch the riveter was in to make the best use of his hammer. A chance to stretch other muscles, relief from the tautness of a riveter's mind.

Joseph was the quiet kind, and when the shift ended he was gone with his Mohawk pals, even though it seemed he had only a few, his tenement mates mostly. Still, it was family, just like other Newfoundlanders were Sam's family.

He asked Joseph early on, a day's work over, what the others thought of him joining a separate gang.

Joseph shrugged. 'Nothin'.' And that was it then, enough said.

Sam laughed and hung his hand on Joseph's shoulder for a while. From the start he had worked at getting Joseph to go for a drink in Brooklyn before heading home. Maybe someplace in Park Slope where the Newfoundlanders had settled, or North Gowanus where the Mohawks had the places they rented.

The gangs were often on the subway train together, as far as the Pacific Street station. 'You fellows all come along,' he said to Joseph and the couple of his Mohawk friends. 'It's only Union, one more stop. On me.'

They looked at each other, smiled his way and shook their heads.

'*You* come with *us*,' Joseph said. 'On me.'

'Nevis's,' they told him.

They had even less reason to go back to their tenements than Sam did. Their women only ever visited, and then only in summer. More time to drink, less time having to keep a woman happy by being on time for her meals. Like Charlie, who turned them down, figuring he best be going on home to his Madge.

Sam had never heard of Nevis's Grill. 'It used to be Irish,' Joseph told him, as if it added another reason for Sam to go. 'You're Irish.'

'Not lately.'

Sam had told him once that his ancestors had come from County Tipperary to Newfoundland. Joseph had a hard time with that. He knew about Labrador. He could never figure out what Newfoundland had to do with it. Could never quite figure out where Newfoundland was. As bad as the Americans that way.

'Many Indians in Newfoundland?' one of the Mohawk fellows asked him as they were walking the couple of blocks to Nevis's.

Sam shook his head. 'Lots in Labrador. Me, I could be half Indian, who knows. Half Indian. Half Irish.'

'Half foolish,' someone said. That got them all laughing, and got the evening started off right.

When they reached Nevis's the place was already packed with Mohawks. A big crew of them from their own job, but an equal number from jobs on Wall Street. Nothing nearly as high as the Empire State, but at fifty and sixty stories, nothing to turn away from either.

Sam was surrounded by them, the odd man out. He liked it. Liked it more that he would have at the table of Irishmen at the other end of the room, even though he could have passed for one of them. He was holding his own where he was, making friends in what had the look of a closed circle.

They all had their ways of getting booze and lots of money to pay for it and whatever grub they wanted. Making a time of it among themselves. Left alone because of who they were and what they did. Nobody in the place had to be told they worked high steel. If they had the look of Indians, the face, the hair and eyes, then they worked high steel, something others had no nerve for. Not the others in the Grill, for sure, as rambunctious as they were.

Before long the tables were filled with food—steak and chops and sausages, French fried potatoes, and stewed corn. They complained about the corn. Never found any place in New York that knew what to do with corn, they said. Missed their *onenhsto*. Would do anything for a taste of it right now.

'No *kakhwakon*,' the oldest-looking fellow said. 'No *kakhwakon*.'

Sam glanced at Joseph.

'He says there's nothing good to eat.'

Sam thought it hilarious, the way the fellow was bolting down what was on his plate. They all ate too much to get drunk fast, but enough to loosen Joseph's tongue a bit, enough to get him talking about his family back in Québec. His wife and two kids. Wished he didn't have to be away from them, but there it was, Mohawks liked being on the move, liked not knowing where the next job was coming from.

'You got a wife, Sam? Never talk about a wife.'

Sam shook his head.

'Woman?' Pause. 'Nothin'? Sex woman?'

Sam shrugged, which could have meant anything. Feeling the booze like they were, it didn't matter.

Joseph didn't particularly want to know more. Sam told him anyway. He felt like telling somebody, some fellow who didn't care or understand. He'd never heard from her. Not an answer to his letters, neither one of them. He'd sent them in care of the Mission in St. Anthony. They had to have reached her, unless she had moved away. Maybe she went back home to Red Bay. In which case the post office would have sent the letters on to her.

He had even gone to the Grenfell shop on Madison, not long after it opened. In the front window was a framed picture of Doctor Grenfell, surrounded by several of his books. The rest of the window was given over to handicrafts produced by the Mission's Industrials.

He had quickly stepped inside. The shop was small and had the look of a pleasantly furnished parlour. The walls were a pale yellow, here and there accented with trails of blue-stenciled flowers. A tall, mirrored credenza stood against one wall. An oval rug covered much of the hardwood floor, a pair of Windsor side chairs at one edge. In wall cases and covering wooden tables were the items for sale—embroidered lunch cloths and tea cozies, bone carvings, wooden toys, knitted scarves and mittens, beaded sealskin slippers, and much more, including a thick pile of hooked mats. A few such mats were affixed to the walls, their images just as Johnny had described them: wild birds and caribou, sailboats, dog teams traversing winter landscapes, all images drawn by Wilfred Grenfell.

Eventually Sam introduced himself to the woman behind the counter and asked if she knew of an Emma Belbin in St. Anthony, whom he understood worked with the Grenfell Industrials. The woman was hesitant, Sam no more than a stranger off the street. But after he told her he was from Newfoundland and had been a close friend of someone Emma knew, the woman admitted that yes, Miss Belbin was the person who arranged for the handicrafts to be shipped to the shop.

That was all he needed to know. He looked about the shop a while longer and left.

He told Joseph only a bit of the story. Enough to see that Joseph was having trouble getting his head around it. It was the liquor as much as anything.

'Know what?' he said to Joseph when they left the Grill, hanging onto each other in the few moments before they separated and turned for home. 'Joseph, 78th fuckin' floor! Fuck the Chrysler. Monday we're drivin' rivets on the highest goddamn building in the world.'

The liquor talking again. There was nothing wrong with that, the next day off work and nothing to do but drive himself crazy in the house with Charlie and Madge.

'That right?' Joseph said, as if the gangs hadn't been talking about it for a week.

'And me and you—we're fuckin' part of it.'

Joseph nodded. Not a drunk nod, a sensible nod. 'Goin' home now,' said Joseph. 'Goin' home to sleep.'

It was close to twelve o'clock before Sam dragged himself out of bed, after Charlie came into the room. 'Makin' sure you wasn't dead, b'y.'

Charlie would never say much. Madge said more than enough for both of them.

'You and the Indians had a good drunk, did you, Sam? What time did you crawl home? Didn't notice I left some supper on the stove? Didn't care, I suppose.'

'I wasn't hungry.'

'What do Indians eat, anyway? Same as us?'

It was the last thing he wanted to deal with—Madge and her questions. With Madge there was a straight answer to everything. So straight it drove him mental.

'Food, Madge. They eat fuckin' food.'

Charlie looked up. 'No need, Sam. She was only askin'.'

'Shouldn't be hanging around with Indians, Sam,' Madge said. 'Making you more snotty than you already are. Stick to your own kind. That's my advice.'

'Nobody asked for your advice.'

Charlie stared at him again. Sam stuffed his cigarette in the ashtray and jerked himself away from the table. Back to his room for his wallet and then out the screen door.

Jesus, Mary and Joseph. He had to move out. Find a place somewhere. Move in with some of the lot who just came from Newfoundland. It had gotten so bad he hated his days off, rather have his time filled up with work. It was August and hot as hell in the streets and what do you do with yourself when there's silly fuckin' Prohibition. At least in Newfoundland they had the bloody sense to do away with it.

What do you do but find a fellow with a bit of something, or crawl away someplace to try to get away from the heat. Coney Island or Prospect Park.

Sam made his way down Union Street to the Plaza. He stopped for some reason—not that he planned to or even wanted to—and took a second look at the gigantic arch and statues. It was another war in another time. Although his war had its statue, too, inside the Park, down by the Lake. He had sometimes stopped there and from a distance looked at the plaques and the trail of names of the three thousand Brooklyn boys who got themselves killed. He never thought it could be so many, not with the Doughboys only in the war for the last two years of it.

The one in Prospect Park should have meant nothing. Except that the bronze statue of the soldier, surrounded by the angel of death, was carrying a rifle that seemed to be missing its barrel. From a distance it looked like a sniper's rifle, the old SMLE.

Today he had to stop and take a moment for Johnny. Stop because it made him think of Emma. He could have another woman if he wanted one. But not Emma, not likely, ever.

'You recognize that fellow? You think he knows you?'

The words came from someone on a bench nearby. Not a bum, not a down-and-outer.

Sam shook his head. 'Not me.'

'I buried a dozen just like him.'

'You in the war?'

'And you, too. I can tell the ones what was when they come by. Not many do, but I can tell them. They're the ones thinkin' what lucky bastards they are. That it could have been them the angel got in her clutches.'

Sam sat with him on the bench. Got to talking because he had nothing better to do. After a while got to wishing he'd never stopped to talk because it only dragged up the old stuff. He told him about Johnny.

It all meant something. If you'd been to the war it meant something.

'Where you from, pal? Not from Brooklyn, that's for sure.'

Sam told him. Told him what he was doing in New York. Impressed the fellow. A fellow was always impressed by someone working high steel.

'Haven't seen you at the Armory, pal.'

'Never wanted to.'

'Think about it. We'll fix you up with whatever you want. Whisky? Rum? Cognac?'

Sam laughed. Had to admit he had trouble getting his hands on good rum. He missed that about home. He asked the fellow what he did to make a living.

He hesitated. Not for long. 'An operation.'

'A speak?'

'Not exactly. An operation.'

'Where you bring it from?'

'Some island belonging to Frenchmen. Saint Pierre.'

'Off Newfoundland. Jesus, I know right where it is. Always was a hell of a spot for smugglers.'

'Crawlin' with booze,' the fellow agreed. Warehouses full of the stuff. 'You heard of Rum Row? Someone runs it ashore in Jersey. We truck it into New York. Simple. As long as we keep the Coast Guard off our ass.'

The fellow's name was Milton Jacobs. They agreed to meet again, two vets with something in common besides war. Sam agreed it would be the Park Slope Armory. It came with the promise of the best drink of rum Sam would have since leaving Newfoundland.

The 14th Regiment Armory took up most of a city block, and with its towers and turrets and vast brick exterior it resembled a fortress. It still drew a few of the "red-legged devils," famous during the Civil War, but most of the vets who showed up now were from the Great War, although they would never call it that in front of a man who fought in the Battle of Bull Run. A bronze statue of a Doughboy, with his rifle in full form, bayonet and all, stood on a pedestal at the foot of the steps to the main entrance. 'I haven't got much time for this one,' Milton told Sam. 'He ain't got the hot air blown out of him yet.'

Most of the interior of the Armory was taken up with a drill hall that seemed to go on forever. Milton said it could hold ten thousand men and Sam didn't doubt it for a second. 'What the hell will they do with it when we all die off?'

He led Sam to one of several rooms devoted to specific fighting units. Milton had been part of the 23rd Infantry and inside the dark, wood-paneled chamber were a few of his army buddies, the ones who found reason to come together. Just as plenty more, Sam suspected, found reason to stay away. Sam had no trouble fitting in. The promised rum greased the process. It seemed Milton had set aside a special cache for his friends at the Armory, likely the reason the rest of the rooms had drawn fewer numbers than their own.

On the table was a bottle of dark *Rhum Negrita*, something he'd not seen since he was last in St. John's. When Sam told them he fought in Gallipoli, it was met with mindless silence. The one fellow who had heard of it knew only that it was a monumental waste of good men. 'What was the war for any of us but a way to get ourselves killed?' another of them said, looking at Sam, even though there was not one among them who would want to think he had fought in a war that accomplished, as the fellow said, 'fuck all.'

That was a lifetime ago.

'No soldier ever put war behind him,' the fellow said.

Never did, true enough, and here in Brooklyn, where Sam thought himself most able to be rid of it, he again gave in. And in the process got flaming drunk.

Milton got him home, by which time he had vomited in some alley, recovering enough to say a proper goodnight and thank-you. Beyond the front door was a different matter. Madge, a sight in her flimsy nightdress, arms folded across her breasts, hair strewn past her shoulders, stood at the bottom of the stairs. There, she said, to make sure the door wasn't left open.

'Charlie,' she called, 'come and get your ass of a cousin to bed before I throw him back outside.'

He got to bed on his own, nothing to do with Charlie. Even if he was sick again, he cleaned it up in the morning and washed the bedclothes. Madge had no reason to bellyache, which didn't stop her from doing exactly that, lousing up his cup of coffee.

'Enough, Madge,' he said, holding up a hand to her face. And when she was about to say something else, he cut across her. 'I heard it the first time.'

'Not that you're about to heed any of it.' She started in on her boiled egg.

'I'm moving out, Madge. You won't have me to complain about. Course that won't stop you. You'll find something else.'

'You got no place to go,' Charlie said, without emotion, without taking sides. It was a fine line that Charlie walked. A fine, spineless line, Sam thought.

'I'll find a place.'

'Good,' said Madge. 'Peace and quiet for a change.'

'That'll be the day.'

'And what is that supposed to mean?'

'Means that mouth on you never slacks. And never will.'

'Enough, Sam,' Charlie said.

'Tell her that.'

Charlie rose out of his chair and walked across the kitchen. 'I said—enough.' Bluntly, with no life behind it.

Sam shook his head and grinned. It was as much as saying that Charlie was an asshole for marrying her, that he had one hell of a woman to deal with the rest of his life.

Charlie drew his fist and, before Sam recovered from the surprise, lashed him across the mouth. It toppled Sam to the floor.

'Jesus, Charlie!' Sam scrambled to his feet, a hand covering his mouth. It hadn't done any damage. No broken teeth, no blood. But a hell of a sore jaw.

'I said—enough.'

Madge was silent through it all, chair pushed back, hands in the pockets of her housecoat, her eyes breathing satisfaction.

That was the end of it for Sam. In fifteen minutes he was at the door with everything he owned in a suitcase and canvas bag. 'I'll see you on the job, Charlie. And don't be fuckin' late.'

He got a room at some hole-in-the-wall hotel that would have to do until he asked around the site and found someone willing to offer him a place. With any luck there'd be a Newfoundland gang with a spare room he could have, a gang that'd be happy enough to save a few extra bucks on rent.

Nobody offered. Charlie knew it, which made it worse. It was bad enough having to work alongside of him, both pretending there was nothing different between them. Joseph sensed their disagreement straightaway, although he didn't say anything, only caught Sam's eye during their break for lunch.

Sam stared off at nothing. Strife within a gang wasn't good for business. Not that Joseph was about to bring it up directly, though when he saw Sam and Charlie go their separate ways after work, he called after Sam and nodded him to one side.

It was Sam who did the talking. Joseph deserved an explanation, before the fellow started having thoughts about looking for another gang. Sam knew it wouldn't take much, not with more Mohawks showing up every week looking for work, looking for someone with experience to make up a foursome. He didn't want to be losing Joseph.

'You lookin' for a place? You move in with us.'

Sam hadn't expected it, but neither did he think it could ever work. 'You fellows got your own way of doing things.

I'm an outsider. Besides, it's you askin', not the rest of your crowd.'

Joseph went straight to where the others were standing, smoking home-rolls, waiting for him to finish with Sam. He returned, with as much satisfaction as he ever showed. 'Sure. Whenever you want. We got a spare room. Twenty-five a month.'

Sam chuckled and shook his head, not to say no, but because Joseph's persistence surprised him. 'Let me think about it.' He shook Joseph's hand, nodded to the others, and walked away then to do just that—think about what it was he should be doing. One thing he did know for sure. He wouldn't be spending many more nights in the flea-bitten hole of a hotel.

The next day broke clear and sunny, one of those fall days in New York that left people thinking it must be the best city anywhere, a city even the onset of winter would not vilify. He left the subway station and found his way to 5th Avenue, still not having made up his mind about a place to live.

Charlie was waiting outside the shed where they went to pick up their gear. There was no point in ignoring him. They would have to work it out, for the sake of the gang they would.

'Whata ya sayin', Charlie?'

'Madge says you can come back.'

'Fuck that.'

'I had a talk with her. Don't say we didn't offer.'

'I'm not sayin' anything except thanks, but no. fuckin' thanks.'

'You're pig-headed.'

'And what are you, Charlie?'

'Stick with your friends, Sam. You don't want to end up like you did before.'

Charlie dared to mention it. It grated Sam that suddenly,

after years of saying nothing, that it was somehow a time to do it.

Sam walked away. He looked back. 'You goin' to work, asshole, or should I be lookin' for someone else?'

Afterwards, when it was all over, Sam flat on his back, ten feet below where he lost his balance, he blamed it on Charlie. At first Charlie said nothing. It was ten feet, but it could just as easily have been seventy-seven stories, and Sam knew it. He came away with a cracked rib and hardly anything more. The last fellow to do that trick had wrecked his brain on a bundle of plumber's pipe.

'Get him to the hospital,' the foreman said, though Sam was already on his feet, shaking it off. He was surrounded by a dozen men, the three others in his gang among them.

'I'm all right.' But it didn't matter what he said, how quick he was to come up with a reason for the fall. Then he told him, 'You weren't doin' your job, Charlie. You fucked us up.'

Even as he was saying it he knew it wasn't right. A riveter makes his own rhythm, he can't depend on the catcher always making the catch, always getting it to the bucker-up. A good riveter is not distracted by the catcher having to make a second try.

'The hospital, Sam. It's company rules.'

'You're not blamin' me,' Charlie called past the foreman. Agitated now, in a way none of them had seen him before. 'You're not blamin' me. War fucked you up. That's what they all said. War fucked you up!'

The foreman blocked him before Sam took a second step toward Charlie. Had Sam by the arm and turned in the direction of the elevator before Sam did anything but curse, and wince in pain, the shock of the fall worn off.

'You're a liar, Charlie!' The words went nowhere, didn't even reach his cousin, who was gathering up Sam's riveting hammer from a spot a few feet away from where he had landed.

Joseph saw it all, knew as well as anyone what went wrong. Sam was distracted. He should have noticed there wasn't a rivet coming through, and, when he did, it was too late. He had shifted his weight upright, so fast it forced him to grab onto the beam. He swung inward, past Joseph, who himself had grabbed the beam. There was nowhere for Sam's foot to go but down, and the other one on the plank wasn't going to stop it.

'Jeeesus!' he had yelled, the other two left jerking to keep their balance.

It was all luck. The way he landed, what was there to cushion his fall, what wasn't there to wreck him. Steel workers had fallen a lot farther and lived, and fallen a lot less and been killed. Only in the hospital, with the doc's fingers passing over every square inch of his skull, the insurance fellow from Starrett Bros. & Eken there in the room to make sure he was doing a thorough job of it, did Sam admit how close he had come to smashing himself up for good.

The fractured rib would ground him for a while. 'Come see me in a couple of weeks,' the doc told him, strapping a bandage across his chest. 'Right away if there's any sign of headaches or dizziness.'

'One lucky bastard,' the insurance fellow said to Sam on the way out.

Sam agreed, when it came to life and death, luck he'd always had.

'The way it happened,' he told Milton, 'makes me think I'm

not right for steelwork anymore.'

'You've lost your nerve?'

'The bucker-up is gone off with another gang. The other two joined up with two more to make a new gang. That leaves me high and dry.'

He hadn't moved in with Joseph and his buddies. There was no point to it. And he wouldn't be back with Charlie and Madge, that was for sure. It was Milton who helped him find a new place, not far from where he himself lived, which was why Sam was spending his time with the fellow, going on his liquor runs for something to do. Not for pay, because he was no help, not with his rib trying to heal.

'Tell you something, Sam. You want another job, you come in with me when you're ready to get yourself back to work.'

Sam liked what he was seeing. He liked the drives for one thing, getting out of the city. The Jersey shore wasn't Newfoundland, but it was saltwater. It had some of the smell, some of the saltwater sounds. Most of what he saw was after dark, although that likely made it better.

The booze came ashore in small boats—skiffs, yachts, tugs, houseboats—belonging to anyone and everyone willing to take the chance. They had a dozen or more favourite spots where they beached and unloaded, never the same two nights in a row. Milton set his pattern, first with the van's headlights, then with a flashlight beaming different colours. All the time he and his partner on the lookout for cops. Given that the boats made it past the Coast Guard on their weak-kneed prowl, the chances of cops showing up were remote. Still, caution was the word, and the quicker the crates got from the boat into the van the better. And better still once the pile of furniture covering the load was aboard, and Milton was back on the main road, his Jefferson & Bros. moving van tight into traffic. It was only then that Milton relaxed long enough to take notice of the grin across Sam's face.

'The city wants its drink,' said Milton, 'one way or another. Might as well be me as the next fellow. I'm not complaining.'

As far as Sam could see there was money to be made, better money than he was making at the steel, and that was ace by anyone's say. Milton wouldn't tell him how much, but, from the difference between what changed hands and the price paid for booze at a speak, any fool could see life was good. And as far as Sam could tell, if Milton's luck ran out he'd pay the fine, repaint the van with a new name, and start in again. Even that was no concern to him. He wasn't saying, but Milton had his cop friends, and he made life a little easier for them. After all, times were tough all around, and when you could help a fellow out, that was good, for him and for you.

Sam saw the doctor again and came away with a clean ticket. The insurance fellow liked what he heard, and told Sam to give himself another week to loosen up his muscles and then show up for work. It meant starting over with a new gang, which would never have bothered him enough to quit, except Milton had made him an offer. He went to the foreman with one hand on his rib cage and told him that with more time he'd be back. The foreman was hardly buying it, not with the doctor's report in front of him and the string of men desperate for work. But Sam had his line and he stuck to it. He left the site with his reputation intact. If it didn't work out with Milton, he'd have a job. No foreman would laugh off a riveter as experienced as Sam.

At the Armory that afternoon he raised his rum to Milton and the pair shook hands. Starting on the next run Sam would be his man on shore, the one to help guide the incoming boat past the rocks and shoals. Sam knew his way around boats and that would be a bonus to the whole operation. As for Sam, he couldn't wait. And as for his wage, Milton only nodded and told him he'd talk money when the job was done.

The day after the first run, Milton showed up with a wad of bills that he tucked in Sam's hand when none of the others were looking. 'Go home and count that.'

No questions asked. Get the job done, sleep 'til noon and in the middle of the day take a walk to the Armory. Before long the rooms he could afford to rent had a kitchen separate from the sitting room, and off it a balcony where he could sit back after lunch, his feet on the railing, light up a Lucky Strike and leaf through a fresh issue of the *Daily Mirror*.

The operation had its sweat. The crates gave him grief the first few runs. His grimace and a brief torrent of curses got him through, and after that it got easier. Before long, with four runs under his belt, Sam had the swing of it, as good, Milton told him, as anyone he'd ever hired.

A few more runs and Milton was grooming him, though he didn't see it at the time. Milton had something bigger in mind—a second van, Sam in charge. He had Sam do the driving to the Jersey shore a couple of times, just the two of them, Milton doing the talking. Business had slacked off from what it once was, now that more of the booze from Canada was coming through the Great Lakes. The way Milton talked, there was a way to get deeper into what was left of the Rum Row operation.

The next time they met in the Armory, Milton put it to him and Sam agreed without a second's hesitation.

'You can't be getting cocky, Sam. The feds are tightening the screws. Get caught now and we're fucked.'

'You deal with the cops, I'll take care of the rest.'

Sam sat back, folded his arms, a drink in his hand, and a smile across his face wider than any that had been there in months. There was big money to be made, and when he had enough he had big plans to set in motion.

EIGHT

LIKE anyone who ever left Newfoundland to find a job, Sam had it in his head that one day he'd go back for good. Even though he knew the high steel men who did go back because they missed home quickly discovered they missed the money even more. Most of them showed up in the city again and got used to it. Before long they had kids growing up in Brooklyn, kids who had no wish to be living anywhere else.

There was no work to keep a man in Newfoundland. They were calling it a Depression now, not that the price of fish had ever allowed a man a decent living. Sam had been sending money back to his father in Harbour Main since his first paycheck. It always shamed his father to be taking it, hurt him that he couldn't make do on his own, even though it was only himself and Margaret in the house. That was the word from Margaret, she being the one who could read and write and manage a letter.

For now New York was the place for Sam, although even

in New York there was no telling how long the work would last. The city was looking grimy. The line-up at the soup kitchens when he drove through Times Square stretched longer by the day.

Sam liked what he was up to. Working the illicit side of Prohibition was daredevil business, but he hadn't yet seen much to alarm him, certainly not enough to swear off it. There were days when he missed the high steel and wondered about going back to a job on the Empire State, but that passed, his wallet growing steadily thicker.

Milton liked how he handled the responsibility. He spoke the language of the men who crewed the boats, and didn't lose his nerve the few times they smelled the cops and cut the operation short. Milton had coached him well, had made certain he always had an escape route in his head should anything turn foul.

A week into the operation Sam worked a deal with the owner of a Highlands beachside estate for use of the road through his property. The fellow knew the game, and had cut a secret door into his barn for temporary storage if there were more crates coming off the boat than a van could handle. He drove a hard bargain and Sam made no argument. Milton's was a class act. There was plenty of money to go around, to keep the operation well oiled and everybody smiling their way through the nights of getting the booze where it needed to go.

A Coast Guard cutter was somewhere off shore, but the rummy's timing was dead right and it struck the beach with the cutter miles away. What Sam hadn't counted on was the pair of shoremen on beach patrol, parading over the sand in their gumboots and mackinaws, long-handled flashlights in their hands, only switched on when the idiots were practically in his face.

The gang shouldering crates dropped them onto the sand and stood in wait, ready to pounce on the pair or make a dash for the van and the boat, whenever Sam gave the word, although it was clear the rummy, bow dug into the sand, wasn't going anywhere fast.

Sam was mad as hell but not about to show it. Two days before he had tracked down the chief of the shore station, and laid five one hundred dollar bills in his hand. Now here they were, a pair of his shoremen, green as fucking grass by the look of it, nineteen and not a day older, either one of them, and nothing but a goddamn nuisance. They would have to be dealt with, for there was no telling what was crawling around in their thick heads. At least there was no worry about guns. The Coast Guard didn't trust shoremen with anything more than Very flare pistols.

'Gentlemen,' Sam said, 'and what brings you out this fine night?'

'Y'all up to something with those crates?'

Jesus, did they come any wetter behind the ears? Where did the Coast Guard dig them up? It was true what Milton had said—some of them were nothing but hayseed Southerners.

'And what would give you that idea?'

The pair smiled, in unison.

'And where might you call home, gentlemen?'

'North Carolina.' Accent thicker than a wad of tobacco.

'Bit out of your territory, aren't you?'

'Yes, sir. The Coast Guard came our way recruitin' and we figured, what the heck. Let's see us New York City!'

Now Sam was the one smiling. 'Anything we can do to make your job run a little easier, say the word.'

What happened next would depend on what the hillbillies did with their flare guns. Either shoot them off and bring a gang of officers with real guns from somewhere along the shore, or keep them tucked nice and safe in their holsters.

'How kindly of you, sir. Chief Sawyer reckoned you was a gentleman and he was right.'

'What else did the Chief reckon?' Like stay the hell away from the rummies?

'Not a thing, sir. But we got to thinking, Jimmy John and me—what these gentlemen got is a mess o' crates, a boatload we reckoned, and what would they care if there was a crate or two they didn't have to carry all the way to that movin' van up yonder.'

Sam's smile broadened considerably. 'I would say you boys might be right.'

'Them crates got anything like our daddies' corn squeezin's?'

'Afraid not.'

What they took away was a crate each of the finest Martell, straight from Saint Pierre. Off they went, trudging over the sand, happy as shit. Sam kept an eye on them, saw them veer off into a sand dune. Where no doubt they would bury the crates, a couple dozen bottles the Chief would know nothing about, which would bring the boys a tidy bit of extra cash to spend on a night with the ladies in New York City.

The way Sam had it figured, a fellow like him got into the racket, made friends, kept his mouth shut, all the time knowing the cops are out for bigger fish. For now his life was as good as it was likely to get. He often thought of Emma, tried to get it straight why he still had the woman in his head. Sometimes he seemed to drown in the thoughts of her, nights returning home alone to his rooms, nights when his head was not lost in booze.

He set out to get himself a girl. Her name was Mabel. She adored her name and when she had a few drinks would straighten herself to her full height, peer coyly across the bar at

Sam, extending her hand as if flashing a diamond ring, as if she were Mabel Boll—the heiress, the 'Diamond Queen of the Twenties'—not Mabel O'Leary.

She was a looker, dressed better than her last dollar allowed, and she charmed the air with a Brooklyn accent barely tamed for the clientele who walked off West 41st Street into Joel's Café.

Joel was Joel Renaldo, and his place was far from a café. Joel himself coined the term 'Bohemian Refreshery' to describe it, but everyone called it Joel's. It was just off Broadway, across from the stage entrance to the New Amsterdam.

Deliveries tended to be late at night when the place was pretty well spent, clean-up for the next day in full swing. Sam first noticed Mabel, still halfway fresh, an arm resting on the boss's shoulder. She seemed the only one with a sense of humour, something Sam liked about her from the start.

'Milton sent me,' Sam said to Joel, knowing any stranger this late at night was met with suspicion.

'And what's anyone named Milton got to do with me?'

'Johnnie Walker, seventy-five crates. Hennessy, forty. Champagne, seventeen.'

'Seventeen?'

'The b'ys got careless.'

Sam had slipped into Newfoundland dialect. It must have been the saltwater, the boat from Saint Pierre. 'The boys, the crew aboard the launch—not too swift on the numbers. And there was no time to go back for the other three.'

Joel knew he would have to live with it. 'Piper-Heidsieck?'

'You got it.'

'You got my Crème de Violette?'

'The purple stuff? You got it. Twenty-five crates.'

'That's half the order.'

'The launch couldn't take any more. Figured nobody needs fifty crates of that stuff, whatever it is.'

'I damn well do.'

'I'll have it for you, pal, next trip.'

Once the liquor was unloaded and stored in the deep reaches of the basement, Sam found out what Joel Renaldo was up to with all those bottles of purple liquor. Sam stood at the bar, a cigarette in one hand, a fancy-stemmed cocktail glass in the other, its Blue Moon to his lips.

'Joel's trademark,' Mabel told Sam, standing within sizing-up distance. 'This ain't your two-bit joint.' Sam had figured as much the minute he stepped through the door.

The Blue Moon wasn't Sam's drink, though it fit the place. Upstairs, where Mabel led him, was their spiffy dining room, where the Blue Moon looked right at home. The back wall was covered with framed caricatures of what Mabel called the big cheeses—singers, songwriters, actors, actresses.

'Miquel sketched these. Come see.' She led him closer, past the bare tables and stacks of chairs, around the fellow on his knees polishing the floor. Many of the sketches were signed by the big cheeses themselves, with a personal note to Joel. Mabel's forefinger jumped between several—Eddie Cantor, Fanny Brice, the Gershwins—and then to Mabel Boll.

'Ain't she the queen bee,' said Mabel.

But that wasn't all. She drew Sam deeper into the room, into what looked to be a smaller private dining area. Mabel pulled back the beaded curtain. A white-haired, bearded man, scribbling in a notebook, looked up from a table. Sam couldn't figure it. He could have been in a monastery all his life, except for the vest and suit and the glass of booze next to him.

'Everything okay, Mr. Markham? I'll let you know when it's time.'

'Thank you, Mabel. How sweet you are.'

She smiled, kissing the tips of her fingers and flicking them into the air as the curtain fell back in place. 'He's always the last to leave. Joel has a soft spot for him.'

Sam hadn't done anything to hide his puzzled look.

'Edwin Markham.'

'Who?'

'The poet.'

Sam shrugged.

'You got no culture, fella. You can't be showin' up here with a brain like a brick.' It had worked its way through her Brooklyn accent without an ounce of irony. Sam laughed.

It was what captured him in the end—her rough-and-ready, unflappable talk, no matter who was at the other end of the conversation. Sam spent most of the next afternoon in haberdasheries, getting himself outfitted in clothes he would never have pictured himself wearing. He returned to Joel's that night, walked uncomfortably up the stairs, straight into the din of the dining room, and into her line of sight.

It caught Mabel in full flight. Brought her to a dead stop. She looked him up and down. 'Well now, Mr. Kennedy, ain't you the dandy.'

Sam straightened his bowtie, hoping he resembled George Bancroft in *Thunderbolt*, only younger.

'No sweet thing hanging on that arm of yours?'

'It couldn't be just any dame. I'm waiting for the right one.'

'Really?'

'And if I wait long enough, perhaps after she's done work...'

'That's taking a chance.'

'I'm a betting man.'

'Are you, Mr. Kennedy? Unfortunately every table in our establishment is filled.' She smiled, kept him waiting for a moment, then extended a hand and smoothed his shoulder. She leaned into his ear and whispered, 'You just got lucky. I can arrange something.'

Mabel fell back into her hostess role, with enough charm to fill the dining room, flavouring it with her snappy candor, leaving the patrons ripe for Joel to start the free flow from their wallets, likely beginning with Blue Moons all around. Through the hubbub she directed that an extra table be set up in the rear of the room. It was so close to the kitchen door that waiters loaded down with dishes were constantly having to dance around it.

It added to the bustle, fit the mood of the place. The waiters didn't complain, which meant it was all in an evening's business. When Joel himself showed up—impeccable in a steel grey, high-collared, double-breasted suit—Sam got no lesser treatment than if he had stepped across the street after finishing up at Ziegfeld's *Follies*. Which meant it was fast, friendly and straight to the point. Joel had his attention on a dozen things at the same time.

'Whisky,' said Sam. 'On the rocks.'

'And to eat—chili con carne?' said Joel.

Sam had never heard of it. 'Bring me one.'

All the time Joel was keeping an eye on his singer—a shy girl bedecked for a Spanish fiesta, whirling her way between the tables, singing '*You made me love you, I didn't want to do it, I didn't want to do it.*' A man with a violin, his multicoloured ruffles a match for her own, trailed two steps behind.

There was no end to the diversions. The duo had hardly retreated when a tango-dancing couple appeared, decked all in black except for a few touches of crimson, including a rose emerging from the woman's hair. A fellow—hair greased, shirt agape—played the bandoneón in the shadows, while the couple, fiercely intense, skirted the dining room. Several times the music rose sharply, then stopped, a cue for the couple to halt mid-stride and pose seductively in front of a particular table, before dashing on, the music blurting aloud again.

A waiter delivered a glass pedestal dish holding a mound of balls, of something which looked like watermelon, only harder, with a circle of shrimp hanging off the rim. 'Mr. Renaldo offers his compliments,' said the waiter, and dashed off to deliver the two other dishes he was carrying.

For a moment Sam mistook it for the main course, then sizing up the progress of meals at other tables, decided it couldn't be. He ate it all, one piece at a time, and with gusto. The waiter showed up and whisked away the empty dish.

A white porcelain plate holding a white porcelain bowl arrived, and Sam was struck with doubts about what now lay in front of him. He shook out his napkin and spread it across his lap. With a spoon, he delved cautiously beneath a mound of grated cheese and into something reddish that wasn't quite soup and wasn't quite stew.

Mabel slipped by to check on his progress. 'You ain't going to find that dish anywhere else in New York City,' she announced with a flair that declared the food to be thoroughly high class.

'I'm not used to spice.'

'Get used to it.' She smiled at him and pursed her red lips. She leaned her head toward a boisterous table on the far side of the room. 'Miquel and Diego, the Mexicans, of course they love chili con carne. The table next to them—hop heads and boozers. They haven't a clue what they're eating. And see those fellas in the corner, they're here every night. They write for the newspapers. Can you imagine? I tell them, write something as good as Mr. Markham, then you can call yourself writers. They think it's very funny.'

Suddenly a yelling match spilled from the back room, swelling over the considerable noise of the dining area. Mabel was off like a shot. When the yelling didn't subside, Sam pushed himself away from the table and went in search of her.

He found Mabel standing between the poet Markham and some drunken stiff who had barged into the room unannounced.

'The bastard owes me money!' the fellow blared.

Mabel stuck her face squarely in his. 'Shut your mouth you obnoxious twit!'

Sam caught the twit's arm just as he was about to lay a fist into Mabel. Sam wrenched the arm into his back and dragged him aside. Down an unlit hallway, to a small back door which Mabel threw open. Sam rammed the fellow through it and landed him in a heap in the alley.

Back in the room the poet summed it up. 'You were a godsend, young man. I thank you, for I don't know to what lengths the derelict would have gone, even though I have never seen him before in my life. You deserve the best these unsavoury times allow.'

Mabel was impressed, for it seemed that Edwin Markham was rarely effusive.

'Mabel, my dear, what good have we to bestow on this gentlemen?'

It was the start of Sam's fraternization with Edwin Markham and his fling with the man's sweetheart. Markham took to Sam in a way a father might to a neighbour's son he admired more than his own. Once it was revealed that Sam had gone to war, the attraction grew even stronger.

Markham told Sam, 'My interest is man in his most wretched states.'

He had Sam recount his war experiences in France, all the while jotting notes in his journal. At Markham's request, Sam returned several times purposely to sit with him and answer his questions. Sam was reluctant to do it, but he couldn't ignore how it pleased Mabel. What Markham wanted were details of the mud and vermin, the endless hours in the trenches, the way it all played on a soldier's mind.

'Have you killed a man?' Markham asked him, when the poet seemed close to exhausting his questions.

'Likely I have.'

'A defenseless man?'

Sam wouldn't answer.

'Because he was the enemy, anything more?' Markham said.

The poet's impatience exposed a strain of righteousness that quickly worked itself under Sam's skin.

'One cannot escape the realities of the modern world.'

'I went to do a job and I did it. The Turks and Germans the same.'

'But we must question the ethics of that job, or the world will never be free of conflict.'

'Have you been to war, Mr. Markham?'

'No, sir, I have not. I was a boy during the Civil War. And beyond my years for yours.'

'Then you are a fortunate man.'

Sam stood up to leave.

'Please, I have no intention of questioning your motives. You had honest ones I have not a doubt.'

As Sam remembered it he had no motives.

'You went then,' said Markham, 'and thought yourself the better man for it.'

'I did, sir!' declared Sam and in such a decisive manner that it put an end to their exchange.

'He'll write a poem about you,' Mabel said to Sam when the two were alone a week later in his rented rooms. 'He's got loads of poems about me.'

'What kind of poems?'

'Love poems.'

'He is in love with you?'

'Of course.'

Sam took it as a game.

Mabel shouted, 'Don't laugh! He's a great poet and you're an idiot. Name one poem he's written. Name one.'

Sam shrugged.

'You don't know nothin'.'

'I know you're a swell girl, and I'll show you what I know. I just need the chance.'

'Is that right, chump? What have you got on your mind that half the men who come into our establishment haven't got on theirs?'

She persisted in calling it an establishment. It drove Sam crazy.

'You want a little coochie? Is that what you're after? Well, ain't you just another bear trailin' the honey.'

Of course that was what he was after. And of course she knew it. It annoyed him that he would have to work harder than he predicted to get it.

'You got a future, Sam? I ain't gettin' involved with a fella what got no future. He don't have to be rich but he gotta have a future.'

The goddamn thing was she was serious. 'I got a future, Mabel.' Wanting it so bad he could have been panting. 'What the hell, Mabel—I got so much future I fucking well don't know what to do with it.'

She shook her head and lit a cigarette, frowning. She combed her hair back through her fingers, then used the same hand to languidly rub the back of her neck. 'I like my men serious. I like 'em cultured.'

'Hell, Mabel, you're a complicated gal.'

She smiled between draws on the cigarette, taking his words as a compliment. For all her talk there was a lot to like about her still. She was a magnet and played it for all it was worth. Played it at a level most Brooklyn girls could never hope to reach, and did it with a smile.

'Sam, sweetheart, you got to work for it. You can't be licking the cone like it's Sunday afternoon in the park. You can't expect to be handed the sweetest fruit you're ever likely to get in your whole life just by being Sam. Show me Sam with class. Show me Sam with more than fancy new Andrew Jacksons sticking out of his wallet.'

'You like music, Mabel?'

'Ain't that an insult?'

'You like it high class, Mabel? You like *art*?'

He said *art* like it was something exotic, as if he were opening the palm of one hand and in it lay a golden figurine.

'Try me. Get me excited.'

He got her excited the following Sunday afternoon, walking up the steps of the Brooklyn Museum, Mabel chic in the lambswool jacket she had picked out and he had bought for her. Arm in arm with Sam, in the trench coat he had purchased for his first evening at Joel's.

They were a swank pair and they made the most of it,

sashaying from gallery to gallery, stopping in front of what particularly caught their eye, leaning against each other and pointing out details and declaring just how wonderful it all was.

They lingered particularly long in the Egyptian Galleries, in front of a glass case containing the painted limestone sculpture of Neb-sen and Nebet-ta. Sam held Mabel tight and read aloud, '1400 BC. Neb-sen was a scribe in the royal treasury. Nebet-ta was a songstress in the temple of the goddess Isis.'

'Ain't that swell, Sam? Don't that make you shiver? *Songstress in the temple of the goddess Isis.*' Mabel gazed on the two seated figures in their elaborate headdresses and jewelry.

'Like you.' Sam tightened his arm around Mabel's waist. 'Nightingale in the Bohemian Refreshery.'

'Jesus, Sam, you're corny. I can't sing a note.'

'Look, one of buddy's hands is hidden. What's it doing stuck behind her back?' His own hand drifted from Mabel's waist to her rump, held there, then gripped one of her buttocks.

Mabel emitted a curse, jabbing Sam in the ribs with her elbow. He groaned audibly.

'Smarten up.' She disengaged and strutted on. Sam caught up with her and cautiously slid an arm around her waist again.

She didn't protest, and eventually she eased herself against him. 'Keep it clean, Sam. Don't be a fucking idiot.'

Sam began weaving stories about his time in Cairo. It kept her close to him. The Regiment on its way to Gallipoli, him riding a camel to the Sphinx, the gang of soldiers filing through the Egyptian Museum. 'This is nothing compared to what we saw, Mabel. Pharaoh stuff you wouldn't believe.'

'Really, Sam?'

'Gold. They used gold like it was paint, Mabel.'

'Real gold?'

'Of course real gold. You heard about the mask of Tutankhamun? Pure, solid gold.'

Gold excited Mabel. Got her heart racing. Set her off, Sam discovered. And no telling what might be the consequence. He savoured the thought of it as they sat in the foyer listening to musicians from the Brooklyn Conservatory. He wondered where he would go to purchase a gold bracelet.

'Mozart's *Eine Kleine Nachtmusik*,' the conductor said it was, and a pair of violins got Sam's heart racing too, the music filling the marbled space and sending Mabel into her seventh heaven, her hand gripping his, her eyes closed as if it was her favourite piece of music ever.

'Oh, Sam,' she whispered when the piece ended, 'this is divine.'

He couldn't say the same about the sex. The gold bracelet got in the way of his heaven, knocking against his testicles on a couple of occasions.

'I'm sorry. Did that hurt?'

Not particularly, but it did mar the moment. He sank himself into her again, gently moving her hand out of harm's way.

'Sam?' she said, when he was drawing reasonably near his peak.

He moaned a feeble 'What?'

'Sam, do you think I suit short hair?'

'Depends where.'

'Oh, Sam. You're such a kidder.'

She wasn't into it. The climax was slipping sorely out of reach.

'For fuck's sake, Mabel, forget the hair.'

'Sam, that's not nice.'

'I'm sorry, Mabel.'

The room's radiator had been malfunctioning all afternoon. He lay, a ruddy, steaming mess atop her. Heat made him especially horny, and the open bedroom window did nothing but confuse the situation. At inopportune intervals a frigid breeze blew across their naked selves.

'Sam, love, think of poetry. Think of your heart swelling at Mr. Markham's words.'

'Fuck Markham.'

She dashed away from the bed at that. Glared at him from across the room. 'Say you're sorry. Say it and I might believe you.'

'I'm sorry, Mabel.'

She rushed into her clothes, all the while crying, her heart severely compromised.

'Sorry is not good enough. You don't mean it,' she blurted through her sobs.

'I do, Mabel. I do.'

She stood over him in a bright, boldly purple dress that clung to her mercilessly, her feet wedged in heeled slingbacks, applying red lipstick with one hand, wiping tears with the back of the other. He sat naked on the corner of the bed, his palms tight against the top of his head.

'No, you don't, Sam Kennedy. No you *don't*. Take that dick of yours and stick it where the sun don't shine.'

She slammed the door behind her.

Either she would never have anything more to do with him, or it was an act—her turning on the waterworks at will. He decided it was the second, and a few days later, when he made his next delivery to Joel's, he went in search of her.

Joel was all business. Word had made its way to him. And, as Sam expected, Mabel gave Sam the cold shoulder. He was sure he could win her back.

'How is Mr. Markham?'

'Ask him yourself. He's in his room. I told him what you said. In one of our intimate moments.'

'A poetry reading, Mabel?' Sam marched to the back room, with more spit and determination than Mabel likely believed he had in him. He dashed aside the beaded curtain and stepped inside. The curtain jangled back in place.

'Mr. Markham, how are you?'

Markham looked up quickly, pen in hand. 'I'll have a word with you young man.' Markham's look hardened further.

It reminded Sam of approaching the aged Father O'Donnell, for his mandatory lecture when Sam was eight, prior to his First Communion.

'We're not sure of you, Sam. We thought we had you figured out. You need some direction, my man.'

Sam had fallen violently from grace. 'Mabel likes to talk,' he told Markham, with his arms spread wide, as if he were addressing the entire world that surrounded Mabel. 'She doesn't always get it right.'

She burst through the beads. 'What's he saying about me? What's he saying? Don't believe a word of it!' She planted herself behind Markham's chair and set a hand firmly on each of his shoulders.

Fuck, thought Sam, perhaps they don't truly have an ounce of common sense between them.

'Take my advice, Mr. Kennedy, and forget the dear lady...' At which point he laid a hand against one of Mabel's. 'And get yourself on the straight and narrow.'

'Shove off, Sam,' Mabel declared. 'Find someone your own type, some floozie from Newfoundland.' Pronouncing the last word correctly, as he had taught her.

There was a long silence during which no one moved. Markham reached into a satchel that lay on the table and withdrew a book. He opened it to the title page and wrote a few words. He snapped the book shut and held it out to Sam, his aged hand quivering slightly. Sam accepted the book.

'Good-bye, Mr. Kennedy.'

Mabel said nothing. She gripped Markham's shoulders more tightly.

Sam turned and left the room. He left Joel's and, although he didn't anticipate it at that moment, he would not step inside the establishment again.

The next day he felt a severe tug back to the Empire State.

It made no sense, giving up the wads of money. Yet every time he passed the Empire State and saw the crews driving closer to what had to be the end, he was left to fight the urge to be working when they topped it out, made the final thrust skyward. If only for a few seconds, he wanted to be the highest steelman on the highest building ever built.

He said so to Milton. He needed a couple of weeks, that was all. Milton was not convinced, and was not about to relent. He liked things the way they were, liked how Sam had made it clockwork. There was no time to train another man. Milton would have to take up the slack himself.

'Men on the streets begging for jobs and you're telling me you want a sonofabitch of a holiday. The cops got my number, but they don't got yours. Don't fuck me up, Sam.'

Good sense wasn't in the cards. 'Some things are more important than money.'

He was sounding like a grousing priest, and Milton was not about to give it the courtesy of a reply. He stared at Sam, his temper ready to flare again. He drew back. He left it to Sam to either dig himself in, or slip away and do the job he'd been hired to do.

'I quit.'

'Jesus.'

'Your ass'll soon be on the curb anyway, Milton. Prohibition ain't lastin' much longer.' It shut both of them up. Sam spread his hands as if he were somehow the innocent one.

'The war fucked you worse than I thought.'

That was the end of it. Sam walked away.

'You don't need me, Sam, that's what you're telling me? Well I'm telling you—don't come looking for me when you're standing in the goddamn breadline, without two fucking cents to rub together.'

The foreman's shed was a madhouse. Like it always was, only worse now that the end of the steel work was only weeks away.

The fellow remembered only too well the fall Sam had taken. Right away he knew Sam was lying. Sam kept it up anyway. 'Got my strength back last week, honest.'

He remembered Sam's reputation. All he had time for was that. 'Who was in your gang?'

Sam told him. The fellow jerked through some papers. 'Mohawk's the riveter now. Bucker-up made a fuck of it a few times. I'll haul him out, put the others back in. Show up in the morning.'

The foreman was on to something else and Sam was out the door.

Sam was feeling decent about what he had done—a good job making good, honest money. Besides, he'd saved a sweet chunk of what he'd made delivering the booze.

He left the site, and walked on to Madison Avenue.

He stopped in front of the Grenfell store, as he had thought about doing for weeks. He stood at the window and looked at the display, braced himself to go inside. A poster caught his eye, propped up on an easel amid Grenfell's books.

The man himself was coming to New York. Part of a speaking tour of the eastern states. At the Mecca Temple on 55th Street. Sam memorized the details, and immediately opened the door.

He nodded to the woman behind the counter, the woman he had spoken to the first time he had been in the store. She was arranging a small stockpile of new merchandise.

'Yes?' Her tone hadn't changed. 'Mr...Kennedy.'

'Good day,' he said. 'I was wondering if you had heard from Miss Belbin recently?'

'No, I haven't.'

He knew it wasn't true. He began walking about the shop, as if he were looking to buy something, as if it were the main reason he had come in.

'I did notice in this last shipment a mat with her name attached.'

He stopped at the pile of hooked mats, and began looking through it. Perhaps the mat had been sold. He asked.

The woman found it immediately, withdrew it from the pile and set it on the counter. The design of the mat was unlike any of the others. 'I'm not surprised it hasn't sold. It's rather odd. The label calls it *Fish on Flake*. It means nothing to us.'

Sam looked at it more closely. It was all of a pattern, a stylized repetition of split fish in subdued tones—browns and beiges, contrasting with white and touches of coral. He considered offering an explanation—the traditional

Newfoundland enterprise of drying salted codfish, outdoors on a platform of sticks, a flake. He chose not to, and instead said to the woman, 'I want to purchase it.'

'Are you sure? You haven't looked through all the others.'

'This is the one.' He made something of a show paying for it, peeling a ten-dollar bill from a folded clump of money, straightening it with pressure from his thumb down its centre, before setting it on the counter.

She rolled the mat into a bundle. 'Shall I wrap it?'

'Certainly.'

She wrapped it in brown paper, Sam standing motionless across the counter from her, adding to her discomfort. They said nothing more, until the paper had been tied and the mat placed in his hands, together with his change.

'Good-bye.'

His eyes fell on hers for a moment, then he turned and left the store, the cylindrical package under his arm.

NINE

THE Shriners' Mecca Temple rose above West 55th Street, a building more at home in Morocco than Manhattan, its façade patterned with brightly glazed tiles, its huge red terra-cotta dome topped by a scimitar and crescent. Sam thought it odd, but nothing he encountered in New York City surprised him anymore.

He followed the crowd into the lavish auditorium, and sank into the last remaining front-row seat in the lower balcony. Above him soared a vast honeycombed ceiling, accented in gold, set off by a host of orbicular chandeliers.

Sam was uneasy. He had nothing in common with the men and women edging him on three sides, and he wasn't sure what, if anything, he would gain from the scene about to reveal itself on stage. It was a relief when the lights dimmed. Into the spotlight came two men—one to introduce Grenfell, the other the man himself.

The applause for Grenfell was long and robust, befitting the figure before them—oddly distinguished, bearing a rugged face and stance that indicated a man who had spent much of his life in the out-of-doors.

When he spoke it was with the chumminess one might expect of a meeting between old friends. 'I have come to tell you about the world to be found along the far-flung seacoasts of northern Newfoundland and southern Labrador. There I have found the most industrious and hard-working people I have ever known. A people needing help to live a decent life, with proper medical care.'

It was something in which everyone in the audience took comfort, for their dollars—the money they had deposited into the collection bins as they entered the auditorium—was about to do good deeds.

Then, just as every soul was relieved, guilt stared them in the face. Onto a large screen behind the Doctor, lantern slides projected the sorry state of poverty within the remotest reaches of the Mission. Not a single person could have been left untouched by the sight of barefoot, desperately clad children outside squat, sod-roofed huts.

The Doctor's experience had taught him the wisdom of lingering, not on hardship, but rather on the ability of the Mission to overcome hardship. He particularly liked telling the story of little Kirkina. Although she had long ago grown into a woman, hers was a tale that never failed to fill every heart, no matter the size or the temperament of the audience.

Two-year-old Kirkina, in an isolated cabin deep in the Labrador wilderness, had suffered a severe case of frostbite. With gangrene setting into her legs, her trapper father severed both limbs with his axe to save her life. Days later the man fell through ice and drowned. Hopelessly maimed and with a mother too sick to care for her, Kirkina was brought to Indian Harbour, where the Doctor encountered her for the first time. Kirkina was embraced by the Mission.

'Some of you would know Dr. John Macpherson. John worked with the Mission in Labrador and when he and his family returned to the United States, they brought little Kirkina with them. It was here in New York that she went to school, where she walked about with her new artificial limbs. Kirkina eventually returned to Labrador and it is there she lives today, a happy, productive human being, saved from a life of misery by people such as yourselves who have been so generous in your support of our great Grenfell Mission. And some of you know of Dr. Elliott Salomon, another of the fine young men who gave of themselves for the Mission...'

The man spoke for ninety minutes, his ramblings taking him from sled dogs to eye surgery, from the dire need for dental instruments to the caribou-hide slippers for sale in the shop on Madison Avenue. He talked of hospitals and nursing stations, of cooperatives and handicraft Industrials. He spoke without a note, and when he decided to bring it to an end the audience was as pleased to be in his company as when he began. They filed out of the auditorium, searching their pockets and purses for more money to add to what they had already entrusted to the collection bins.

Sam, like every person in the audience, was filled with the need to help. For him it went beyond money. The business of the afternoon had been his people. If not exactly his kin, then people who lived a meager life not far off what he had once known, not far off what his own father still knew. He remembered a summer as a child when he himself had gone barefoot, when the price of fish fell particularly low and the merchant refused to extend them credit beyond anything but food.

He hung about the foyer anxious to speak with Grenfell. The man emerged from the inner reaches of the building to autograph copies of his books. Sam waited for the interminable line to thin, several times stepping outside, smoking, walking aimlessly about the sidewalks, until he returned to find the line near its end.

'Doctor Grenfell, sir. May I have a word with you?'

Sam's cadence caught his ear. 'You're not from New York.'

'Newfoundland.' Sam quickly introduced himself and explained what had brought him to the city.

'And do you miss the island?'

'I would like to go back. Would the Mission have any work?'

Grenfell looked at him with some curiosity, for most often it was a young man on the cusp of finishing medical school who approached him after a lecture, or a wealthy supporter of the Mission anxious to volunteer his son for a summer of rough work to make a man out of him. Sam was far from either.

'We don't have much call for high-steel workers in St. Anthony.'

'I'm a handy man on any construction job. I know my way around boats.'

'Have you driven a dogteam?'

'I can learn.'

Grenfell had no doubt he could. He had seen such a trait in plenty of Newfoundland men—agility in taking on manual tasks, especially if they involved getting about in the outdoors.

'I'm very keen on what you were saying about cooperatives.'

'And why is that?'

Sam told him about his father's life in the fishery. 'Get me involved,' he said to Grenfell. 'Teach me what to do and I'll do it.'

'I'm not sure you would stick it out. After New York, there's a lot to get used to.'

'I made it through the war. I can get used to anything.'

The change in the man was pronounced. Grenfell looked at Sam with an intensity that hadn't surfaced before.

Sam had known Johnny, that was the clincher. And Archie Ash. He, too, had worked for the Mission. Grenfell went silent for a moment.

'If you show up, I'll see what I can do for you,' he said in the end, quickly shaking Sam's hand, though not before he retrieved a booklet from the table and handed it to him. 'Here, read this.' Grenfell allowed himself to be ushered away for dinner, following which he would catch a train to Philadelphia.

Sam was left standing alone. The exchange had given him plenty to consider, had put the Grenfell Mission within his reach.

He glanced at the booklet, before slipping it into his coat pocket to read when he returned to his lodgings. *Labrador's Fight for Economic Freedom*, the cover said, by Sir Wilfred Grenfell.

There was one piece of business left for Sam in New York— the final stretch of work on the Empire State. It would be his invisible mark left on the city.

When Sam showed up to start work Joseph welcomed him as if the original gang had never split.

'Joseph, and how the hell are you?'

Joseph smiled more broadly and shrugged.

As for Charlie—the two would tolerate each other, and never act like it was anything but a job. No risks, no chances, safety first, and that was all that mattered. Ray was Ray, his aim from down below as accurate as ever.

The estimate was two weeks to topping out, two weeks of all-out effort to bring an end to the steel work. Everyone was feeling the fervor of stretching past any building ever erected.

Their labour was single-minded. It had only taken a day back on the job for the order of work to reconcile itself and for the four of them to lock back into the team they had once been. They rarely spoke, except when they paused to survey their efforts, to be certain nothing had been missed, before moving on, edging the next beam in place, ever upward.

The main structure was topped out at the 86th floor. Beyond it rose a tower that ended in an open-air observation platform 102 stories high. Through the centre of the tower was a metal shaft that would eventually extend through the platform's conical dome, and there taper to a mast for mooring dirigibles. It was amid the curved steel shaping the dome that Sam and Joseph eventually found themselves, two of the chosen few gunning in and securing the rivets of what would become the inhabitable limit of the Empire State Building.

They were given the go ahead to climb the derrick that for now ran through the centre of the dome, a bucket of hot rivets following behind on a pulley. Joseph had inherited the rivet gun when Sam was off the job, and led the way along the girders, Sam tight behind, the iron bar of a wrench in his hand. Raw-nerved monkey men clambering about the pinnacle of steel.

On the uppermost part of the dome Sam purposely broke the routine and forced Joseph to take in the moment with him. They would never be any higher.

They did something they rarely did—looked down and around, filling themselves up with the expanse of the city.

Their steelworkers' eyes fixed on the skyscrapers filling Manhattan. They were far above the Woolworth and the Singer, the Bank of Manhattan Trust and the New York Life, and best of all, a good twenty-five floors atop the Chrysler. Its glinting Deco cap of terraced stainless-steel would never be matched. But height was what mattered to steelmen.

Sam jerked his thumb in the direction of where the mooring post would sit. 'The nose of German Zeps, perched right there. Believe it?'

Joseph shook his head. Neither of them did.

'They killed your buddies, in the war.'

And now he was building a place for them to dock their airships.

Joseph grinned his stupid, sweet grin.

'You an Indian from Québec and me a Newfoundland bayman, on top o' the fuckin' world. Whataya think o' that?'

'I think you're crazy.'

They laughed and gripped each other's free hand, the one they normally used to steady themselves, and in their grip made an alliance, if one that would likely never manifest itself again.

Al Smith showed up after that. One time Governor of New York, the man who ran against Hoover for President and lost, now head of the corporation that built the Empire State. He shot in a rivet of solid gold. Sam caught his eye, as if to say yes, hadn't the men done a fine job, and weren't they all proud to say they were the team that did what couldn't be done. The steel work was complete and it was still only the 21st of November.

And when the Empire State Building opened on May 1, 1931, it had been thirteen months start to finish.

The day it opened Sam was home, in Harbour Main,

oblivious to the ceremony. Otherwise he would have been there alongside Joseph and the multitude of men who had worked the Empire State and who had come together to revel in the day.

He'd made it to Harbour Main in time for Christmas, the first Christmas he'd spent there since the year he'd returned from the war. He showed up with a good deal more than a few dollars in his pocket, keen to make it something special for his father and Margaret.

Sam had given them little notice he was coming—a telegram sent from Port aux Basques while waiting to board the train that would take him across the island. He left the train at Avondale and walked the last few miles, over a road he'd walked dozens of times as a raw schoolboy. He was hardly dressed for mid-December, and the suitcase was a nuisance, but when he came in sight of Harbour Main he shed all the discomforts and let himself be restored with the sentiment he felt for the place.

It was borne of the freedoms of youth to be sure, and in time a cynicism would set in, but for now he was coming home with family to welcome him.

His father was at the kitchen table when Sam came through the door, having drunk tea half the day to pass the time before his son turned up. Margaret was on the daybed, resting. She'd just finished peeling a bowlful of carrots, potatoes and turnip, ready now for the pot, along with cabbage, salt beef and peas pudding.

'Blessed Jesus, Paddy, and what are ya at?' A smile across Sam's face as broad as sunshine. He wrapped one arm around his pale, arthritic father, the other around the bone-thin waist of his sister.

There was plenty to be thankful for. Sam's safe return for a start, always that, because his life in New York was so far removed from their own in Harbour Main as to be incomprehensible. Sam's health and strength, so much more tangible than anything they now knew. The fact he survived the war, when so many hadn't, had been a miracle to set him apart in their minds, only reinforced by the tales of what he worked at in New York. Sam filled up their mundane lives as soon as he stepped inside the house. It brought tears to his father, something Sam hadn't seen since the day in 1919 that he stepped back in the house in his uniform.

It had been a harsh fall, with a harsher winter bound to follow. The price fishermen were getting for their saltcod had dropped to less than $5 a hundredweight. Not many years before it had been three times as much. The price for herring was no better.

A few local men had been hired at the iron-ore mines on Bell Island, but his father's age and poor health had put it permanently out of the question. He and Margaret survived on fish and bread, and the vegetables that filled their cellar. Harbour Main, thank God, had good grounds for growing vegetables and that more than anything would keep them, come March, from joining the lineup to be put on the dole.

Sam had never seen his father in a worse state. His spirits lifted when the tears passed, spirits that couldn't go much lower according to what Margaret told Sam when he and his sister were alone. Margaret herself was hardly much better. She had always been a nervous sort, never wanting to leave home, not even to be a nun as it turned out, and never wanting a man as far as Sam could tell. What satisfaction there was in her life came from taking care of her father. For all those years now just the two of them.

Sam often wondered about Margaret, what she could have made of herself if she'd had the will. When she graduated with her grade eleven the priest tried to convince her to apply for a course in stenography at Littledale in St. John's, the college run by the Mercy Sisters. No trouble getting a job once she finished, and the nuns would look out to her, Father Dwyer had said, so she needn't get nervous about being away from home. Margaret wasn't convinced. She worked for a time in the merchant's general store, and did well at it, too, with her head for figures, but that lasted no more than a couple of years. She hadn't done anything since, so far as Sam could tell, except knit, read and cook, keep the house spotless. And go to Mass.

'Monsignor is worried. He's seen the change in him. Father's wearing away to nothing, Sam. And he won't go to Mass anymore. Monsignor don't know what to make of it.'

His sister's life was built around the Church. It played into every thought she had, everything she did, as if, without it, there would not be a world for her to live in. As much as it irritated Sam, he knew he couldn't complain, knew Margaret's life might be in ruin without it.

Sam preferred the house when it was filled with people. Once word was out that he was back, there was a steady stream of them—aunts and uncles and all four of his cousins who lived within walking distance, their wives and husbands and children. They all came with the same story, what a hellish year it had been, that it could only get worse.

Sam had brought bottles of dark rum, Milky Ways and Baby Ruths, and Camel cigarettes. For the moment at least, their troubles were set aside. On Saturday evening Billy Woodford showed up with his accordion and an even bigger crowd of them sang and danced and scarfed down pea soup and bread until daylight. Crawled away somewhere, those not living in the harbour, for a few hours sleep, before they all got up, washed themselves and paraded off to Mass. Margaret in the lead, with her father propped up against Sam, crippling along behind.

Sunday dinner then, a brace of rabbits as tasty as ever graced the table, Margaret no more proud than if the Lord had personally smiled down on them, the Kennedys, together and liking what they did have, and not forgetting who they had to thank for it all.

His cousin, Albert, was living in St. John's, and when, several months later, Sam couldn't escape the frustrations of life in Harbour Main any longer, he made plans to visit him and to look for a job to tide him over to the time of the first coastal boat run of the season to St. Anthony.

Paddy didn't want to see him go. Margaret less so, he was thinking, with him ruining her peace and quiet the way he had. He had spent the summer and fall fishing with his father. He expected little and there was little to be had. When winter came again Sam passed his time in the woods, cutting spruce and what little birch he could find, hauling it out on a wood sleigh with the help of one of his uncles and his uncle's horse. Wood enough for two winters. They stacked the spruce upright to dry, leaning the lengths against each other in a conical fashion, like a tepee. They built the stack deliberately in view of the kitchen window, so every day his father and Margaret would have reassurance they wouldn't be done in by the cold.

Sam sawed and split what was left of the wood that had been cut the winter before, and added it to the pile in the shed. Plugged away at it by himself most of the time. It was hard work and not often did the sun shine to make it any better. Still, he liked the icy stillness of the place in winter, the sweetly acrid smell of wood smoke, the way the snow swirled over the vegetable grounds, the occasional voices of children playing. He'd often sit against the wood horse for a smoke break and the mug of tea Margaret had brought out to him, and wonder what was in store now that he had cut ties with New York. He had plans, but every place, it seemed, men and their plans were being sunk by the weight of the Depression.

Nobody said as much, given all they had to worry about themselves, but Sam suspected that in some houses in the Harbour there were people close to starvation. Where he went cutting wood he set rabbit snares, checking them every day, and the few rabbits he caught he left on the doorsteps of the houses Margaret had told him were likely the worst off. Left the rabbits and knocked on the door and went on again, having been warned by his sister to keep his distance for fear of tuberculosis.

The government did nothing to help. Those on able-bodied relief were given a monthly allowance of six cents a day, and not everyone who needed it got that. The tightwad of a welfare officer—deciding who qualified as if the money were coming out of his own pocket—set people to cursing the government at every turn, but even that was no comfort.

By early March, Sam was walking the snow-crusted road to Avondale, on his way to catch the train into St. John's. It pulled into the station five hours late. The thirty-six miles and eight stops took another hour and a half, getting him into the city well past midnight. He made his way up Water Street, connecting eventually to Livingstone. Albert was waiting up for him.

The kitchen was lit by a single candle and the house felt like ice. 'We couldn't keep the fire in any longer. The coal got to do us 'til the end of the week.' Albert's first words, an apology. Only then did the cousins shake hands.

His wife, Elsie, kept the house clean, but with three youngsters—and from what Margaret had said, another on the way—she hardly had the energy to do that much.

Albert no longer had a job. 'There's no business. I'll be hired back when there is, that's what Mr. Leamon said.' That was four months ago.

All Sam could think was that the youngsters must have had a miserable Christmas. 'What are you living on, Albert?'

'I does the scattered odd job for Mr. Leamon. Shoveling his steps when there's snow, storing in his coal. He pays me some in cash and the rest in coal. Mrs. Leamon always has a little something for me to bring home. Elsie takes in a bit of sewing when there's any.' He was getting the pittance of government relief, but even that had him worried. 'What if the officer gets wind of what Mr. Leamon is doing for us?'

The next morning Sam was seated in the same spot at the kitchen table, across from Albert, the two having a smoke, Elsie making tea, the three youngsters huddled around the stove and dancing from foot to foot, trying to get into their clothes. Sam had spent the night half frozen himself, in the same bed as six-year-old Jack, the kid knotted in a ball at his back, complaining that Sam was letting in the draft every time he moved.

Sam had promised them a treat, brought all the way from New York City. It rested on the table in a paper bag, there for when they were dressed and had settled down, Elsie told them, as silent as mice. And when it was revealed—a Tootsie Pop for each of them—they were staggered with excitement. They had never seen such a thing, as Sam expected, for he had been told that it was something new even in the candy stores in New York.

He instructed them to take off the wrappers. 'Now hold on the stick and lick.' They did so, nonstop it seemed, until Jack had reached the centre and they all stood in amazement. 'Now that's the part you chew.'

Which is what Jack did, although reluctantly, for he realized he would be left with nothing but the empty stick. The time came when the other two had licked down far enough that they would have to do the same. The kids held off until they had struggled into boots and their scraps of winter coats, and were gone then, through the door to find other kids willing to watch them chew the centres, just so they could relish their envy.

'You heard what the bastard Squires has been up to?' Albert said when the three children were out the door. 'Lining his own bloody pockets with government money, from you crowd what fought in the war.'

The bastard in question was Richard Squires, Prime Minister again after being kicked out of office once, accused of taking $5000 from the budget of the War Reparations Commission. Sam had heard about it, and had been as incensed as the next fellow, but hearing it again in St. John's where it had all happened, the Colonial Building a ten-minute walk away, stirred his blood a second, stronger time.

Squires' accuser was Peter Cashin, the onetime Minister of Finance, himself wounded in the Great War. Sam had crossed paths with Cashin in France, had known him to be a good officer, a decent fellow.

That was bad enough, but the latest news out of the Colonial Building was worse. Albert had been on the street and back again before Sam was out of bed, and there was almost a satisfaction in telling him what he'd heard. 'Now the bastard says the government debt is so bad they got to cut back on the war pensions.'

Because Sam had come back from the war in one piece and all of it eventually in working order, he had never been eligible for a pension. But he had fought alongside plenty who returned home, missing limbs, or with the parts they did have forever disfigured. The poorest of buggers with lifetimes ahead of them and no chance of jobs.

Sam knew that the stream of oaths he was about to emit would do nothing to endear him to Elsie, so he held back, only to burst loose later that day when he showed up at the Veterans' Club on Water Street. The club was crammed with broken men livid at what their government was about to mete out to them.

'Not enough that we wasn't fuckin' killed.' The sentiment of the hour, made all the more conclusive by free flowing liquor. The talk was of a march on the Colonial Building, something to show Squires and his crowd that they weren't going to stand for it, not them who had nothing more to lose, who had already lost it all the day they came off ships in St. John's Harbour, back from the war, crippled or on stretchers. 'All fuckin' heroes, Sam. You remembers. You was there helping us off, you lucky sonofabitch.'

When the march ended it had grown to more than veterans, to a general swarm of the steadfast and exasperated, long-coated men, hands in their pockets, standing solemnly before the hulking Ionic columns and limestone walls of the seat of government. Scattered throughout the crowd were ardent women, feckless youth and young children. They made an uncompromising grey sea of citizenry, of all classes, all religions, totaling ten thousand.

There was no expectation of a riot, certainly not from the delegation of lawyers and merchants standing in the portico, there to deliver its fastidiously worded petition. But the delay in admitting them proved fuel to the legions of men behind. When the door was finally opened and the delegation let inside, it was quickly shut again, the mob left chomping for more. The mass of men engulfing the steps and portico, Sam among them, grew more raucous by the minute. Their roar rang through the walls and into the ears of government, spiteful affirmation of the petition handed at that moment to the Speaker of the House.

When the delegation finally emerged, their job done, the roar failed to die away. The delegation and their marching band moved off. The mob remained, rallying around their Union Jack.

It had no intention of dispersing into the late afternoon dreariness. The turning point to violence, the call for a battering ram, was spontaneous, from a mass with a mind of its own. Sam was in the middle of it, raging with the loudest of them, his hands one of several pairs wrapped around the five feet of iron bar. Now driving its jagged end against the massive doors.

Policemen mounting the steps were shoved aside. The constable on horseback in the crowd below was hauled to the ground. The horse tore off through the crowd.

The door splintered, the roar a crescendo! The policemen guarding the inside rushed out to defend their own. Wielding batons, as frantic and lost to the moment as the rioters who countered with bare fists and fence pickets, and rocks to bash the windows.

Glass rained down, inside the building and out. The mob dodged it both sides, plowing past the door and into the heart of the building. Intent on ransacking whatever they could.

Sam cared nothing now. Relished the release of what

curled his guts. Stood, arms dangling, weaponless, in the office of the Prime Minister. The secretary stared Sam in the face and fled. Sam laid hold of one end of Squires's desk. With all his strength, upended it. Flung whatever files he could lay his hands to. Dug out the drawers of the desk and sent paper flying, heaps of it fluttering to the floor in shameless disarray, heaps more through a broken window, to scatter through the chaotic air and drift vacantly to the ground.

The Colonial Building was in shambles, though the attempt to set fire to it had been curbed. Some wisdom prevailed and the rioters left the structure intact, ganging instead for the man himself. Deep in the bowels of the building Sam and a few more came upon a locked set of double doors. They drove their shoulders dead against them, the thuds harder and louder until the doors gave way.

It was not Squires behind the doors, but a fellow with reams of salvaged paper in his arms.

'He's escaped! He's made it out of here!'

The others streaked past the fellow. Sam slowed down, stared wildly into his eyes, jerked the mound of paper from his arms.

Outside, the riderless horse rounded the corner of the building, darting about frantically, cutting Sam's advance.

Sam sank to the grass, the horse weaving circles around him.

He groped for his wallet, fumbled it open, pulled out the photograph. The sky surrounded and sheltered him. Drenched and blinded him.

Distant chaos settled over him like a shroud, and over that layers of dirt, repeated and repeated until Sam was sunk beneath it, the colour of dirt, desperate for air.

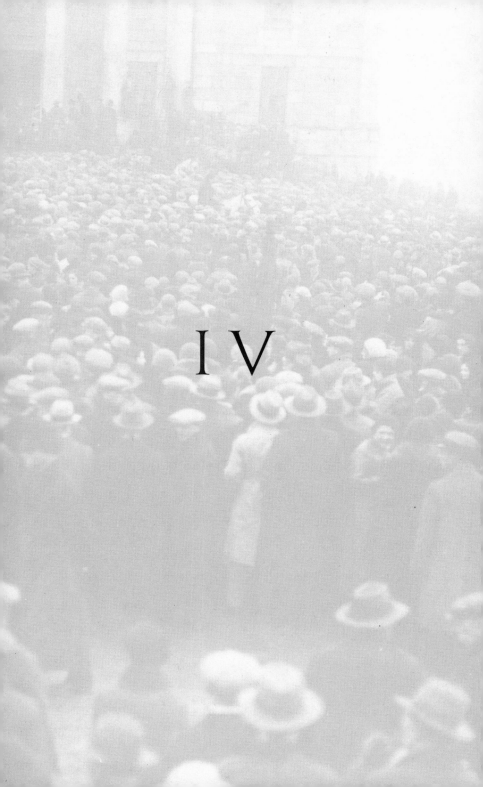

IV

TEN

HE wandered several hundred miles by train and coastal boat in anticipation of the moment he set eyes on her. For an instant his heart swelled. The woman opening the door was the photograph. But then she wasn't. He stood with a broken smile and told her his name.

'And how may I help you, Mr. Kennedy?'

The woman's features were fresh, pleasantly rouged by sun and wind, framed by light brown hair that curled slightly, cut stylishly short. She wore a long-sleeve dress, a miniature floral print in yellow and blue, drawn neatly at her waist with a belt. Her name was Rhoda Dawson and when she spoke it was with an English accent.

'I was told I would find Miss Belbin here.'

'But I don't believe she is expecting anyone.'

He straightened up a bit more, and brushed unruly hair from his forehead. 'A friend, of a friend. From New York.'

'I see.' She turned him about in her mind. Then moved

back to allow him past the door.

She walked silently ahead of Sam down the hall, slowing as they neared the entrance to the sitting room.

He stopped. Across the room was all the reason in the world for his journey. Emma Belbin turned his way, startled for the time it took to draw herself upright, away from the wooden mat frame. She set aside the small, smooth-handled hook she was holding in her hand.

'This is Mr. Kennedy.'

Miss Dawson was about to add something more when her friend nodded slightly. A sign she had some knowledge of the man. Miss Dawson's uncertainty dissipated, reluctantly.

'I'll be sketching in my room, Emma, should you need me.' She ignored the man standing next to her, turned and continued down the hall, out of sight.

Sam was alone with the woman whose image he had clung to for so long. Years of preconception disappeared. Emma drew the edge of her hand to her mouth and suddenly she was no longer the youthful soul who had embedded herself in his mind. Older now, less the vision, unquestionably real.

Her face was no less lovely, in the way that it had aged, her skin warm and smooth against her cheekbones, her eyes as clear, a bright blue-grey he saw now.

Emma sat stiffly in the wingback chair, its dark paisley in contrast to the pale mint of her dress. Sam stepped closer, but stopped abruptly.

'Did you receive my letters?'

She looked aside, as if thinking that if she were to wait long enough, he would no longer remain in the room.

'I should have written again. I should have, to tell you I was coming.'

At no time had he any intention of doing so. What if she had tried to dissuade him? What could he possibly have done then?

'Why *have* you come?'

It was not the voice he had imagined. Higher pitched, less rounded. Perhaps it was the question. He hadn't imagined the first words he would hear from her would be a question.

Why had he come? For now a single reason was enough. From his coat pocket he withdrew it. He stepped closer and held it out to her. It was soiled and discoloured. She looked at the envelope, finally stretching out her hand and taking it. The address was barely legible.

'He wanted me to deliver it. If he didn't make it through the war.'

More than sixteen years ago now.

'I'll come back when you have read the letter.' He needed to be bold. If she were not to dismiss him outright. And polite and solemn. 'Johnny was my very good friend.'

The seconds passed, haltingly. 'You realize how difficult this is. It was a great hurt when Johnny was killed.'

'I wished it had been me.'

Emma looked into his eyes, hers intensely focused, darker than before.

'I'm sorry it took so long to deliver it.'

'You could have sent it by mail.'

'Johnny insisted. He made me promise to deliver it myself.'

At that moment the front door to Blackburn Cottage opened, and within a few seconds closed again.

A teenaged boy appeared, his frame broadened by a grey, home-knit sweater. Sam was numbed. The fellow could have been walking across the open fields of Pleasantville. Sam looked to Emma and then back again to the boy.

'John, this is Mr. Kennedy. He was a friend of your father's.'

Sam brushed back his hair with his fingers once more. 'I am glad to meet you.' He held out his hand.

The young man held out his, with some awkwardness, as might be expected of someone his age. He tightened his grip. His hand had been worn by more than school work. In height he was the equal of his father, and likely the equal in strength. His clear, tawny complexion indicated a love of the outdoors. Even the fragment of a smile was a reminder of Johnny.

'John was born just before the orders that sent his father to Gallipoli.'

'I didn't know.'

'I'm surprised he kept it from you.'

'I remember now,' said John. 'You two were in the same Company. You were mentioned in the letters.'

'Many times,' his mother said.

She waited several moments before looking again at Sam. 'You were the only one in the Regiment he ever did say much about.'

Sam left the house not long after, when he was sure there was an expectation he would return. Even if the boy more than his mother was the reason for it. John was filled with questions about his father.

It would take time. He wouldn't crowd her.

She had been left with a son. It was true.

Sam was restless. He had trouble sleeping. He had a separate room, but the crowd of college boys in the dormitory were up all hours talking, the first few nights at least.

Grenfell had been impressed with his initiative in reaching St. Anthony. A job followed, something that would fill his summer until Grenfell found other work for him, at the

Mission's cooperative. That was the plan. He put Sam in charge of the local batch of summer volunteers—gung-ho young college lads who arrived each summer for six-week stints at the various Mission outposts. WOPs Grenfell called them—Workers Without Pay—even if the letters didn't quite fit.

They were from New England most of them, a lean, sinewy lot, burnished of any coarseness, their hair unruly, but full of style, teeth unfailingly polished and straight. The lads were the boisterous, fraternal kind, perpetually high-spirited, generally willing to take on whatever was asked of them and without a scrap of trepidation.

Some crews he directed to construction jobs and repairing Mission property, others to handle the Mission's incoming supplies, unloading them, carting some to warehouses, re-distributing others to vessels destined for stations farther along the coasts. Sam's job was to keep the strapping Ivy Leaguers occupied and out of trouble. It was outdoors work mostly, and Sam had always enjoyed knocking about in the open. For the several hours each day he was on the job, his head cleared.

The landscape settled in his blood. Sam was suddenly the Newfoundland man telling the American college boys what to do, fellows whose fathers could have bought him and spit him out a hundred times over. He worked side by side with his crews, not expecting anything of them that he wouldn't do himself, working up a dirt-grain sweat, cursing when sweat didn't get the job done. He pushed and pushed to force to the surface whatever was beneath their amiable Christian exteriors.

Trench diggers. Pack slaves. Workhorses slogging water and provisions. He speculated if these fellows would have had the gumption for war. Likely they would, he concluded, re-calling the tales of the Doughboys from Brooklyn. War would have driven steel up their rears, like it did everyone who joined up.

Their talk was baseball. Dodgers fans, a couple of them, but most fervent for the Red Sox. Sam liked the game, though he had never played it growing up, liked it well enough to spend more than a few Sunday afternoons in Ebbets Field. Phil Todt had been his man. Sam had liked the look on his face when he was guarding first base. Todt was gone now, traded to Philadelphia. And no odds, what with Sam figuring he'd never see Ebbets Field again.

Sam made sure they all got a straight up taste of Newfoundland. Within the confines of the Mission, palling around with themselves, it could have been anywhere they had turned up. Sam had them cross the harbour, make themselves known to fishermen furrowed by lives spent on the saltwater, men up before daylight and gutting fish by lanterns at midnight. Men who through it all kept a smile and a raw wit.

Here, too, the price of fish was the worst in years, with little hope of it rising any. 'We got our pride, b'ys. Hope to Jesus the market comes back, that's all you can do. Tie a knot in yer dick so's you won't have any more youngsters to feed.'

The fishermen laughed at that, and so did the New England lads, though by then they were distracted, their nostrils fouled with the odour of fish guts, and the cod oil baking in the sun. Sam had them knocking about the dank sheds, thick into the splayed and gutted fish packed in bulk salt. And outdoors, club-footing about the fish flakes.

It was the girls who were embarrassed having them around, girls the same age as the Mission boys staring at them bent over their work. Girls knowing that not one of those handsome fellows, as good as any dreamed of in *True Romance*, would ever be looking with any interest on their bare legs or the curve and strain of their summer dresses. Not considering that in their arms was a half dozen sun-stiffened slabs of salt cod, gathered in because black clouds were in the distance, moving fast, threatening to blot out the sun.

They stacked the fish in circular piles, to be covered with oil-treated tarps until the rain was over or the threat abated. There was an art to stacking the fish, of overlaying them to stabilize the pile. One of the older women, Flos, stood by the growing mounds to be sure it was done right.

Flos was far from embarrassed in front of the Americans. 'Ye here for the summer? Seeing the sights, are ye?'

'Yes, ma'am.'

'Ye wouldn't want to be at this, I daresay.'

'I wouldn't mind,' one of the fellows replied, to be good about it.

She was caught by the cut and spiff of their clothes. Easy-going it was, but nothing any of their men would wear. So clean and unpatched. Nothing cut and sewed from Mission clothes, castoffs likely sent from wherever it was the college crowd lived.

'And what are ye fellows goin' at once yer back home?'

'I start my first year of medical school.'

'Law school,' said another, with no animation, a quiet statement of fact.

'I'm pleased for ye,' she said. 'Ye'll do good.'

She said no more, turning her attention to the fish and the girls, and now a batch of half-grown boys called in because the rain clouds were moving toward them even faster than expected. The boys were barefoot, and more agile about the fish flakes than the college lads in their oxfords.

'Would you like some help?' the would-be medical student asked.

'That's very kind, sir. I rather ye comes back a doctor, sir. That's the most help ye could be.'

'Perhaps I will.'

'And then again ye might have had enough of us crowd.'

His smile was not a commitment, nor a rejection. Time would pass and in due course someone, though perhaps not that particular fellow, would arrive in St. Anthony from foreign parts and give the people their medical care.

Sam led the young men on, over the road to where they all could get a good view back across the harbour to the Mission buildings. A couple of them had Kodaks and the others posed, first in clownish fashion, but then more seriously for their mothers and fathers back home.

They were caught in a great downpour as they rowed back to the Mission, though they didn't seem to mind, and did, in fact, take some pride in getting soaked to the skin by the cold rain and not complaining.

Sam slipped into Emma's life. Gradually, tentatively, as his confidence and her sympathies permitted. He was more assured, even as his expectations of her were being traded for other expectations, more vague, less sensuous.

It began with regular visits to Blackburn Cottage, for Sunday supper. The invitations stood despite the suspicions of the Industrials supervisor—a stout, flinty Scot whom everyone called by her surname, Pressley. It was clear she thought Sam could be conducting whatever business he had with Emma elsewhere. Instead, Sam arrived near the end of each Sunday afternoon and stayed into the evening.

The first conversations through the Sunday suppers were stiff and self-conscious, despite the fact that stories about catwalking the heights of the New York skyline couldn't fail to interest them, even the irascible Pressley. Neither could his accounts of the city's brassier events. He'd seen both Lindbergh and Amelia Earhart, he told them, in ticker-tape parades down Broadway.

So just why had he given up New York for a Newfoundland outport? Hadn't he said he'd gone to New York to get away? There had to be things about the city he was missing.

'New York is not all it's cracked up to be.' It sounded lame and insincere, but he pressed on as if it were nothing. 'Amelia Earhart started in Newfoundland,' he said, 'when she flew the Atlantic. Lindbergh flew over St. John's on his way to Paris.'

He started again. Searching for his regular self, when they didn't know what his regular self was. They saw him flounder, the odd one out, and then, embarrassed for him, pulled him into their lives with the Mission.

Through it all Emma was the listener. While others took charge of the conversations, Emma was subdued, conscious of showing too much of herself, realizing each word and gesture was being scrutinized by the unknown man across the table.

Their exchanges were few. 'Have you flown yourself?'

'No.'

'Perhaps working at such heights is not unlike flying.'

He wondered if her speech had been the same when Johnny knew her. She had little trace of an accent.

'Johnny spent eight months in New York.'

He likely knew more than she did about Johnny's time in New York. Sam kept it to himself.

The boy showed no such reticence and Sam had answers to all his questions, later in the evenings when the three of them were in the sitting room, his mother at her mat hooking, the other women somewhere else in the cottage. The questions were about the training in Pleasantville, their best times, that and Scotland. The other questions, about the end, perhaps they would come later. Sam was shaping his memories for the young fellow. If he stumbled it was because he wanted to get it right for him. He was being decent and genuine, and Emma had to see he was, looking over at them from time to time and holding back.

When the talk turned to sniping, the boy couldn't get enough. Of the way it was in the nest, a working pair of best pals. It excited him.

So much so Sam suddenly stopped and turned away from it. John looked no more than a kid, like they had, with a mind not meant for the wretched brunt of war.

He entered the Loom Room, not far from the cottage, catching sight of Emma bending over a small stove. She was wearing trousers tucked snugly into hide boots, and a blue cotton smock. On her head a cloche hat, raffia circled by a band of striped cotton.

She stood up as Sam approached, looking as if his sudden appearance was not completely unexpected.

Resting on the burner of the stove, with steam clouding from it, was a large enameled dishpan. Emma donned a canvas apron and a pair of workman's gloves.

'An experiment.'

Floating in the dishpan was a bubbling crust of lichen. Emma worked a wooden paddle through the water, which had turned an uncommon reddish-brown.

'We skim off the lichen,' she said as she did just that, ladling it into another bowl. 'And add a small strip of white flannelette to see what colour we get.'

There was a measured cordiality in her voice. She peered at the cloth as she swirled it about in the hot liquid. Every few moments she inspected its colour, using the paddle to lift it just above the water. When she was satisfied the colour would go no deeper she allowed the cloth to drain, then plunged it into the pail of cold water and fixative that rested on the floor near the stove.

She squeezed out the flannelette and examined it for how well it had taken the dye.

'Warm,' she said. 'Rather like some heathers I've seen.'

She led him to a mat pattern laid out on a worktable. He couldn't tell what the image was until she explained—a sealskin stretched inside a wooden frame, drying in the sun. One of Rhoda's new patterns. Emma shuffled strips of fabric from one segment to another, debating aloud the merits of each combination. She eliminated some and recombined them with others. 'We like to take time to experiment,' she said.

He proposed a walk, along the Tea House trail, to gather more lichen. He knew he should have held back, but couldn't, not with her acceptance of his being there, her seeming at ease with him.

On his second asking she agreed, and the following Saturday afternoon they met at the entrance to the Loom Room and set off on a trail that eventually narrowed into woods and led uphill to a lookout, where hikers sometimes stopped for a respite and boiled a kettle for tea.

She wore a jacket of quilted cotton, and a skirt this time, to the edge of her walking boots. A long-strapped bag made of canvas duck crossed her chest and rested at her side. It would hold the lichen.

She kept a respectable distance between them, yet the

slight animation in her voice led him to think it might be something of a game. He launched into more stories about the life he had left behind in New York, knowing it would hold her interest, for he could tell she would have travelled more if she'd had the resources. She told him there had once been plans for the Grenfells to send her to Berea College in Kentucky to study weaving. It hadn't worked out.

'I've been in the Grenfell Shop on Madison Avenue,' he told her. He had been waiting for the best moment to reveal it.

'Really? I choose the merchandise and arrange for it to be sent.'

'Then you should go and see the shop for yourself.'

'There was talk of it, but not the money.'

They walked on. Comfortable in the silence, it seemed to Sam.

They had not gone much farther when some vegetation caught her eye.

He leaned closer to her. He kissed her lightly on the lips, resisting the compulsion to wrap his arms around her. She forced herself away.

She said nothing, continuing the walk.

'Are you surprised? You're an attractive woman.'

'And you're impulsive.'

An observation more than a criticism? 'You have been on my mind for all these years.'

'Please, don't.'

'It's true. Ever since Johnny showed me your picture. You must believe that. It's true.'

'Please.'

Her plea did no good. 'You have to know,' he said. 'You have to realize what I am telling you is true. What reason is there to keep it from you? None.'

'You mustn't.'

He knew perfectly well what the letter he had delivered to her said. It was two brief pages. Johnny had said if he were to die, then he wanted her to try as hard as she could to find happiness. That the man who was bringing her the letter was as good a man as himself and she was not to feel guilty if she fell in love with him. Hadn't he seen the letter with his own eyes? That is what it said. He knew. He had committed it to heart before resealing the envelope.

She had hurried some distance ahead, but he caught up to her, careful not to get too close.

'I know it's been hard, me showing up so unexpectedly. But Johnny wanted you to move on?'

He stepped closer. She looked at him, not with anger, not fright. 'How would you know what I want? Johnny is gone and I don't have that life anymore.'

'But we could make what you do have better.'

She held up her hand, compelling him to keep a distance.

They had not gathered any lichen, but neither did Emma rush back, away from him. The silence between them intensified, his hope holding on.

The walk ended where it began, at the entrance to the Loom Room. Her poise had given way to a stiff, plain-spoken manner. Sam left her, offering a careful smile as he walked away. She did not respond. She remained cautious of him, but the step had been taken, and there would be no drawing back.

Sam came again to supper the following Sunday. John was at the house of a friend. Rhoda was being particularly talkative, and Pressley was being Pressley, so the focus at the table shifted away from him.

Rhoda, he learned, had come to St. Anthony from England on the spur of the moment, several months before, with little knowledge of Newfoundland other than it was the home of the Grenfell Mission. It turned out the Mission had a place for her talents. Her background was in the Arts and Crafts Movement, as a designer. Her parents did enamels and jewelry, some of which appeared on the breast of Queen Victoria.

Much of the supper talk was about the tourist vessels, the *New Northland* and the *North Voyageur*, the first due the following week. This was something untried, the Clark Steamship Line out of Montreal cruising to the "alluring North," as the advertisements referred to it. It was the first of several trips scheduled for the summer and early fall.

'Visit the fishing villages, fur trading posts, and the havens of the famous Grenfell Mission,' Pressley quoted in the severest tones of her Scottish accent.

'Oh, dear,' said Rhoda, 'we've become exhibits. But as long as they spend their money. Buy, buy, buy. Let the cash box be filled!'

'How hopelessly crass,' said Pressley. 'But realistic.'

'Will anyone buy when the stock market has sucked away their fortunes?' Sam inserted.

'Of course they will!' Rhoda declared. 'Art buoys them up. They want to feel good about *something*. They'll all want a souvenir!'

'We'll see just what sells and what doesn't. This will be the test, Dawson.'

It was an obtuse reference to Rhoda's unconventional new mat patterns, another of which stood on a frame in the corner of the room, one that Emma had been working to finish in time for the influx of tourists. It was a circular mat depicting a wreath of stylized, intertwining wildflowers.

'I love Rhoda's patterns,' Emma said, in defense of her friend.

'I purchased a hooked mat at the Grenfell shop in New York,' Sam told them. '*Fish on Flake.*'

Emma looked at him in surprise.

'Truly?' said Rhoda.

Sam nodded.

Rhoda was vindicated. 'There now. If a man chooses *Fish on Flake* then surely it indicates that tastes in mats are evolving.'

'I cannot believe you wouldn't have chosen something more...manly, Mr. Kennedy,' said Pressley. 'A husky dog. Or a sailboat at least.'

Rhoda laughed out loud.

'The women who make the mats dislike the patterns,' Pressley announced, to no one in particular.

'Not all of the women,' Emma said.

Pressley soured more, mild as the comment had been.

Rhoda was relishing the moment. 'And did you think yourself an oddball, Sam, to be appreciating the hooked mat in the way you did?'

'*Oddball*, Dawson. What a perfectly horrid word. Where do you come up with them?'

Sam reached inside his coat pocket and produced a small book. 'If enjoying art and poetry are oddball.'

'Of course not.'

'This is for you,' he said, turning to Emma. 'I was told you like poetry.' He stretched his hand across the table.

'Poetry—how perfectly crack-pot!'

'Dawson, please take control of yourself. Well, tell us what it is, Emma. Who wrote it and what it's about.'

Emma read the title page aloud. '*The Man with the Hoe*

and other Poems. And he has signed it. It says, *Look. Listen. Edwin Markham*.'

'Truly? *Look*? *Listen*? How utterly sublime!' declared Rhoda.

Pressley was at the end of her rope. 'I have not heard of the man!'

'I've met him.'

They were clearly impressed. 'He must be American, is he?' said Pressley.

'Of course he's American,' Rhoda said. 'Read us one, Emma dear. Read us *The Man with the Hoe*.'

When she had finished there was a deliberate pause around the table, as much for her part as for the poem.

Sam smiled and nodded. The book was not mentioned again.

ELEVEN

GRENFELL liked what he saw in Sam, liked how well he matched the job. Everyone Grenfell ever hired for the Mission presented him with a challenge: that of instilling his own daredevil thirst for doing good. Sam was proving an easier subject than most, since he had ample daredevil qualities to start.

'The chaps like to swim?'

'They're thinking the harbour water is a bit cold, sir.'

'Nonsense,' said Grenfell. 'And you, Kennedy?'

'The icebergs put me off.'

Sure enough, the next sunny day Grenfell had the lot of them in their wool swimming shorts treading the frigid, brilliantly blue water, clambering onto the flat expanse of an iceberg, one of several that lingered near the harbour entrance, on their way south from Greenland.

Sam, with Grenfell's approval, had recruited John to go with them. Sam had mentioned it to the young fellow the previous Sunday, after supper, out of earshot of his mother, as something of a lark for them both. It would tighten the bond between them, and get John thinking of himself in comparison to the American fellows, of himself beyond the boundaries of Newfoundland. In Sam's view, a fellow needed that, needed to put himself up against the outside world, demonstrate he could be every bit as smart and tough.

And there they were, he and Sam, in the thick of it, roaring and laughing with them all in the ice-charged sea water, the most reserved to the most boastful, to a man coated in goose flesh, frolicking like fiends, thoughtless to the danger of the iceberg cracking apart or flipping over. Showing Grenfell they had the balls for it. With the sixty-seven-year-old Grenfell diving from the iceberg into the midst of them and stroke for stroke back to the boat, the last man aboard.

'Sir,' shouted one of the Boston boys, 'bloody swell, sir!'

The crews would go back to New England with their stories, to be recalled many times into the future, no matter if they ever set foot in Newfoundland or Labrador again. The Mission would never fade from their minds and, as doctors and lawyers and businessmen, they would write cheques to it for the rest of their lives. Not only that, Grenfell's Mission made men of them.

Sam, rubbing at the cold as hard as anyone, was less sure of how to peg the man. Sam wasn't awestruck, wasn't blind to Grenfell's failings, but in the end such things didn't matter. Sam had learned to do good and along with that, with John smiling and huddled next to him, thought of himself as drifting closer to something settled in his life.

His optimism came to an abrupt end the moment the boat turned toward the Mission wharf. Standing at one end of the wharf was Emma, her arms planted firmly against her chest, her impatience at the length of time it was taking the boat to reach the wharf surpassed only by the fury in her eyes. They were planted firmly on Sam and her son, straying from them only long enough to dwell momentarily on Grenfell, who remained oblivious to it all.

Sam saw to it that John was the first out of the boat. Though the young fellow was no worse for the excursion, and beamed with pride, he had not been able to quell the shudders that ran intermittently through him.

By the time Sam stepped onto the wharf, Emma and her son were on their way along the path to Blackburn Cottage. Sam ran to catch up with them.

Emma turned and faced him. 'Just who gave you permission to take him along on your little escapade?'

'Mother, it doesn't matter. I'm fine.'

'I'm sorry,' said Sam.

'You're sorry. He could have drowned. He's practically frozen to death.'

'I'm fine,' John said, quivering still.

'He's my son. I had a right to know.'

'Mother!' Then came the boy's trump card, the reasoning that couldn't be faulted. 'Doctor Grenfell said it was fine.'

Emma held back, only for a moment. 'It was Doctor Grenfell who talked your father into going off to war. It was Doctor Grenfell who could only say he was sorry when Johnny didn't come back!'

She rushed off, leaving her son and Sam standing together, neither with anything to say to each other. John turned and followed his mother.

Sam stood alone, peering after them, emotionally fouled.

Three nights later he showed up at Blackburn Cottage as he had been doing for weeks, as if nothing unusual had transpired. A brazen assumption, but what was he to do but put the past behind him and push on. He couldn't let a Sunday go by. It would make it all the harder for her to find her way back to him.

There was no pleasing her.

She wouldn't come to the door. She had sent Rhoda to fend him off.

'Emma would rather not see you right now. She is still upset. Perhaps in a few days.'

'May I speak to her please?'

'No, Sam. She'd rather not.'

'Emma,' he called past Rhoda's shoulder. 'Emma! I would like a few moments please.'

'Sam, you are not listening.'

His calling out brought Pressley to the door, only too happy to take the matter in hand.

'Mr. Kennedy, this is entirely inappropriate.'

'I only wish to speak with her. Emma!'

'I must ask you to leave this property.'

'John,' he called, 'would you ask your mother if I may speak with her?' It was a simple request. He was being perfectly polite.

'If you do not leave this instant then I shall have to report this entire episode to Doctor Grenfell.'

The Doctor had nothing to do with it. It was between himself and Emma.

At that moment John appeared, against the wishes of his mother, as her voice in the background made known.

John led Sam away from the women, down the front step and along the path away from the house.

'My mother doesn't want to see you. Not now.'

'I don't understand.'

'She's not ready to talk. I'll give her a message if you like.'

A message? His only message was he loved her. He wanted to marry her.

'Tell her I have something I want to say to her. Tell her I'm sorry.'

'You must go away. You can't be coming around here, not now.'

'Another time?'

'Yes, another time.'

Sam put a hand on his shoulder.

'Is that a promise?' he said. 'Will you give me your word?'

Swear on the memory of your father is what he wanted to say.

Sam was gone then, wandering aimlessly until people he encountered on the roads and the wharves inquired if there was something wrong. He chain smoked the home-rolls that filled his silver cigarette case, each time smartly clicking the case shut and slipping it back in his trousers pocket. Shaking his head, forcing a smile and walking on, as if people wouldn't think he was anything but normal.

That night, in bed, he wallowed in the mud of war, crawling to free himself, summoning conviction to find a way through to some immaculate ground. He and Johnny, firing that clear, flawless, consummate bullet, once and for all.

Sam and Emma did meet, not long after. Alone, although the other women were in the kitchen, and John, the peacemaker, who had been with his mother and Sam long enough that Sam could see they were on reasonable terms again, eventually wandered away to his room.

Emma was wearing a summer dress he had not seen before, a shade of blue that did wonderful things for her eyes.

Sam had gone over in his head everything he wanted to

say. The world could be crazy, but he knew if he had a plan and followed it then everything would be so much better.

'I'm reliable, Emma. You know that. I'm good at my job and Doctor Grenfell has never had a complaint. In New York our crew was one of the best. I was a good soldier. Johnny would have been the first to tell you that. I know how to size up a job and do what has to be done. I won't let anyone down. All I need is the chance. Everyone makes mistakes, but that was long ago in the past.'

'Sam...'

'If you took time to know me you would see there is nothing to worry about, that I would treat you well, because I would, I would with every ounce of life in me, you have to believe that, because I know it for a fact. And John, too. We could be the best of friends and I could show him how to do things like his father would have. And all the other things that go with making a relationship between the two of us, me and you, all those things I would do right. You have to believe me, Emma, because it is true.'

'Sam, let me...'

'I just have to say that I have seen a lot of the world and if you want to go places I could go there with you. If you want to go to New York, we could do that. Or St. John's, but if you want to stay right here we could be as happy as we would ever want to be. I love you, Emma. I do. With everything that is in me.'

There were tears in her eyes. His words had made her cry and that was alright, too. Couldn't he just wrap his arms around her and reassure her that they had each other and that was all they would ever need?

'Sam, I can't do it. I can't be that person, just because you want it. You need to be happy, but I can't be the one to make you happy, just because you want me to.'

'Johnny wanted it.'

Did he shout? He didn't mean to if he did.

'I'm sorry,' he said quickly. But it was true. She knew what was in the letter.

She stood up, walked over and sat on the settee next to him, definite in her action, her emotion.

'I know this is hard for you. You want something that is impossible.'

'It's not impossible. You want to make it impossible. For some reason you do.'

She was sitting next to him and he needed to kiss her. Whether she knew it or not he needed to and if he didn't he would go crazy and it would be pounding at him. She shouldn't have sat next to him, not if she didn't realize what he would have in his mind. Besides, it would do no harm, only good. Affection was only good. He knew enough of what hatred did, from the moment they clambered ashore on the beach at Suvla, he knew. Hatred blew past his brains. Blew out the brains of everyone who came within his crosshairs. The sweet, unknowable bastards. No, it was affection that would win out in the end. It would be a kiss and nothing more. He wanted more, he thirsted for more, but a kiss was all. A tender touch of his lips to hers was all. He would never be more gentle.

Sam leaned his head toward hers. For an instant their lips touched, before she fell away from him. He took it for an invitation to rise above and sink into her. Their lips had only touched again when she was squirming away from him.

'No,' she said in his ear. 'No, Sam.'

She hadn't understood. She needed to give into it. Let herself fall in love like she was meant to do. If only she would.

She pushed against him and when he didn't withdraw, she called to the other women.

When they came running from the kitchen Sam was sitting upright and Emma had pulled herself to the end of the settee, in tears.

Sam jumped to his feet, rushed past them, and past John who had just appeared. Out the front door and along the path, away from everyone.

He ran all the way to the shoreline and along it, to where he imagined the rocks gave way to sand, stumbling until he fell and lay there alone, the surf striking the shore, his memories in retreat.

TWELVE

IN the late spring of 1933 Sam boarded the Mission boat *George B. Cluett* heading north. He had passed the fall and winter months in St. Anthony, although he had come close to returning home to Harbour Main after a letter arrived from Margaret telling him Paddy had taken another turn for the worse. In the end he made up his mind that Margaret was the one to deal with their father, that she was well enough suited to the task even if he was now close to being an invalid. Sam wired her money.

When the summer volunteers had gone and before the Grenfells headed back to the States, Doctor Grenfell had turned Sam over to the manager of the Spot Cash Cooperative. Mr. McNeill was known to have the patience of Job and at times, dealing with Sam, he needed it. Nevertheless Sam earned his keep. After work was over for the day Sam withdrew to the dormitory, where he was the sole occupant. He rattled around in it all winter, with only his employer dropping in from time to time to check he wasn't going stir crazy.

He wasn't. He set in a few batches of home brew as a way of saving extra money to send to Margaret. He read and drank his way through the winter.

From time to time he encountered John in the Cooperative. The words between them were few. John was sent by the women of Blackburn Cottage to do their shopping, although eventually Pressley showed up in the store, and Rhoda, though never Emma.

He did see her at a distance, and in church at Christmas and Easter, when the whole town was there. He made no attempt to make eye contact with her. It would have only confounded the situation further. She appeared as composed and collected as Rhoda, who occupied the seat next to her. And equally as smart in a beret and tailored coat, its collar trimmed modestly with fur. He wondered if she was thinking he might also be in the congregation. But never once did she look behind her, even when the service ended and she made her way to a side exit.

Sam was destined for Labrador. During the winter Grenfell had sent a letter instructing him to make his way to Cartwright on the boat's first run, and there put himself in the hands of Miss Stewart who was in charge of the Mission. She had work for him.

He didn't know what to expect of Cartwright, other than the fact it was along the coast of southern Labrador, considerably smaller and more isolated than St. Anthony. It had a nursing station and a school, but no hospital. It had Miss Stewart, from Ottawa in Canada, and Nurse Berthelsen from Denmark. There were two Mission buildings, the larger made up of the dormitory and staff quarters, together with the nursing station. The other, the school, also housed the Industrial and the clothing store. During the school year the dormitory was home to upwards of fifty children from all along the coast. Miss Holden, also from Canada, was the principal.

It was St. Anthony on a smaller scale.

When the *Cluett* sailed into Cartwright the school children had gone back to their homes for the summer, and rooms were being readied for the four Mission volunteers soon arriving. Sam was given accommodations in the building's staff quarters.

Miss Stewart was tall and slight, a model of efficiency. Her temperament hardly wavered, despite the multitude of demands thrown her way.

'You speak Italian.'

'I'm afraid not,' he said, confused by her assumption.

He had lived near Italian families in Brooklyn, and drank with the fathers. He could manage a few words and phrases.

'Then you understand enough to communicate with them?'

'Them?'

'Has Doctor Grenfell not told you? We are being invaded by a contingent of the Italian Air Force.'

Miss Stewart was at once amused and horrified.

'They are stopping here en route from Italy to the Chicago's World's Fair, to refuel and spend the night.'

She was serious.

'Two dozen airships and their pilots, led by General Italo Balbo, the Minister of the Air Force. They're calling it the Italian Armada. They're out to impress the Americans.'

And nothing that he could fathom for the moment.

The airships would arrive from Iceland, the village of Cartwright their first point of contact with North America. The Mission's dormitory was the only building along the Labrador coast that could accommodate so many people. Arrangements between the Italian government and the Grenfell Mission had been in place for months, and soon a small steamship, leased by the Italians and renamed the *Alicia*, would plant itself in the harbour loaded with gasoline and supplies, flight mechanics and a bevy of air force officers ready to execute every detail of the visit. And, as it turned out, Italian newspaper reporters, enough to exhaust Mr. Moores, Cartwright's Marconi man, on a daily basis.

'I understand Italian men can be quite intimidating,' Miss Stewart said.

It had seemed to Sam on first meeting her that no one, Italian or otherwise, could ever do enough to intimidate Miss Stewart.

'I'm to act as a buttress?' Sam said.

'So to speak.'

The affair would be topped off with a grand banquet in the dining hall of the dormitory. The cooks aboard the *Alicia* were to prepare the meal but the hall had to be readied and wine set in. The thought of a banquet room full of wine-soaked Italian airmen had set Miss Stewart permanently on edge.

Sam's years in New York paid off handsomely. The only protracted dispute involved the large framed photograph of Benito Mussolini, looking menacing in his military garb, which the Italians wished to fix to the wall behind the head table. Sam insisted that a photograph of Doctor Grenfell also be hung, and, although it was given a portion of the wall, it could hardly compete with the size of Il Duce's portrait or its garlanded frame.

The procession of aircraft when it did finally appear in the clear blue August sky astonished every last person in

Cartwright. Twenty-four Savoia-Marchetti S.55 flying boats. Unlike any aircraft ever produced. A pair of cigar-shaped hulls, which also served as pontoons, joined by a wing spread of eighty feet. Booms stretching behind, holding up double-fin, triple-rudder tails. Side-by-side cockpits looking out from the wing sections wedged between the hulls, and, on struts above it, twin tandem engines mounted back-to-back.

Cartwright would not see the like again. Nor the like of Italo Balbo.

It was as if Mussolini himself were heading ashore. Boisterous applause from the crew of the *Alicia*, very near adulation, greeted the General and his airmen as they stepped out of the dories and onto the Hudson's Bay Company wharf.

That evening, on the Mission side of Cartwright, the entourage passed under a triumphal bough arch, past a facing pair of ten-foot high pine replicas of the Fascist emblem, the Axe and Fasces. In wait on the dormitory steps were two local children dressed in Italian costumes that had been sent aboard the *Alicia*. One presented Balbo with flowers, the other a bureau scarf embellished with needlepoint of polar bears, a gift from the women of Cartwright to the person they imagined as the General's long-suffering wife. A gift more likely to end up, Miss Stewart whispered to Sam, in the hands of his mistress. Balbo removed the cigar from his mouth long enough to rub the tops of the children's heads and pose for a photograph.

Miss Stewart endured, repeatedly taking solace in the fact that the fliers would be gone by morning, leaving behind substantial income for the Mission.

The cooks from the *Alicia* had prepared pork stuffed with dried tomatoes and prosciutto, on a layer of linguine. The toasts were long and frequent. Sam injected several robust repetitions of *'grazie mille!'* The cheers encouraged him to dig deeper. He responded with rounds of *'Il vino—eccellente! Eccellente!'* It exhausted his public vocabulary. The effort was embraced with gusto, however, and as the evening wore on *il vino* took charge, raising the noise level considerably. Soon conversation gave way a rousing stream of patriotic songs, *"Fratelli d'Italia"* the title of the first, at least those were the words shouted the loudest before the singing commenced. Sam understood hardly a word of the next, except the name of Mussolini, punctuated by straight-armed salutes and shouts of *'Eja, eja, alalà!'*

The operatic fliers, drunk as pigs and not far off their demeanor, eventually careened their way through the hallways to their rooms for the night. The slightly more sober crew of the *Alicia* departed to supervise the task of refueling the Armada. The Italians had hired the townspeople of Cartwright and their boats for the transport of the fuel, a vast stockpile of which was brought from the Mission wharf to the airplanes in every manner of container, all under lantern-light. The harbour was alive with flickering trails of light and a brew of languages. Beautiful, if it hadn't been so precarious an undertaking. But everyone survived, and with stories that would no doubt be retold in the kitchens of Cartwright for decades.

Early the next morning the flying boats again filled the sky, next stop Shediac, New Brunswick. The *Alicia* steamed away shortly thereafter and Miss Stewart emitted a deep sigh of relief, although the Mission would be a duller place by far.

Sam had barely time to collect his breath when, incredible as it was, another, simpler airplane, a single-engine Lockheed Sirius, descended on the village. This one contained no less than Charles and Anne Morrow Lindbergh.

For a brief few days Cartwright was starting to feel like the centre of the universe.

The Lindberghs were heading north to Greenland, and then making a complete circle of the Atlantic, a trip of several months, to scout flying routes for Pan American Airways. Their plan had been to intersect with the Italians, but they missed them by a day.

There was a second reason for their trip, one the Lindberghs chose not to speak about. The women of the Mission staff did, among themselves, although always quietly and with great care that the couple didn't suspect it of them. The kidnapping and death of the Lindbergh's young son had taken place only the year before, and the FBI investigation was still filling the newspapers and radio broadcasts in North America. The couple had left to escape the hounding of the press. They had deliberately chosen the most remote of stopping points.

Unlike the Italians, they showed up in Cartwright with little warning. They had no need of Mission accommodation, having booked into the modest saltbox Cartwright called its hotel. After the first day, with the fog settling in, it was inevitable that the couple and the Mission should come together. The Lindberghs knew a good deal about Grenfell and shared his pioneering spirit.

Word reached Sam that they would be joining the Mission staff for their evening meal. It would be a table of a dozen or more. A fire in the fireplace, geraniums in the windows, more blooms on the table. Besides the regular staff were the summer volunteers, including an earnest young fellow from Princeton, who at the moment Sam entered the room was deep in conversation with the famous aviator.

Mrs. Lindbergh had chosen a seat at the far end of the table, next to Nurse Berthelsen, attracted, it seemed, by the nurse's European roots. Mrs. Lindbergh's manner was generous. She appreciated the energy needed to make a life in a foreign outpost.

Sam took the seat opposite her. When the nurse's story had come to its conclusion, Sam stretched his hand across the table and introduced himself.

'The first thing you must tell me, Mr. Kennedy, is how you came to be here. I envy the solitude, the sense of untamed wilderness.'

He wanted to think her interest was as earnest as she made it seem, but he had doubts. More likely, the Mission staff was a diversion, something to fill the Lindberghs' time, take attention from the fact that when fog settled into Cartwright it could well be around for several days. The Mission and its mix of workers were as urbane as the couple could hope to find.

'I came to assist with the Italians.'

'Charles was so disappointed to have missed them.'

'The Italians are mad,' Sam said decisively. 'Altogether mad. I expect they will be a great success in Chicago.'

Anne Lindbergh didn't quite know what to make of him. She smiled charitably.

Sam recalled the commotion when the word reached New York that *The Spirit of St. Louis* had landed in Paris. The city went wild. He had just finished work for the day on the New York Life Insurance Building, when suddenly every fire engine in the city seemed to be on the street, sirens blaring in unison with the clamour of ships' horns that filled the harbour. Lindbergh was instantly the greatest of heroes, celebrated across the world. The ticker-tape parade down

Broadway to welcome him home drew four million people, Sam among them. It was doubtful if there was a more famous face anywhere.

Madness of a different kind. And hadn't Sam been caught in it as much as anyone who lined the street.

Lindbergh noticed that another male had joined the Mission table. Shortly after Sam began explaining to Mrs. Lindbergh how he had spent his time in New York, her husband headed their way. His long arm found its objective. The two shook hands, and Lindbergh was soon adding his appraisal of the construction of the Empire State Building.

'I'm doubtful if the Germans ever seriously considered mooring a zep to that tower. Totally impractical. The wind on any given day would render it outright treacherous. Can you imagine disembarking from a swaying dirigible a quarter of a mile up in the sky, onto a gangplank two feet wide? Solely an excuse to raise the tower even higher.'

'To trounce the Chrysler, Mr. Lindbergh.'

'Absolutely.'

Sam and Lindbergh had landed on common ground.

The fog was going nowhere.

Sam took Lindbergh on a tour of the village. He was surprised to discover how relaxed the aviator was once it became clear that the local people were not in awe of him. So remote was Cartwright that many of them had never heard of the man, and were more interested in his airplane than its pilot. Lindbergh admired people who survived in harsh climates by their own resourcefulness. The North Atlantic fishery was not something he had ever experienced and he was eager for Sam to expound on it in more detail. It reinforced their alliance.

They talked of other things. Inevitably, the Great War.

Lindbergh had spent the war in high school and on a farm in Minnesota, with a father who was desperately opposed to America entering the conflict. Yet, war could be the story of gallant men, and Lindbergh very much admired gallant men.

Lindbergh especially admired the aviators, of course, and spun out what he knew of Rickenbacker and von Richthofen. 'The Great War,' Lindbergh said to Sam, 'was a tremendous boon to the advancement of flight. War is the great testing ground of man and science.'

It was the first irritant between them. There was something gnawing in the fact that the pronouncement came from someone who had never donned a uniform.

Lindbergh would have been in one, had he been the age. He made that clear. And likely would have been a flying ace himself, for that matter. Or just as likely dead, Sam was tempted to say.

'You, Sam, from what I can see, have a sense of daring. And undoubtedly no fear of heights. You'd do well in a cockpit.'

And that was the great thrill of Lindbergh's company. The man's world was limitless, the paths he might take hardly able to keep up with his imagination.

Sam went with him to the Lockheed Sirius when Lindbergh rowed out to check if its mooring was still secure, that no rain had found its way through the cockpit window. The window had been giving Lindbergh trouble on the flight into Cartwright.

He encouraged Sam to take to the cockpit and was pleased to see how easily he slipped inside. Lindbergh leaned over and gave an explanation of the instrumental panel. Sam sat consumed by the moment, for he would likely never be so intimately touched by fame again.

Their time together stretched to part of three, then four days, by which point Lindbergh's interest in Cartwright had more than exhausted itself. Sam left him to his own devices. On the fifth day there were signs of clearing inland, enough that Lindbergh decided to take to the air, if only to venture in the opposite direction from which he needed to go. He would have to return to Cartwright, until the fog lifted offshore. Still, it meant he was going somewhere.

He and his wife headed over the Mealy Mountains and down Hamilton Inlet to the village of North West River, returning that same evening, impressed with the contrast in Labrador's climate and landscape. But the following morning the weather conditions hadn't changed. Lindbergh had reached the limit of his patience.

He came in search of Sam, with the notion they take the airplane on a short jaunt inland to go fishing. Anything to use up a few more hours. Sam escaped his Mission duties and was at the wharf within a half hour, fishing rods and a supply of dry flies in hand.

The rear cockpit was open to the four winds, a leap beyond the Empire State, into the fringes of the clouds. And the world below him—his own in the way New York could never be. Stoic black spruce fringed by undulating marshlands. Cut by a gray-blue tapestry of rivers and ponds, lapsing into bedrock. A great swath of fantasy come true.

They chose a landing site and Lindbergh splashed down, easing the Lockheed to a sheltered shoreline, where Sam, slipping onto a pontoon, then leaping ashore, secured the airplane to several sturdy trees.

The interior of Labrador was renowned for its fresh water fishing. Its speckled brook trout were hardly to be believed— six- and seven-pounders taut at the end of a ten-pound test.

Lindbergh, no expert with a fly rod but in dire need of a challenge, took to it doggedly, until his catch of fish was nearly equal Sam's own.

The pair had set themselves in the natural world in the way few outsiders could ever hope to, for the moment inseparable from wilderness. The unspoiled interior of Labrador was something Lindbergh envied and might never again have within his reach. In that Sam took satisfaction.

Their alliance had quietly slipped into rivalry. It churned Sam's notion of himself. In Sam's sudden gaze, Lindbergh was a man, a supremely accomplished one, but no more than himself at his core.

Their talk was of flight, its compression of time, seeming to foretell a future without boundaries. It was talk of the Italian Armada of airships that had passed through Cartwright.

If the Italian fliers were a marker, Sam was far from certain the future was a clear-headed one. To his mind, Balbo and his pilots had been all too self-assured, sniffing about for adulation. Yes, mad as all hell.

'I have to say I admire what the General has done with his air force,' Lindbergh said.

'They pranced ashore like gamecocks.'

Lindbergh laughed. 'Italians are impetuous, but they are not foolhardy.'

And the Germans? According to the Italian reporter Sam had befriended it was the Germans who were on everyone's mind in Europe.

'Wonderfully efficient. Extraordinary engineers,' said Lindbergh.

Sam paraphrased the reporter. 'Hitler has shut down all opposition parties. Jews are in constant fear of being arrested. In May, university students held a massive book burning in Berlin.'

'The German people have made tremendous progress, pulling themselves out of the defeat of war. Ultimately, I have faith in the common man.'

'Then you need equal faith in his leader.'

Lindbergh dismissed Sam's opinions. Sam had not travelled the world nor shared tables with its leading minds as Lindbergh had. Sam's knowledge of Germans was down the sight of a rifle. It no longer counted for anything.

'I should think the world has learned its lesson,' Lindbergh added.

'You're optimistic, Charles.' It was the first time he had used the name. 'I can't say I am. I've seen too many people die. I've killed some of them myself.'

It drew Lindbergh up short, if only for a moment. He looked at Sam warily, seeing a man who had deliberately and unnecessarily crossed a boundary. Lindbergh had no time for histrionics.

'In which case you know the value of peace more than most.'

Sam was a fool to argue with the man. There were countless other things to admire in him. But such logic did not take hold. 'Peace has no value unless honourable men are behind it. From what I know of Hitler he would just as soon cut your throat as look at you.'

Lindbergh smiled at his naivety, his use of the vernacular. 'And how have you come to this conclusion?'

'I look. I listen.'

'Have you visited the country?'

'Have *you*?'

'I have not. But I may well do so. Unlike yourself, I assume.'

'Fuck that, Lindbergh.'

It threw the man off balance.

'War is a hell of a price for optimism.'

Lindbergh stared him down. 'Take control of yourself.'

'Fuck control, Lindbergh.'

The aviator turned away from him. 'We better be getting back.' He began disassembling his fishing rod. 'I suggest you...'

'You got the attention of the world,' Sam shouted. 'Use your fucking influence!'

Lindbergh untied one of the ropes that held the airplane to shore. 'Get aboard please.'

Sam grabbed him by his plaid shirt and yelled into his face. 'It detonates in four fucking minutes!'

Lindbergh rammed his fist into Sam's jaw and sent him to his knees. He towered over him, saying nothing.

Eventually Sam gathered his rod and took it apart. He helped collect the fish they had caught. He climbed aboard the airplane and into his seat as Lindbergh pushed them away from shore.

The airplane broke free of the water, the engine noise its loudest.

Sam rose in his seat, forced his head out the open window.

He screamed Johnny's name, the echo blaring into his friend's beloved wilderness.

THIRTEEN

THEY looked an alien pair bundled in their fur-collared, one-piece flying suits, all pockets and zippers, heads tightly covered by leather aviator caps. Across their foreheads rested wide, rubber-framed goggles. They posed easily for the few cameras to be found in Cartwright, Anne Lindbergh a fraction of the height of her husband, both beaming despite how overheated they must have been. They were not dressed for mid-summer in Labrador, but for the temperatures they would find high in the atmosphere, and which would prove steadily colder as they neared Greenland.

It was still early morning. The Hudson's Bay Company wharf was crowded with townspeople. Its usual business of codfish and salmon had come to a halt. The fishermen in their oilskins and the warehouse workers in their coveralls gathered for a succession of cigarettes. The Mission staff stood together, more aware than most of how remarkable it was that they had spent a week in the company of Charles and Anne Lindbergh.

Sam kept his distance, his head still resounding from the impact of Lindbergh's fist. The space between aviator and onlooker had been reset. The man was again Charles Lindbergh, unquestionably fixed in his role as the pioneer of flight, leaving all others to stand captivated by their own moment in history. In his flying garb Lindbergh was even more the giant of a man among a community of lesser men.

As the couple boarded the open boat to be rowed to the airplane, they raised their hands to everyone assembled. To a person the bystanders fixed their eyes on the pair. The Lindberghs climbed aboard and into the cockpits, first Anne and then her husband, only their heads left visible.

The Lockheed turned slowly and cruised toward the outer harbour, to catch what little wind there was. The engine noise lifted, the airplane building up speed until it skimmed the surface, labouring to rise above it. The struggle went on for so long it seemed the flight might have to be abandoned, but at the last moment the airplane broke free of the water, and began its climb, drifting into the sky above the open ocean. The people of Cartwright stood on the wharf, intent on it until it turned to a pinpoint, and then was gone from their lives.

Within a few days Sam was gone as well, aboard the coastal boat heading south. To where, he wasn't sure. St. Anthony, Harbour Main, New York?

'Sam, you are not yourself,' Miss Stewart had said to him on his return from the fishing trip. Whatever his self was.

'He bloody well admires those Italians,' he told her in the kitchen of the dormitory, while she tried to calm him down with tea, while the nurse examined his bruised jaw.

'The Lindberghs are distraught, Sam. They have lost a son.'

Sam's head was in a different place. He was being loud again. 'That scruff of a reporter from the *Alicia*, remember.

You like this life, no?' Sam mimicked. 'Constantly at this table, smoking putrid little cigars and drinking coffee. *What do you do to amuse yourself, you young miss, when there are no visitors in the long winter? Ah, you are of some religious order? Ah, no, I have seen you smoke cigarettes and you do not wear a habit.'*

'*When I was your age I was long months, high, high in the snows, in the war, in the fight at Caporetto. But we had our Regiment, we had our country. We had our people urging us on. You do not have this. I do not understand. Why do you come here, why are you so interested in these people, all so poor, in this miserable place?'*

The two women were silent, co-conspirators it seemed to him.

'Can't you see,' he pleaded, loud again, 'the world understands Mussolini more than it does Grenfell. We have all been witness to something rotting, and the great Lindbergh can't contain his fucking admiration.'

Sam burrowed himself in his room. The coastal boat was due in a few days. He was expected to leave. He was no more use to the Mission in Cartwright.

Miss Stewart came to see him off. She stood alone at the land end of the wharf, her cardigan buttoned tightly, each of her hands tucked inside the sleeve of the other arm. It was evening now and it looked like rain. She was there to be certain he boarded the vessel rather than out of any regret at seeing him go. He held up his hand from the ship's railing. She withdrew one of hers and raised it to him. Within a few seconds Sam disappeared inside the ship. He wandered into the lounge, nodded to the steward stocking the bar and ordered a double rum.

When the *Prospero* docked in St. Anthony he was still debating whether to get off or remain aboard and wait out the few hours until it left port again. From the deck he surveyed what had once been the promised land. The sun appeared from behind the clouds and brightened the rain-soaked village with crisp intensity. He walked down the gangplank.

He walked past a batch of volunteers, all new, all as fresh-faced and incorruptible as the lot from the summer before. He didn't recognize the person in charge. Whoever he was, he was self-assured, durable. Fully able to do as good a job as Sam had done, though no better he was sure. He passed them by without a word.

He had decided on the Loom Room, but as he was going by the Mission's Gift Shop he noticed it was open. He approached the screen door, its scrolling accented a light blue against the white of its panels. He recalled that one of his crew from last summer had done the painting. It had taken him a long time.

Sam stepped inside. The spring mechanism on the door drew it closed with a muted smack. There was no one to be seen, although he could hear a person moving about in the back room behind the curtain. And her voice, 'I'll be right there.'

Sam glanced about anxiously. The shop was filled with hand-crafted goods, set out much as he remembered. One piece suddenly took all his attention. On the wall behind the counter was the hooked mat Emma had been experimenting with in the Loom Room. The image of the sealskin pelt had been very finely hooked, in tans and greys and russet. The colours of lichens.

Emma appeared from behind the curtain. She stopped abruptly at the sight of him. She held her arms across her chest.

She was looking older than she had the few months before, and out of sorts. He wanted to think it was the consequence of him standing in front of her, but it was likely not just that. Strands of hair fell to the side of her face where they had been so perfectly in place before. Her dress hung loose and inconsiderate of her thinner frame. She was unsmiling, remote.

'Please don't say you are sorry,' she said. 'I don't want to hear it.'

'I'm on my way south.'

'That's for the best.'

'You have been keeping well?'

She didn't answer.

'And the others?'

Her silence continued for the moment.

'You should go.'

He should not have been attracted to this woman. So far from his picture of her.

He made no move to leave.

'I want to buy the mat on the wall behind you.'

Emma glanced needlessly past her shoulder.

'I would rather you didn't.'

'He would have wanted me to have it,' Sam said. 'We talked a lot about hunting seals.'

Her reply was lost to a quiet intake of air, the edge of her hand rising to cover her mouth.

'He told me he would lie in wait for hours on the ice, until the seal showed itself through its breathing hole.'

Her eyes were closed. He walked silently to the other side of the counter. He stood in front of her and slowly enclosed her with his arms. She shuttered at the touch of him. She started to slip downward through his arms, but she let him hold her upright, drawing the two of them together. Sam sank his head into her shoulder.

When John came through the door they had separated, though only moments before.

Sam walked to where he was standing and held out his hand. John held out his. It would have been more awkward not to. Sam was thinking he might have grown taller, and told him so.

'How come you're back?'

'I'm heading somewhere,' Sam said. 'I don't know where.'

'When I finish school I'll be going too.'

'John,' his mother said.

'I could take training in New York. I could join the Regiment.'

'John.'

'She doesn't want me out of her sight,' he said, provoking her again. 'She thinks I'll end up like my father. She thinks you were a bad influence.'

Emma could do nothing to stop him, except at the risk of her son's temper rising further.

'I'm old enough to make up my own mind. My father wouldn't have held me back.'

'You don't know that,' Emma said.

'Your father is dead,' Sam said, his own temper blunting the boy's. There was reverberation in his few words, as if a padded clapper had struck a bell. 'And if you ever run off to join up, I'll come looking for you and when I find you I'll break every finger on both your goddamn hands.'

In the stalemate that followed Sam walked to the wall and quickly pulled away the mat, rolled it up on the counter, and planted in its place a ten dollar bill. He left the shop, the screen door slapping shut behind him.

FOURTEEN

BY midnight Sam was drunk and throwing up his guts, as much from the rough seas as the rum. He lay in the bunk oblivious to the foul scum circling the cabin floor. When he woke in the morning he cleaned up what he could and changed his vomit-caked clothes. He opened the porthole window and quit the room.

'Where we stopping?'

'Conche,' the steward answered him from across the lounge. 'Coffee?'

The first word cleared his head, as the black coffee should have, but didn't. The steward refilled his cup and went back to sweeping the floor.

Sam had heard Conche mentioned several times when he lived in St. Anthony. The Mission sent a nurse there for a few months each winter, a three-day journey overland by dogteam. Sam wandered onto the deck, the cup in his hand. He peered past the railing to the birthplace of his mother.

It had the markings of a stoic Catholic outport, its lofty,

double-towered church keeping watch over the scattering of square-framed houses, sturdy but unadorned, inhabited without doubt by unrelenting fishermen and their sizable families. Frugal and hard-headed. Salt of the earth, salt of the sea. Bound to an inlet of the Great Northern Peninsula. By coastal boat an overnight sail from St. Anthony.

It being Saturday the wharf was rampant with children, the coastal boat forever a curiosity. A few of them ran bare-foot, scampering after each other. More stood by, in wait of something, without knowing what.

'Any of you Carews?' Sam called down to the assortment directly below him.

A dirty hand shot up. 'Me, sir. Ben, sir. And me sister, Aggie.' Ben looked to be about six, his sister, standing bashfully nearby, was probably twice that age.

When all was said and done, young Ben and Aggie were relatives of Sam.

They led him to their clapboard house, weather-worn to grey. Here Sam discovered their mother standing at the kitchen table, her hair covered and tied back with a bandana, hands deep in bread dough. And yes, good heavens, she had heard of Gladys Carew.

'Your mother, was it? And you from Harbour Main? That's right, that's where she went. That's the story I was told. The poor girl.'

The Aunt Gladys nobody ever saw again. Her family in Conche hadn't known she died until two weeks after she was buried.

The woman's husband, Ronan, showed up for his tea. He and Sam were cousins and they had never laid eyes on each other before. Ronan stood close to six feet. He didn't fill his clothes and his haircut left his face more raw-boned than it needed to be. Still, Sam had hardly known a more welcoming handshake.

Ronan revealed more, he being reared up with the stories.

'Your mother had gone north to Labrador, cook for the summer aboard a schooner and there she met her man.'

Young Gladys had broken her parents' hearts when she went to Harbour Main. So far away and no telling when they would see her again. And, as it happened, they didn't. Within a few years she had died. And not many years after that so had her mother and father.

'Love, I guess. Love and the promise of a future for herself. She was wanting to be a nurse. And by all accounts smart enough to be one.'

Ronan bit into a pork bun and washed it down with tea.

'Didn't you know? Perhaps it's not true then.'

He drew out the time with the tea.

'He promised to take her into St. John's, help her get into nurse's training. And then they would think about getting married.'

It hadn't happened. Ronan shrugged.

'You must know,' said his wife.

Sam looked at her, forming the last bit of dough into a ball and adding it to the two others in the pan.

'She was having a little one. And that was the end of that.'

Sam was on his way to board the boat, when Ronan came calling to him. He stopped so Ronan could catch up. The tentative rake of a man had a proposition.

'Stay why don't you? Stay and catch the next boat.'

Sam hadn't wanted that. He couldn't see how staying would do him any good.

'There's lots more Carews you haven't met. We'll put you up. We'll make do.'

He didn't doubt it.

'You can earn your keep. You any good at the fish?'

Even so. Two weeks was a long time.

'You were in no hurry to get here. No need to be in any hurry to leave.'

He wasn't convinced to stay, but he did stay. It was home of a sort. Home of his own invention, one to shape by his own devices. A home far enough away from home.

He discovered a holy load of relatives, so many he gave up trying the keep straight the connection to them all. The older ones all had the same story—of a promising young girl who left home and never returned. It was embedded in the lore of Conche, for the expectation had been that one day Gladys Carew would return a nurse and live and work among her own people. In their stories 'her man' would have come with her.

Or likely not. Sam couldn't imagine his father outside Harbour Main. He would have been pleased enough when he got her pregnant.

Besides Ronan's father, Sam had two more uncles and a maiden aunt living in Conche. The aunt was the one with the pictures. Her name was Edna and she was not well, confined to her house because of arthritis. Nonetheless, she came alive when she had visitors, especially strangers.

A never-seen-before nephew was a blessed windfall.

'Dear God, you looks like your mother, that you do. I minds her going, as if it were yesterday.' Edna lost all composure.

Sam was left standing in the porch with nothing to do but come into the kitchen and wrap an arm around her shoulders.

'The sun shone out of that girl brighter than it do from the Blessed Virgin.'

Edna hobbled across the room to the kitchen table and inserted herself onto a chair.

'Take a seat, Samuel, my love. Take a seat and tell me how you came into this world and what you have been doing with yourself since you did.'

Edna was all heart and eagerness, with a bustle about her only suppressed by her aches and pains. They talked and talked, and drank black tea and ate blueberry cake.

'Oh, the dear God,' she said when he told her about New York. 'And you born and reared at sea level like the rest of us. You never knows, do you, you never knows what people is capable of once they sets their mind to it.'

Her goodwill sank into him.

'And never married. Course, I'm someone to talk, I is. Nar man, nar chick ner child.'

At that moment young Ben came flying through the door and into Edna's arms. 'Course 'tis like havin' one o' yer own.' She held Ben's head to her bosom and kissed the child on the forehead. 'Aunt Edna could squeeze you 'til she's blue in the face, she could.'

Great Aunt Edna. There was something marvelous in being embraced unconditionally, even if it was simple, childlike.

He gave into it, and stood apart. Guardedly clenched what they held out to him. After a few days at Ronan's he moved into a small house that had been left vacant by a relative who had recently died. His life was about making do. Settling into a pattern, his days governed by the working world of Conche, in some ways much the same as what he knew growing up, but in other ways different.

The fishery in Conche grew out of separate family ventures,

not the credit system of a single merchant. Two brothers might team up, with their unmarried sons and a couple of cousins as sharemen. The brothers had once worked as sharemen themselves and made money enough to acquire their own boat and their own codtrap. The crew caught the fish, turned it to dried saltcod, and sold it themselves in St. John's for cash and supplies. They didn't live and die on credit.

They lived by their wits and hard work. Even so, these days that wasn't enough. With the Depression price for salt-cod, the people of Conche were left with barely enough to keep body and mind together, as in every outport on the island. They gladly left it to the Catholic Church to take care of their souls.

Still, his cousins made room for him in the fishery. Their vegetable grounds weren't as fertile as what Sam had known, but he was a good hand at that just the same.

He spent the winter.

The one thing he missed was some touch with the outside world. He ordered a Philco from St. John's and it came on the next boat, although most times it filled the kitchen with nothing but heavy static. He ran an antenna to higher ground and that helped. In the meantime, he had become good friends with Magistrate FitzGerald, who operated the post office. It had a crank telephone, the only one in the place, and Sam regularly came away from visiting the Magistrate with one bit of news or other.

From what he gathered Frederick Alderdice, who replaced Squires as Prime Minister, together with the whole House of Assembly, had resigned. Newfoundland had abandoned self-government, and put itself back in the hands of Britain.

For months the country had been on the brink of bank-ruptcy. The war debt, the cost of building the railway, the

Depression, low fish prices—all conspiring to sink the dominion. Britain agreed to bail it out, but only on condition that it could set up what it called a Commission of Government. The country was now governed by a troupe of six men, three from Britain and three from Newfoundland, with Britain holding the purse strings.

'We're no longer a country,' said Sam, around Ronan's supper table. The politicians had let them down, more profoundly than he ever thought possible. He told Ronan about the riot in St. John's.

'It can't be forever. We got to get our government back some day. Then you run in the election, Sam. By the sound of it, you got the head for politics.'

It was all so much talk. Talk that went down with a steady few drinks, a bunch of relatives in his kitchen, someone with an accordion then and a few songs from the old country. He had one for them.

Sam wrote to Margaret to let them know his whereabouts. He had no more money to send. Weeks later he received a letter back. Their father was no better, and no worse.

Margaret kept strangely distant from the stories about their mother. She had not told Paddy. It would have been too much for him, she wrote. His heart might not be able to stand it.

Who was Sam to question her? To be telling her what to do? Leave Paddy in peace is what she meant. Leave their father to live out what was left of his life without the old man's questions making it worse for Margaret than it already was.

What about the striking young maid from Conche, her dreams stolen from her? With children she didn't want? Perhaps they had won their mother's heart the moment they were born. They would never know.

Half reared, he and Margaret, by their father. Other lives long past. As was the war, as was New York. There were times, in the woods that winter with Ronan, cutting wood with a bucksaw, colder than he was ever used to in Harbour Main, cold close to frostbite, that Sam knew there was nothing more to be found. Left holding to the crackle of the snow and ice beneath his feet as he made his way from the woods to home and back and forth again, to fire crackling in the wood stove, his wool-stocking feet warming on its oven door. The toast and tea a blessing.

In the late spring Sam heard, his ears straining past the static, that Hitler had purged the Nazi Party of his enemies. And not long after, that he had declared himself Führer of all Germany. Angry black clouds were circling Europe. Newfoundland seemed far away, but Sam knew that if it ever came to war again, the Atlantic would be its corridor.

He and the Magistrate drifted into deep conversation over each fresh batch of news. The two grew into pipe-smoking companions when Conche seemed its most insular. That March they went seal-hunting, not far offshore. For several weeks sealskins were stretched on their wooden frames outside his house, while inside, pinned to the wall, was the hooked mat he had brought from St. Anthony.

St. Anthony was often in his mind. He had all the reason in the world for not going back, though it would have been easy enough when the coastal boat resumed its service. As did everyone else in Conche, he came out to see the boat on its first trip of the season. Strung across the railing were another gang of Grenfell's summer volunteers. Sam had no urge to join them, though he speculated if Grenfell would have given him back his job.

The return of the coastal boat triggered a restlessness in him, one he fought against, without enough success. As the summer came to an end, nearing the time the boat service would soon cease for another year, the restlessness chafed at him even more.

Roosevelt was pulling the country out of the Depression. Employment was on the increase. The seventy-story RCA Building had opened. Nothing was stopping the thirst for skyscrapers in New York. Sam made up his mind to leave Conche.

He would give himself another month, to see Ronan through the fishing season. A couple of weeks later the *Prospero* again sailed into Conche, the last trip south before his own. He had just cleaned himself up at the end of the day when a knock came on his door.

'John.'

'We heard you was here.'

They shook hands. 'Watch the fingers,' John said, with an edge of a grin. He was a stronger fellow, now stronger than his father for sure.

He was on his way to Lewisporte, then the train, then New York. He was nervous. Excited but nervous.

'All set to start training. Machine repair.' Like his father.

Sam told John he would be seeing him in New York. The young fellow smiled broadly. It took away some of the anxiety.

The two sat down for a drink of rum together.

'Don't ever forget where you came from, John.'

There was no need, they both knew.

'But when you get to New York, the first thing you got to do is buy yourself a charcoal fedora.'

John grinned, not knowing what to think. Right there and then Sam put enough money in his hand.

'Wear it, and swank around the streets of New York. Let 'em know you're somebody.'

They laughed. Sam laughed until he had tears in his eyes. He hadn't felt so sweet a moment in a long time.

Before John left he handed Sam an envelope. 'She asked me to give you this.'

Sam set it aside.

He didn't return to it until after John was aboard the boat and it had steamed out of the harbour. Even then he put off opening the letter, until the light had faded completely from the house and he was left alone in the dark with his misgivings. He lit the lantern and sat beside it.

Dear Sam,

The time has past for an apology, from you or from me. But I think it is only right that you know my mind, since you were so eager to share your own.

There will soon be just myself. I will be truly alone for the first time since Johnny went off to the war. He left and I had our son, and now he, too, is going. He will be back for a time, but it will no longer be the same. He is a man now and men grow beyond their mothers. His life could take him anywhere. He has that eagerness to see places, as I once did.

I will be without Rhoda, who has returned to her home in England. I have two sisters, but we were never close. And parents, who I am afraid have never forgiven me for leaving home, and who are now too old to revisit my reasons.

There was a time I believed I had the Grenfells, but I was foolish enough to think I was any more than a nursemaid, or a worker for the Mission. I would need to have been of a different heritage. Or have married any one of the doctors who showed up in St. Anthony.

And that leaves you, Sam.

I knew of you since you first met Johnny at the training camp in Pleasantville. I was fiercely jealous even then. You had the sight of him, and all I had were the memories and his letters. In every one of them he would write of the hours you spent together, and there was a time when I hated the very mention of your name. It was wrong of me, I know, for friends need their friends in war. Yet love is never simple, is it Sam?

You had been the best of friends, but once word reached me of Johnny's death, there was nothing from the Sam Kennedy he had written so much about. I thought you must have met your own end, in another part of the war. There was a letter from the officer in charge the day Johnny died, Lieutenant Steele, a letter I still hold in a dresser drawer and at times take out and read again. His words were carefully chosen, very thoughtful, very kind. They are painful for me, but they have always been a help through a grief that has never truly subsided. It was several months after the war ended, when the official list of the Regiment's war dead was distributed, that I learned Lieutenant Steele, too, had been killed.

And then, all those years later, two letters in quick succession, from Sam Kennedy. As if the years had meant nothing, as if your letters had followed on the heels of the war and you could slip into my life, and be welcomed for doing so.

I chose not to answer the letters. Their intensity aroused feelings I didn't trust. Why, after all this time had passed? What did you expect—that my life had not moved on, that I could pick up the pieces from a shattered romance and readjust them to someone I had never met? As if you and Johnny were one in the same.

My life had altered, as would anyone's after all that time. My employment in the Grenfell home had come to an untidy end, as if it had never existed. My hope of accompanying them on one of their winter trips to the United States, as they had often promised, had vanished. Mrs. Grenfell's only gesture was to pass along some of the baby clothes her boys had outgrown, though not the best of them. She came to see me after the birth, without the children. Not out of any great wish for us to spend time together. Out of obligation most likely.

All that remained was my connection to the Industrials. Doctor Grenfell did see to it that I had an income, enough to maintain myself and John. I wanted to think it was not done out of guilt for what had happened to Johnny.

And over the years that is how I have lived, assistant to whoever has been in charge of the Mission's Industrials. Invariably it was someone brought in from the United States or Britain. I have seen several women come and go, and still I was never offered the position, as if I don't quite measure up, even though I was in charge between the departure of one supervisor and the arrival of the next. I have learned to live with it.

I never married, as you have come to find out. Much to your relief, I assume. For what it is worth, there has been more than one man interested. You should not think I have been waiting idly by, waiting for just such a man as yourself. I admit there have been times when I wished for the permanent company of a man, for the well-being of John as much as myself. Most were young doctors who came to work for the Mission. Some of the relationships lasted months, and in the case of one a year, but in the end they all moved on, back to wherever it was they had left. The fact that I had a child was likely the least of reasons the handsome, year-long Dr. Salomon never once spoke of marriage.

In time the doctors' invitations to keep company came to an end. I grew older, and my appeal waned. It was just as well. Not one of them could ever replace Johnny. I would be forever thinking, as I still do, of the life that should have been, but never was. It was the reason I could never for a moment involve myself with a local man. It made for talk of course, that I thought too much of myself, that I always wanted to be someone I wasn't, that I was too vain to marry a Newfoundlander.

And now, suddenly, there is Sam Kennedy.

Would I be wrong to think you loved Johnny as much as I did? Was there any more than his physical love that separated you from me in his eyes? Our son, of course. But I have often wondered, if Johnny had come home from the war and there had not been a child, what would have become of us.

What would the war have done to him had he lived to see its end? I don't mean to be hurtful when I say that the war made a hell for you. How could it have been any different for Johnny, if he had returned, all those dead behind him?

We like to believe, you and I, that he would have been the Johnny we both knew. I think instead he would have been a Johnny we didn't know.

I would have loved him as much as ever I did. Would you have been able to say the same?

You must wonder why I am writing to you now.

Over the months since we encountered each other for the first time I have asked myself if there could have ever been anything between us. It would seem we are both lost. I have wondered, if there had not been a Johnny in our lives, would we have been drawn together? If we had met at nineteen, the age of John now, would we have fallen for each other? And if there had not been a war. A bold thought. I am capable of boldness, though you might not think it. As the years have gone by I have come to believe that boldness has its place. Life often does not give a second chance.

Then there is the letter you delivered.

I think you know what it says. I think it was written by your own hand. Simple and to the point and easy enough to fashion if you knew his handwriting. Perhaps I am wrong. I would like to think so.

And now what? It would seem we go our separate ways and restart our lives once again.

To you, Sam, I wish you well. I wish you peace wherever
you go. If it is New York, then be good to my boy.
If it is Newfoundland still, my hope is you will find
someone who will be kind and true.

Emma

Sam told no one he was boarding the *Prospero*, the trip
heading north. He'd had enough of good-byes, and who
wouldn't think he might be back when the boat stopped for the
last time on its return.

The same steward gave him coffee in the same place in
the lounge. It could have been that Sam had never stopped in
Conche.

He had. As the boat steamed away, he withdrew the
picture from his wallet. His Aunt Edna had insisted he have it.

She was a good-looking young woman. Bright, he could
easily tell. Lively, he guessed, at the right moment. Full of a
yearning for something.

She was dressed in a blouse and a long, high-waisted skirt.
The blouse was white and embroidered with a chain of
flowers at the neck, embroidered by her own hand he guessed.
She was standing against a lilac tree in bloom.

Her hair swept across her forehead, curled at the sides,
and held in place above one ear by a beaded comb. It was long
enough that it could have been tied back with ribbon. Her
features were small and gentle, but strong for all that.
Her dark eyes, focused slightly away from the camera, warm
and intelligent. She would have had no shortage of interested
men.

He returned the photograph to his wallet, and took out
the other, the lifelong one, the one he had withdrawn so many
times that he could recall the progressive phases of its history,

from pristine freshness to faded misadventure. He held it in his hand a last time, then let it slip from his palm and drift away, downward, coming to settle on the sea, before being folded into the swell and disappearing.

And then the letter. Without its envelope. He held it in his hands, stared at it for a moment. He tore it into two pieces and then into four. They fell from his fingers into the endless water below.

He returned to the lounge and called this time for rum— *Rhum Negrita*. The good stuff, reminding him of New York.

'You know someone in St. Anthony, do you?' said the steward, after Sam had borrowed his cigarette to light his own.

He nodded. 'How long will we stop there?'

'A couple of hours I expect.'

'Long enough.'

'You going on then?'

'Could be. I never know.'

The steward left him in peace, returning to his work. Sam settled in with his drink. The hours ahead turned about in his mind. And turning about them were days and years, all encompassing his private world. Turning about that private world there was disquiet, as there had always been.